DIVINE PURPOSE FOR SHERRI

Kenny Reed

PublishAmerica
Baltimore

To Launa Perry: May God's grace and peace ever abide with you and yours.
Kenny Reed

First printing

ISBN: 1-4137-9469-6
PUBLISHED BY PUBLISHAMERICA, LLLP
www.publishamerica.com
Baltimore

Printed in the United States of America

To my loving Savior, Jesus Christ,
for His granting to me,
through the Holy Spirit,
another medium for blessing others in His name.
What a joy it is to write for those
who enjoy God-honoring literature.

ACKNOWLEDGMENTS

A special thanks to my sister, Pat Keuning, who edited and critiqued the manuscript for this book. She tirelessly taught me many computer techniques and short cuts—sometimes having to teach them a second and third time.

Many family members and friends share the joy of my being published. I certainly want to thank Christian author Bea Carlton for her instruction and kind words during my Novel Writing Workshop, and, of course, the wonderful staff at PublishAmerica.

CHAPTER ONE

Monday, April 16, 1979

Sherri Mosley, since Pastor Richards preached about it, frequently prayed that God would help her find purpose—maybe a special purpose. This day, she moped through the entire morning, feeling especially unfulfilled.

She couldn't shake the notion that her life had become one of enslaved hopeless existence with a husband who insisted that she not work outside the home, though their personal economics suggested they could use the extra income. That circumstance would be more tolerable if only Frank hadn't gradually annulled every one of her friendships even with the other young married women of the church. She had come to doubt Pastor Richard's and Frank's emphasis on her submission—or at least their exaggerated views of the matter. She couldn't reconcile their interpretations with that of scripture that spoke of freedom in Christ and other biblical teachings of love and cooperation between a husband and a wife.

Her concern that Frank had apparently lost all interest in church further fueled her discontent and confusion. He had been spending more and more time with his brother in the evenings. His leaving shortly after supper and returning late nights generated suspicion. She would have spied on him if she had the means. They owned only one vehicle; Frank's new 1979 Chevy four-wheel drive truck. She had few friends—none so close that she would confide in them about personal matters. Certainly not her marriage concerns. How she wished they hadn't relocated to Frank's hometown—Youngstown, Ohio. At least in Morgantown she had a few friends. She felt lost and faceless in the large church she and Frank joined after their conversion to Christ.

A soft steady rain accented the cool but dark spring day. The wet chill gnawed at her bones, making her home seem dungeon-like.

Sherri ignored the ringing of the telephone. Relieved that the caller gave up after ten rings, she sighed, "Not now. Call back later." Minutes later the ringing resumed. This time the caller would not be denied.

"Hello," Sherri moaned into the receiver.

"Sherri, this is Janet. How are you?"

Sherri feigned a semi-enthusiastic, "Fine. How are you? It's good to hear from you." Ordinarily, Janet Pixler was a welcome distraction from her lifeless existence. But she just didn't feel up to conversation. Not even with her long time friend from back home.

"You sound a little down," Janet said quizzically.

"Oh, I just feel the Monday morning blahs."

"Anything wrong?" Janet asked sincerely.

"I don't know. I'm not sure I can coherently convey my thoughts right now."

"I hear you."

"So what's up with you? I really miss you. I hate this place."

"Sounds like you're a little homesick. Why don't you come down for a visit?

"I should."

"Have you heard anything from your Uncle Joseph?"

"I have tried calling him several times in the past few months but he had his phone disconnected. Janet, I'm kind of worried about him."

"Well, the reason I'm calling is to update you."

Sherri supposed Janet would explain that Uncle Joseph disconnected his phone to avoid calls from his ex-wife, Angela. Janet had informed her months ago that Angela had leveled new false charges against him.

"It seems that he has become homeless," Janet continued, missing Sherri's cue about feeling emotionally out of sorts.

"Why would he be homeless?"

"The church he pastored fired him. It's rumored that they considered him an embarrassment. I heard that they didn't want the church to chance being disgraced..."

"Disgraced about what? *They* are the disgrace," Sherri shouted. "That makes me so mad!"

"Maybe I shouldn't have called you," Janet apologized.

"Yes you should have." She then asked, more civilly, "So what is all that about? How is he a disgrace to the church?"

"It's kind of involved, but I'll try to summarize for you. Just hold your peace and let me explain without you exploding. Okay?"

"Okay. Go ahead."

"The *Scoop Weekly* printed an accusatory article following the recent charges that Joseph allegedly threatened Angela's life. They recklessly elaborated on the murder he'd been acquitted of in 1969. Their report created an avalanche of letters to the editor, most of which slandered and judged Uncle Joseph and re-accused him of murdering Spike Cottrell in 1968..."

Hot blood rushed to Sherri's cheeks. Her jaws tightened in concert with every muscle of her slender, shapely body. "That is so ridiculous. I guess I need to write my own letter to the editor. I have a few charges to make against their precious socialite, Angela, and her crowd—including the *Scoop Weekly* staff."

"You know Sandy Jackson," Janet interrupted. "She attends a sister church of Tennant Valley's Grace Chapel. She says that Grace Chapel and the Church Conference offices have been flooded with letters and phone calls insisting that they ex-communicate the Reverend Joseph Short and strip him of his credentials.

"I spoke with Larry Smallwood the other day and he says that Joseph couldn't find work in the area. Reportedly, he has become homeless. Larry explained that Joseph had recently paid off the rest of the mountain of debt Angela had accrued against him. It took him all those years to finally pay them off. He no sooner got his breath from those hassles than Angela and others launched new attacks against him. That ungodly *Scoop Weekly* has really prejudiced the community against Joseph."

"I tell you what," Sherri threatened, "they will all hear from me. I owe a lot to Uncle Joseph. I know him to be a better man than any of those who sit in judgment of him. Oh, that infuriates me! Why do people read that irreverent gossip?"

"That tabloid's slander and misinformation has contaminated every community within seventy-five miles of its headquarters in Morgantown."

Sherri gritted her teeth. "I think it is time for them to be run out of Morgantown. No… Out of the state of West Virginia."

"Hey, Sherri, I have to get back to work. I just came home for lunch. I'll call you when I have more news."

"Please do. Thanks Janet. God bless you. I've got to come down and make things right for Uncle Joseph."

"I want you to stay here with me when you do come," Janet said warmly.

"Okay. Bye."

Sherri busied herself about the house, cleaning and cooking to occupy her mind. She thought more clearly when busy. And she certainly needed to sort through the maze of what if? how to? and who? questions. What if her intuitions do have merit? How will she approach the task that she is determined to take on? How will she explain to Frank the urgent need for her involvement? How can she gain his support in this mission? Who can she trust to assist her? Who even cares?

Dozens of questions buzzed about, dizzying her. The anticipation sickened her. The longer she awaited Frank's arrival home from work the more anxious she became. The house hadn't been this spic and span for months. Fresh pine scent mixed with that of potpourri. A cross breeze floated about the entire house circulating the complimenting aroma of fresh homemade potpie.

Unable to calm herself, Sherri repeatedly paced to and from the front porch, frantically searching the street. Frank seldom came home from work later than 5:30 p.m. He usually called ahead to inform her if he was going to be late. Six-fifteen and still no phone call to ease her worries. She characteristically began to imagine terrible, tragic things. "Where is he?" she mumbled impatiently. "All I need now is for something to happen to Frank."

With her back to the graceful pulsating breeze she whispered, "It's okay, Uncle Joseph, I'm coming." Uninvited tears blurred her vision as she continued assuring her uncle that neither she nor Jesus would forsake him. "Remember, Uncle Joseph, what you taught Frank and me when we trudged through our deepest valleys. 'And we know that all things work together for good to them that love God, to them who are the called according to his purpose.'" The verse repeatedly echoed in her mind. She reasoned aloud, "Could the Holy Spirit be *calling* me to Uncle Joseph's aid?" How she prayed that He speak that message to Uncle Joseph; wherever he might be.

She checked supper to insure its readiness to serve, upon Frank's arrival. She once again appraised the table settings, and then stole away to pray. Fifteen minutes passed before she could utter a comprehensible sentence. She hadn't prayed with such fervency or under such heartache since Frank's near fatal tragedy three years ago. The groaning barely resembled her voice. For every plea she made, an uninvited pessimistic thought raced to counter her hope. Soon she was propelled into a form of spiritual warfare she had only heard others preach about or retell. Never before had she so vehemently cried out threats against the powers of darkness. Nor had she, theretofore, called out so assuredly to God her promises to submit to His perfect will.

"Hey, where are you?" Frank's voice resounded, distracting Sherri from her prayer. She hadn't heard him come home.

"In here," she called.

"Sher, you okay?" he asked gravely.

She wiped her swollen eyes and tear soaked cheeks with the lace of her pillowcase. "I'm all right." She sniffed as she rose from bedside. "I was just praying. Frank," she whimpered, "I wish you would let me know when you are going to be late. All I need now is for something to happen to you, too."

Holding her close and stroking her thick strawberry blonde hair, Frank whispered, "What happened, Sher? And to whom did it happen?"

"Go wash those cruddy hands and come eat," she said half laughing and half crying. Sherri disliked being seen weak or needy. She tried to always put on a strong front. Too often, she had been taken advantage of and mistreated when others saw that she could be hurt. Besides she is thirty years old now. Too old for vulnerability.

"Then, you'll tell me what is bothering you, right?"

"After supper."

As she placed the potpie, topped with fluffy biscuits, on the table Frank said in a tone of slight alarm, "I thought you were just frying burgers for supper tonight. Is someone special coming for dinner?" Sherri hadn't fixed chicken potpie since his birthday two years ago. "Are we celebrating something, or mourning?" he asked sarcastically.

"Someone special is already here for dinner," she teased, hugging his neck from behind and kissing his crown. With a few deliberate bounces to the refrigerator she reached in to retrieve his favorite dessert -- strawberry-drenched cheesecake.

"Sher," Frank asked nervously, "Did doctor Snyder call today with my test results?" He had seen the oncologist at the urging of his family physician. A series of tests were conducted to determine why his breathing had become labored in recent months.

"No, silly. Just enjoy the meal. Oh, I almost forgot. We did get a letter from his office today. It said that they found nothing to explain your laborious breathing. Dr. Snyder wants to run more tests."

Frank hissed. "No need to bother with it now. It has been cleared up for a week now. They should have run all the tests the last time. I'm not trying to make them rich."

"That does take another worry off me," she said softly.

"So then, what is troubling you?"

"I guess I'm just too moody."

"Sher, you don't weep that bitterly and pray so intensely that I can walk through the house without you hearing me unless there is something drastically wrong. You just as well spill the beans now," he demanded. "You're starting to annoy me."

A trickle of tears sneaked down her cheek in spite of her forced smile. "Just enjoy your supper. I'll explain it to you after you've eaten. You know how sentimental I can be, sometimes."

They engaged in little conversation while eating supper. Although Frank grunted his approval of the feast, Sherri could see the frustration building over her postponement of the news. If only she could find a way to present her cause without provoking an argument.

"Okay, Frank. I can't take this silent treatment. Let me get you a piece of cheesecake. Then I'll tell you what's on my mind." She tried to sound sweet but her voice betrayed her resentment.

"You can't expect me to act like all is well," he said angrily. "Am I suppose to put my mind on hold while you contemplate your next move? I can't enjoy dessert right now, Sher. Just get on with it."

If he intended for that remark to sting, it reached its mark. Sherri felt her heart sink. He had always loved her homemade potpies, and would give all he owned for her sumptuous strawberry cheesecake. Granny Short had often said that the way to a man's heart is through his stomach. Frank's delight over her cooking pretty well testified to Granny's adage.

"I don't even know where to begin," she cried.

"Start somewhere," he barked as though he didn't care about her obvious pain.

Sherri's hurt quickly mixed with anger. In an agitated shaky tone she replied, "It's about Uncle Joseph. I don't expect you to understand this, Frank, but I need to go to his aid. You can join me if you wish. Not that I expect you to care for anyone but yourself."

"How can I care for someone's situation when I don't even know what the situation is?" he shouted. They both paused to regain a measure of civility.

"Is he okay?" Frank asked in a strained but calmer voice.

"I don't know. I kind of doubt it, according to what Janet Pixler told me."

"Janet? When did you talk to *that* nosey gossip?" Frank could not be rightly accused of being fond of Janet.

"Telling the truth doesn't constitute gossip in *my* book," Sherri said angrily. "You can't stand her because she told me about that affair you had with Angela."

Frank's lips tightened into a thin white line and his eyes glinted with suppressed anger. "You're exactly right. I don't like that nib-nose. She needs to mind her own business. That little episode amounted to nothing. You and I had just had a huge fight and Angela just happened along. Still mad enough to spit nails I unloaded the whole story on her. She showed me sympathy and…"

"I'm sure she did," Sherri said sarcastically.

Frank threw his hands up in surrender. "Okay. Get on with Janet's news report."

"She called me this afternoon. You know how Janet keeps up with the tittle-tattle around Morgantown."

"Amen to that."

"Can you just hold your criticism until I'm finished?" Sherri snipped. "She said that Uncle Joseph lost his position as pastor and evidently the whole town has pretty well forced him into homelessness. It's a long story. I just need to try to help him, Frank. If I can even find him."

"That's about a four hour drive one way from Youngstown. You can't be running back and forth to West Virginia on a regular basis. We can't afford that. What could you accomplish with no time left in the day since you'd be traveling eight hours? And you certainly are not taking my truck."

"See what I mean?" she retorted. "You're already making excuses. What? Have you forgotten all that Uncle Joseph sacrificed for us a few years back? God knows that your family couldn't be bothered with our problems."

"Sher, settle down. We'll do what we can. But you know we're limited here. I haven't forgotten the sacrifices he made in our behalf. But we have to be realistic. I don't mean to sound unthankful. But what has his predicament got to do with us?"

"I tell you what. You sit here on your sorry butt and don't worry yourself with any of this." Her fury begging to be unleashed, she noisily began cleaning off the table and straightening the kitchen. "It has nothing to do with you, Frank. Just crawl back into your cozy little shell. I'll let you know when it's safe to come out."

"That's your problem, Sher, you always blow up. Go ahead—now is when you stomp off, pouting. You've already begun your insults. Just as well stomp like you always do, to finish your fit." Rising angrily from the table, Frank jerked open the back door and slammed it shut behind him. "Thanks for the lovely meal," he bellowed, his voice penetrating the closed door.

She banged about the kitchen a few minutes then broke down in mournful groaning. "Why do I always make things worse? I've got to get control of this stupid temper. I hate this emotional roller coaster. Good job, Sher. You really accomplished a lot; didn't you?"

Pastor Richards had warned her on a couple occasions that she would run Frank off with her angry outbursts. "How about Frank's inhospitality," she had countered during one such conversation.

"You had better get a grip on that tongue, young lady," the pastor had admonished, altogether dismissing her countercharge.

Even Janet once suggested that her poisonous tongue might have contributed to Frank's turning to Angela.

"Ah," she mumbled, "maybe that is why Frank is so indifferent to Uncle Joseph's troubles… Angela."

Every time that memory surfaced Sherri felt renewed rage toward Angela. The foul treatment she had dished out to Joseph further fueled the resentment.

Frank returned to the house two hours later. Sherri knew instantly where he had been. His navy blue work pants and the light blue work shirt were covered with sawdust. Until recently, the small wood shop out back served as Frank's refuge. Sherri seldom entered that part of his private world. The smell of fresh cut wood and the stinging odor of thinners, sealers, and lacquers repelled her like Raid fends off pests.

The buzzing of power tools could usually be heard when Frank practiced his woodcrafts hobby. Not this time. Sherri had been too deep in thought to notice. Frank had once declared, "she can daydream through a bombing, only to wake up and wonder what happened to the neighborhood."

"Frank," Sherri pleaded from the living room couch, "can we talk?"

"Why? Have you thought of some new insults that won't wait until our next bout?" he yelled defensively.

Sherri held her peace as she contemplated Frank's remark. She hated being like her mother—verbally cutting Frank like her mother always cut at her and Dad.

Frank entered the living room with a tall glass of water in hand and plopped into his broken-down recliner. "Go ahead, I'm ready for the next round of incoming," he snarled. That's what Uncle Joseph used to call Sherri's tongue-lashings—paralleling it with the mortar fire in combat.

"Frank," she said tenderly, "I'm thinking about asking Pastor Richards if he would be able to give us some marriage counseling…"

"I don't have the problem," he snarled matter-of-factly, avoiding eye contact. "You have the problem. I just happen to be married to the *problem*."

"Okay," she said with deliberate calm. "I think I need to get counseling. I just want you to know I don't intend to attack you like I do. Frank, I love you." Genuine remorse gripped at her throat. "Mom always talked sharp like that and I really detested it." Her eyes ran like open faucets. "I can't even stand myself anymore… I feel like I'm losing my mind. I know God has forgiven all my sins but it seems like He has deserted me, leaving me with this disgusting bitterness. I have no meaningful purpose for my life."

"Maybe it's me, Sher. I really don't think I'll ever measure up to your expectations."

"It's not you. You don't deserve the brunt of my anger. I just can't seem to get control." An image of her as Alice Lance drove needles through Sherri's being.

"Sher, if you want to ask Pastor Richards for help I'll consider going with you. I'm not crazy about it, but I'll go."

"No, I think I need to get help on a personal level," she said reflectively as she looked beyond Frank and through the outside wall, to a distant time and place.

They shared apologies and sat talking about things in general—something they hadn't done for several months. They often spoke politely to one another but without a sense of closeness. They argued more than either thought any couple should, especially a Christian couple.

Her resolve to go to Uncle Joseph's aid would not be squelched. Carefully choosing her words, she pressed on. "Frank, I really feel strongly about taking up the battle against Uncle Joseph's adversaries."

He rolled his eyes toward the ceiling and blew air.

Fighting against the urge to tell him how childish he'd become, she said, "I really would like to have your blessing."

"I don't know that I can agree to such a harebrain idea. I'll have to think about it."

"Meanwhile, maybe we can get marriage counseling."

His jaws tightened as he glared at her. "You get us an appointment," he sternly replied. "If the counselor doesn't convince me that it's worth the effort—during the first meeting—I reserve the option to discontinue counseling."

"So, you *will* go with me?"

"What did I just say, Sher? If you're going to be demanding about it I'll not go at all." He then bounded to his feet and marched out the front door.

CHAPTER TWO

Monday, April 23, 1979

"Hi, I'm Joshua McCormick," the counselor said enthusiastically. "You two must be the Mosleys." He met the description given by Pastor Richards. He exhibited peculiarly personable warmth, almost belying his physical stature and the commanding voice.

The office had a homey feeling about it. Reverend McCormick motioned for them to be seated on a small couch as he eased himself into a matching ocean blue upholstered recliner. The furniture showed signs of long or frequent use. A large window at the westward wall ushered in the bright evening sun, illuminating the décor of Christian themes and light oak wood furnishings. The smell of fresh peaches soothed the senses.

"Thanks for seeing us so soon, Reverend," Sherri said with a forced smile.

"That's Brother, Josh, or Brother Josh. Drop the reverend; it's too formal for me. Pastor Richards explained a little about your need but I'd like for you two to tell me what it is you wish to gain from Christian counseling. But first let's pray." He apparently had a schedule to keep, and the Mosleys were fifteen minutes late for the appointment.

Sherri expected Frank to refuse to hold hands in a circle of prayer as Brother Josh reached for each of their hands. He cooperated though he hesitated at first. Frank, on several occasions, had voiced his discomfort with such close contact and he often griped to Sherri about such things. Josh led in prayer and closed with the familiar, "in Jesus' name."

"Frank," the counselor said, "why don't you begin by stating why we are here?"

"Because Sherri thinks we need it," he said with a nervous laugh.

"What do *you* think?" Josh asked courteously.

"I don't think we need help. She just needs to lighten up a bit."

"How so? What does 'lighten up' mean?"

Frank folded his arms across his chest and replied, "Every thing is drama with her. She consistently makes mountains out of mole hills."

Sherri jerked her body toward him and started to correct him, but cut herself short, realizing he intended to ensnare her.

"For instance?" Josh invited.

"Oh, I don't know… Just everything."

Josh looked Frank squarely in the eyes and said, "If we are going to make progress you'll need to be more specific and less evasive."

Sherri felt her body stiffen. She appreciated Brother Josh's discernment, but she knew all too well Frank's propensity toward avoiding such confrontation and taking his frustration out on her when they were alone.

"Okay," Frank growled. "Like our most recent argument. She got a call from her nosey, gossiping friend from back home. Now, she wants to go off gallivanting to who-knows-where. And based on nothing more than hearsay."

Sherri snarled, "First of all, Frank, it isn't mere gossip. Janet's information came from published sources and from people, by virtue of their positions, who are in the know." She then turned toward Josh. "Ask him to tell why he doesn't like Janet?"

Frank stared threateningly at her. "Maybe you better back off while you're ahead, Sher."

She met his glare with a determined gaze into his fiery eyes. "I know this is shocking news to you, Frank, but you no longer scare me. You just as well retract your horns."

"Whoa," Josh commanded. "Both of you take a deep breath and

look at me… For the time being, I want you to refrain from addressing one another. And don't interrupt each other in my counseling sessions." He rose from his chair and walked briskly to his desk and grabbed a set of papers from the lower right drawer. Handing Sherri and Frank each a copy, he said, "Before we go any further, let me introduce these biblical communication guidelines."

Frank's jaw muscles throbbed as Josh read aloud each of the ten items.

"Now, I don't expect you to grasp all ten guidelines, immediately. But I will expect you to make an honest effort to incorporate them, item by item, into your conversation with one another." He paused as he looked questioningly at Sherri and then Frank. "Are you both willing to adopt these guidelines as a personal goal?"

"I'm willing," said Sherri.

Frank slumped back and proclaimed, "She's the one who needs to learn how to properly communicate. I think I do pretty well at it."

Josh pressed him, "But are you willing to accept these as goals?"

"Yeah. But I already practice them," Frank answered conceitedly.

Josh said, "Sherri, it is apparent that Frank, for the moment, can't humble himself to accommodate us. Let me encourage you to do right—regardless of the insincerity of others."

"Thanks, Brother Josh. I'll do my best." She found it refreshing that Josh saw through Frank's façade—unlike Pastor Richards who seemed to always take Frank's side, reproving her without regard for her views or convictions.

Frank sat forward on the couch and defensively remarked, "I suppose you think Sherri is 'Little Miss Innocent'."

Before Josh could reply, Sherri countered, "I know I need help; that's primarily why we sought your counsel." Holding the Communication Guidelines sheet in front of her, she said, "I find myself lacking in many of these. But I will not let Frank think he has them right either."

Josh asked, "Frank, am I reading you right? Do you think you need no personal improvement or character building?"

"I didn't say I'm perfect. I do know that I don't need counseling." He rose angrily and threw his copy of the Communication Guidelines onto the couch beside Sherri. "I'll wait in the truck. Maybe Brother Josh can help *you* get your act together before it is too late."

Josh's face reddened and his eyes tightened. "Frank, sit back down and try to not behave like a spoiled rebellious teenager."

"Okay," he snarled, as he plopped onto the couch, and swung his right foot atop his left knee. "Let's see you work your magic, preacher. You'll soon see that she is not the cooperative sweetheart she'd have you believe her to be."

"I think she has already admitted her faults in a commendable manner." He shifted in his seat and rubbed his forehead. "Let's make another attempt at understanding what prompted the two of you to seek counseling."

Frank flopped his right foot on the floor and shifted toward Sherri. "Last week, I came home late from work. I knew she had something up her sleeve when I realized she'd fixed one of my favorite dishes and my favorite dessert."

Appalled at his condescending attitude, Sherri peered into his eyes, with an angry squint. Suddenly, her eyes widened. "Oh, my! I just realized how conniving that must have seemed... Oh, Frank, I'm sorry. I guess that must have been insulting to you. But I had no intentions of offending you."

Frank offered an arrogant smirk, but said nothing.

"Sherri," Josh asked, "what prompted you to prepare this special meal?"

She recounted the phone conversation that impelled her to urgently strategize to gain Frank's approval of her intended quest.

Frank sneered, "See what I'm up against? When she wants to manipulate me she goes all out to be nice. Ask her when she last cooked a special meal for me."

Through taut lips, Sherri ordered, "Shut up, Frank, and let Brother Josh conduct the counseling session." She quickly converted her contorted facial expression to a controlled menacing grin, and suggested, "Ask Frank when he ever deserved to be pampered and catered to."

Frank sat motionless, grinning victoriously.

"I hope you both are satisfied, now that you've wounded one another," Josh said firmly. "Should I sit on the sidelines while you each go for the kill?"

Frank threw up his hands in surrender. "I guess you can see why we need your advice or guidance or something."

"I'm sorry, Brother Josh," Sherri meekly offered.

"I think you two need to apologize to *each other*. Don't you?"

Sherri inhaled deeply and turned toward Frank. Beholding his triumphant smirk nearly dissuaded her, but she would nevertheless rise to the occasion. "I'm sorry, Frank. Please forgive me."

His smirk widened into a less condescending smile. "Me too, Sher. I'll trade you, forgiveness for forgiveness."

Caught off-guard by the uncharacteristic humility, she stammered, "Uh…Yeah… Um… Okay." Could his considerateness be some sort of ploy?

"Maybe Brother Josh can give us some direction concerning your uncle's situation."

Josh replied, "No disrespect intended, but I think we need to deal with *your* problems before taking on those of relatives."

He spoke too lovingly for Sherri to take offence to it.

"Well," Frank politely sighed, "her uncle's predicament is what actually brought our need for counseling to light for us both."

"Really? Maybe we *should* discuss this."

"I guess it wouldn't hurt to talk about it," Sherri muttered. "But I don't see how it is going to help Uncle Joseph any."

Josh paused as if to reflect on what Sherri said. "I don't either, Sherri. But I suspect, from what Frank said, it is the straw that nearly broke the camel's back. Would you agree with that analysis?"

"Yes. But only because Frank doesn't seem to care about Uncle Joseph's plight," she said with a tone of resentment.

"Frank, how do you answer that statement? Now be mindful of our purpose here and politely correct it if it is a misrepresentation or misinterpretation of fact. If it has merit, attempt to explain yourself to Sherri."

Frank fidgeted in his seat and focused on a spot on the carpet in an apparent effort to come up with the right words. "I don't know," he said with a blow of air. "Maybe we should just leave it be and go on to what you had in mind, Brother Josh."

"That's just it," Sherri scorned, "you can't admit that you're selfish. And you expect me to be like you. I'm not like you, Frank." Sherri's face reddened. She leaped from her seat and stomped to the door.

"Sherri, sit back down and hold your tongue a minute," Josh commanded.

She slunk into her seat, sulking.

"I tell you what," Josh announced, "let's pray and ask God for patience and invite the Holy Spirit to take control of the situation." He bowed his head not waiting for a reply from either of them.

Josh prayed for the fruit of the Spirit to be developed in the hearts of the two. He specifically asked the Lord to help Sherri with her apparent need for temperance.

Incensed, Sherri wanted desperately to interrupt Josh's prayer. How dare he single her out in his prayer! Why is it always her fault? What did this preacher think? That Frank is flawless?

Without warning, the Holy Spirit washed over her. "Heavenly Father," she said so intensely that Josh paused, "I don't handle conviction so well. Please, help me to open my heart to the fruit of the Holy Spirit." She sobbed heavily as she tried to continue her audible prayer, unconcerned that she confessed in the presence of others. Soon, peace engulfed her, rendering her speechless. The room fell silent. Finally, she promised God that she would no longer live in the flesh, asking for His help to fulfill her vow.

After they prayed, Sherri and Frank both sat still and hushed. They both stared off in deep thought until Josh interrupted.

"I hate to close this session right now," Josh apologized, looking at the wall clock. Sherri followed Josh's glance to the timepiece. At the tips of the minute and hour hands, miniature, gold, praying hands glistened from the clock's soft perimeter lights. A message printed in white writing reminded, "...Pray without ceasing."

"I'm a few minutes late already for a board meeting at the church."

"We'll be on time from now on," said Sherri. Looking apologetically at Frank, she said, "I'm sorry, Frank. I really mean it." Taking his hand she promised to work on controlling her temper and her tongue.

Frank caressed her more meaningfully than he had in several months. He stood and reached to shake Josh's hand, apologizing for being late and for causing him to be late for the meeting at church. "So, when are we to return for our next session?"

"Same time, in exactly two weeks. Then we'll take up the matter of Uncle Joseph. I'll expect you both to put yourselves wholly into the counseling process. Meanwhile, your homework assignment is to read and study the various scriptures concerning your respective roles as husband and wife. I want each of you to keep a notebook. Record, in your own words, what those scripture references specifically say to you."

Sherri surveyed Frank's face to determine his mood. He hadn't said much since they left the counselor's office. No tension showed on his husky face with its strong square chin. He wore neither a frown nor a grin as he drove quietly toward home. She seldom saw Frank so expressionless. Married ten years and still she could not read him at times. She stared more noticeably, unintentionally unnerving him.

"What?" he asked dryly.

"I didn't say anything."

"No, but you sure are piercing my soul with that questioning look of yours," he snarled.

"I'm wondering what kind of mood you're in," she replied softly. "I'm not sure how to take you half the time. Especially, these past several months."

"What is that supposed to mean?" he asked defensively.

Suspecting she may be walking on proverbial eggshells, Sherri gave herself time to think what she should say instead of speaking as quickly as usual. She certainly didn't want to destroy what progress they might have made.

"I really appreciate the way you acted in the counselor's office,

Frank." Her compliment, spoken more sincerely than she knew herself to be capable of in recent months, surprised Frank as much as it pleased her.

"An unsolicited compliment?" he asked sarcastically, flashing his dimpled smile while keeping his eyes on the road.

"I guess that is something else I need to work on," she replied reflectively. "We use to compliment each other a lot. What happened to us, Frank?"

"Remember how your uncle used to tease us about being so mushy," he mused. "'You two are going to turn to mush.'"

She remembered all right. She also recalled the rest of the tease that proved to be somewhat prophetic. "Trouble with mush," Uncle Joseph would add, "is that unless it is well sweetened, kept warm, and stirred frequently, it will become sour, stiff, and unappealing."

"Frank, what did you think of Reverend McCormick?"

"I don't know. He seems to be pretty good at what he does." He paused as if in deep thought.

Sherri waited patiently for him to continue his remarks.

"I'm not sure," he said slowly, "but I don't think this counseling thing is for me."

She felt something pull her heart to her stomach. "I thought, from the way you responded to it—especially those last few minutes—you were getting something out of it." Wearing her hurt like a weather-beaten ornament, she stared out her side window to hide the tears that burned mercilessly.

"Maybe our marriage is beyond repair, Sher."

Frank's matter-of-factness drove the pain deeper. An emotional whirlpool overcame her, paralyzing her for the remaining twenty-minute drive home. How could he be so calm about such a thing? How could he be so untouched by such a statement? Surely, she hadn't done *that* badly. Could he have slipped into infidelity again? Why else would he speak so unfeelingly about their marriage?

Sherri hadn't realized they were home until Frank barked, "Are you going to sit there all day? Or are you coming in?"

She followed him into the house and remained standing as he plopped triumphantly into his recliner. "What is your problem?" she demanded, her voice shaking from the dual emotions of anger and hurt.

He coldly replied, "I just don't care anymore, Sher. I think I want out."

"You want out," she screamed. "Then, get out. I'm tired of walking on thin ice around here. I love you, Frank, but I will not beg you to stay where you are so obviously unhappy."

Stumbling numbly to the bedroom, Sherri threw herself onto the bed, weeping. She heard the slamming of the front door and then the rush of the truck engine. "Oh, God," she cried, "What am I to do?"

Waking fifty minutes later she felt rested and clear-headed. She reasoned that she'd be free to search for Uncle Joseph without having to appease Frank at the same time. She grabbed her Bible from the nightstand. Propping her head in the palm of her left hand she leafed through its concordance to find the scripture advice about the unbelieving, departing spouse. But Frank professed Christ. How God had blessed them since Uncle Joseph led them to Christ! How could they have gotten so far from His will? "There it is," she exclaimed. "But if the unbelieving depart, let him depart…But God hath called us to peace."

She labored to make sense of her failed efforts to maintain peace in their marriage. She had suppressed her own friendly disposition in hopes of dissuading Frank's frequent unfounded accusations that she invites flirtation from other men. Even relationships with other young women had become targets of Frank's ridicule. He had so vehemently opposed her activities with the women's fellowship group at church she'd too often made excuses for not participating and they all gradually drifted from her.

"I refuse to remain in this prison," she declared. Bouncing from the bed she said, "Frank Mosley, you will *not* cut me off from the only two people who've ever cared a hoot about me."

CHAPTER THREE

Tuesday, April 24, 1979

"Oh come on, Janet, answer the phone," Sherri commanded.

"Hello," Janet answered breathlessly.

"Janet?"

"Yeah. Sherri?"

"You sound winded."

"Just came in the door from work," Janet said excitedly. "I'd planned to call you as soon as I got home. You aren't going to believe who I saw this morning near the courthouse square in Morgantown."

She choked backed the tears as she guessed, "Uncle Joseph?"

"Sit down," Janet pleaded. "I have good news, in that I know he is at least alive and still in the area." Her voice became more solemn. "But, I almost didn't recognize him. If it weren't for the distinctive limp from his combat injury I probably would not have even noticed him."

"Is he okay? Are you sure it was him?"

"His curly red hair is about shoulder length and unkempt now, but I knew him. He even has a scraggly beard; red, as you might expect. You know how neat and well groomed he always kept himself. It is hard to believe, but I know who I saw."

"Did you talk to him?"

"No. I dropped off a neighbor downtown on my way to work this morning. I thought about parking and catching up with him. But you know how hard it is to find a parking place along High Street. I made another trip around the block and he had already gone out of sight."

"Janet, is the offer still open for me to stay with you if and when I need to, while I try to help Uncle Joseph?"

"Of course. Are you finally going to come? I'll even help what little I can."

"Frank and I had another round yesterday on the way home from a counseling session. When we got home, he told me that he wants out of the marriage."

"Sherri," Janet politely advised, "You know if Uncle Joseph knew you were abandoning your marriage just to come to his aid, he would not be pleased."

"I'm not abandoning my marriage," Sherri retorted. "Don't start acting like Frank."

"Easy, girl. I'm on your side."

"I'm sorry, Janet. This whole mess is driving me crazier than two tomcats with their tails tied together."

"Have you told Frank you were coming?"

"Sort of. He didn't even come home last night. I haven't heard from him all day. I suppose he went to work this morning. He is so double-minded!"

Janet blurted a laugh and explained, "It is funny that you should say that. You know I don't attend church. But just the other day I recalled a sermon I heard your uncle preach. A few years ago he appeared as a guest speaker on a local TV program. He read from the Bible that a double-minded man is unstable in all his ways. I can still see him reeling his body—crippled leg and all—in illustration."

"That must have made an impression on you for you to remember it yet."

"Well, that is when I had reached my wits end over James."

"Oh, yeah, that two timing hypocrite from Fairmont."

"You got that right. Listen, when are you coming?"

"I don't really know," Sherri said with a heavy sigh. "But I have made up my mind that I am going to do this with *or* without Frank. Janet, I love him and want desperately to keep this marriage together, but I cannot forsake Uncle Joseph just because of Frank's heartlessness. I'll keep in touch and let you know something soon."

"Okay. Meanwhile, I'll do what little snooping I can for you and see if I can't make contact with Uncle Joseph."

"He always loved being Uncle Joseph to everyone. He'd be pleased to know that you still call him that."

"I know. He is such a good person. Look, I've got to go. Call me as soon as you know what you are going to do."

"Okay, and thanks, Janet. God bless you."

"You too. Bye."

Sherri turned the kitchen radio on and tuned into a Christian station. The first song, about a blind man tapping along and someone saying to him, "Friend, I feel sorry for you," and the blind man's reply that in heaven he'll "see just like you," captivated her. When they sang of the cripple dragging his feet down the street and his reply that he'd walk in Hallelujah Square, she drifted off to Morgantown.

The vision of Uncle Joseph, dirty and dressed in rags, squeezed her heart until she felt faint. She imagined his once five foot eleven inch frame with thick broad shoulders now thin and stooped. His left leg dragged behind his laboring skeleton.

The slow, warm leaking of her eyes seemed almost soothing. Her heart then lightened with the vision of Uncle Joseph walking down a glittering golden street past a square filled with sparkling jewels. His new body straight, he strutted gleefully without even a hint of a limp. The radiance of his face, when he shared his faith on earth, now reflected against each precious stone as he passed.

"Heavenly Father," she whispered, "please keep Uncle Joseph safe and well. Remind him of your promises. Help me to keep the faith and to trust that all things work for good to those that love you and are called according to your purpose. In Jesus' name I pray. Amen."

A whispering spring breeze wafted from the open front window drying the salty tears from Sherri's face. The thin lacy white curtains danced gently, resting occasionally against the window screen, and then resuming their performance. Street traffic hummed by reverently. Distant voices of children at play floated by like rhythmic lullabies.

Soon she drifted off to dreamless, restful sleep.

Sherri jerked from her nap on the couch at the sound of slamming metal. Her stomach knotted when she saw Frank step onto the front porch.

He clumsily opened the screen door and staggered in. "You still here?" he roared, slurring his speech.

She sprang to her feet in anticipation of Frank's wrath. He hadn't drunk since his conversion three years ago. A distinct sour brew, carried by a faint draft, attacked her nostrils. Sucked into the dark memory of an abusive drunken husband, she felt adrenalin, like an electrical shock, shoot through her.

Frank lurched toward her, poked his finger in her face, and then drew back with an open hand to slap her.

She locked onto his wrist with her right hand and brought her left hand to assist in a self-defense move that surprised them both. Instantly she spun him around, hurling him facedown to the floor, and followed through with a pin to the linoleum.

"Don't ever think you can get by with knocking me around again," she growled through gritted teeth.

Frank yelped like a whipped pup. The pain forced involuntary pleading. "Okay, Sher. Ah! Okay, let go."

"I'll let you up, Frank," Sherri promised. "But if you make one wrong move, I'll break your arm next time." She wrestled with the temptation to do serious harm while he remained under her control. A sense of appreciation for Uncle Joseph's self-defense instruction from years gone by sent chills up her spine.

Frank rose slowly and swaggered to his recliner, shock still registering on his reddened face.

She stared searchingly at him as he slumped into his recliner across from her. His bloodshot eyes glared at her in disdain.

"You know what?" he gruffly announced, "I want you to leave. I've talked it over with some of my friends and family, and they don't like you either."

Sherri desperately struggled to suppress the volcanic aching in her soul. With a cry of agony she asked, "Why are you doing this? I've tried my best lately to become a better wife to you." She wanted to say more but refrained, hoping to calm the inner convulsions.

"And don't start bawling," he snarled. "I'll be back in a couple days and I want you gone. It's over, Sher. Just get out."

Frank wiggled to his feet and staggered to the door. Turning once more toward Sherri he slurred, "Go find that hotheaded bum uncle of yours and give my regards to Angela." He pushed open the screen door and wobbled to his pickup truck.

She sat petrified for several minutes trying to convince herself that she'd soon wake from a nightmare to find all is well. Even the cross-breeze that had helped quiet her spirit, now forsook her.

"Almost there," Sherri sleepily said to herself. The mountain road snaked upward from State Route 7, getting progressively steeper. How she loved this part of God's creation! The trees had already started to leaf at the base of the mountain. She swerved and braked to avoid running over a young raccoon scampering across the road in a sharp turn of the Summers' School Road.

Besides the raccoon, her headlights lit upon five deer and a lone skunk in her ascent to Janet's home. No wonder they call this wild, wonderful, West Virginia. She'd almost forgotten how much she loved God's creatures. Well, except the likes of polecats.

She pulled onto the narrow Nicholson Loop. Soon she'd be at Murray Road and Janet's house. The last time Sherri visited Janet—two years ago—she had to wait two hours while a dozer cleared the two feet of late-winter snow from the Loop to Janet's farm. The "Mountain" had received two feet of snow, with six-foot drifts, while only a few inches lay on the ground in Morgantown, a mere seven miles away.

Sherri eased the rental car next to Janet's Jeep CJ and quickly shut off her headlights. Should she wake her or just sleep in the car until morning light? She slowly exited the vehicle to stretch and enjoy the view. Nicholson Loop and many of its side roads offered an awesome overlook of the entire Morgantown area and even into southwestern Pennsylvania. The soft distant runway lights of the municipal airport atop a lower hill at the edge of town quietly cooed for her notice. The cool mountain breeze delicately massaged her face. Even the air here seemed kinder. Maybe she did the right thing after all.

The sudden flash from spotlights on the house startled her. An undistinguishable face peered through the corner of a curtain and then disappeared just when Sherri thought to wave. She stood in the illumination wondering what delayed Janet.

The front door opened abruptly and Janet called, "Scare me half to death, why don't you! Get in here, girl."

Sherri raced to Janet's open arms, reminiscent of a lost child scurrying to her rescuing mother.

Embracing her, Janet exclaimed, "My goodness, Sherri, you are shaking like a stubborn leaf in a late fall wind storm."

Sherri wept uncontrollably as Janet ushered her to a living room chair.

"Sit here while I get us a glass of Pepsi. It's okay now. You're home."

The sincerity of Janet's comments propelled Sherri into more sobbing. She couldn't remember when she last felt so accepted. Fighting back the self-pity, she sniffled, "You know what? I don't think I have ever felt at home in Ohio. There is just no place like home. I can't count the times I wished I could do like Dorothy and just click my heels and declare myself 'home.'"

"Well, I'm sure happy to see you," Janet said gleefully. "Of course, I would have straightened the place up a bit if I knew you were coming so soon."

"Then, it wouldn't have that homey feeling. What is a home without a little lived-in appearance?"

"Lived-in is one thing, but clutter of neglect is quite another."

Sherri giggled, "You are such a neat freak. I can still hear your mother calling you Jumping Janet. Or my favorite, Janitor Janet."

"Speaking of Mom; I'm so appreciative for the wonderful funeral service Uncle Joseph did for my parents. They really loved him and would have been so proud. My dad thought nobody could measure up to Joseph Short. 'Not like those stiff shirts and self-righteous boasters I grew up around,' he'd bellow."

"Did they ever make an arrest for the hit and run?"

"They found the car that hit them. But it had been reported stolen. Whoever ditched it must have taken great pains to remove all fingerprints. The trooper who investigated the case said that they apparently even vacuumed the car and washed it thoroughly inside and outside." Janet wiped a lone tear and whispered, "Eighteen months and still no hard clues."

Sherri admired Janet's even temper when talking about such tragedies. Why couldn't she be so steady?

"My goodness," Sherri exclaimed, "we've been yapping for three hours. It's three in the morning. And you have to be at work in a few hours."

"Relax, girl. I'll just call in and take a day off."

"You can do that without getting into trouble?"

"Sure," Janet teased, "they'll understand when I tell them that some Buckeye kept me up too late, reminding me of the silly things we use to do."

"I tried calling you but you must not have been home. I couldn't stay another night in *Frank's house*, since he told me to get out."

"He didn't?" Janet gasped.

"He did. He gave me two days to get out and he left to go who-knows-where. So I packed up my stuff and called a car rental dealer. They even brought the car to the door. I loaded up, grabbed my secret savings and skedaddled."

Yawning, Janet suggested they get to bed and pick up where they left off when they wake.

CHAPTER FOUR

Wednesday, April 25, 1979

"Hello," Janet said after the third ring.

Sherri looked at the bedside clock. Eight a.m. and she could easily sleep another hour.

"Yea, she's here," Sherri heard Janet say sarcastically. "But she's asleep. Do you want to leave a message?"

Sherri rushed to the living room to receive the call. She knew it had to be Frank. She reached and Janet waved her off with a let-me-handle-this look.

"Let's get something straight here," Janet said angrily. "First off, you don't order me to do anything. Secondly, this is my phone. I'll hand it to whomever I wish and only as I wish, Mr. Mosley. Now talk to me like you have a little sense or end the conversation."

Sherri's heart raced as she tried to determine how she should feel. On one hand she felt victorious, leaving without saying good-bye. Yet she longed for the love she and Frank once knew—apparently a desire not shared by him.

"Let me see if she is awake and if she wants to talk to you," Janet said. Holding her hand over the mouthpiece, she asked Sherri if she wanted to talk to him. "If not, I'll tell him you will call him when you're ready to talk."

Sherri took a deep breath and reached for the receiver. "Hello," she squeaked and then cleared her throat. She hated how Frank could make her choke up with uncertainty.

"It didn't take you long to leave. Couldn't wait to get out of my life, huh?" Frank's uncanny way of turning things around often made her feel like the villain.

"In case you don't remember your drunken display of disgust with me," Sherri politely scolded, "let me fill you in."

"I was angry and drunk, Sher. You know I didn't mean for you to leave."

She reminded herself that she must not let him make her feel guilty for *his* actions. "Frank," she said with pretend composure, "Until you get over whatever the problem is, I'll abide by your decision for me to leave. After all, I have to go find that hotheaded bum uncle of mine. Remember?"

"Hey, Sher, that was the booze talking," Frank barked.

"No, Frank. You did the talking with the *help* of Satan's brew." She felt a rush of confidence she seldom experienced when arguing with him. She nearly spit from an explosive giggle at Janet rubbing her eyes while acting out a baby's whining.

"You think something is funny, do you?" Frank yelled. "I'll show you funny. You aren't the only fish in the sea."

Sherri slowly hung the phone on its cradle. "I guess he didn't appreciate my sense of humor. Or yours." Her voice crackled with mixed emotion.

"Sorry. I just couldn't help it. I'm mad at him for treating my friend so disrespectfully."

"You have no blame in this troubled relationship," Sherri explained. "Frank has been looking for someone to open the corral gate so he could run wild. I guess it just bothers me that I am not woman enough to tame him, or at least not for long."

"I thought he got saved when you did?" Janet questioned. "If Jesus can't change him, what makes you think you will?"

"Oh, Janet, don't talk like that. Don't accuse God of not doing His part."

"I'm not accusing God. I am simply saying that if he is no more devoted to the Lord than that, you'll not convince him to change. Nor will any other woman."

"I can't claim absolute innocence in our relationship either," Sherri said, staring at the floor. "I've had a difficult time controlling my temper and there were times when I cut Frank deeply with my *Alice Lance* tongue."

"How *is* your mother?"

"I don't really know," Sherri said, misty-eyed. "She has never forgiven me for witnessing in Uncle Joseph's defense back in 1969. She is convinced that her baby brother killed Spike Cottrell. Even she and Daddy have had problems over her insistence of Uncle Joseph's guilt."

"Why would she be so headstrong against her own brother?"

"She claims that since Uncle Joseph suffers such hellish nightmares from his experiences in Vietnam he is capable of most anything. Especially since he has a bad temper. Like *she* is void of any faults!" Sherri's muscles tightened. Her eyes burned with fury. "Let's talk about something more pleasant."

"Okay. How about some breakfast?" Janet walked to the kitchen as she motioned for Sherri to follow.

Sherri had often said that nobody could cook a good country meal like Granny Short except Janet Pixler. She felt renewed resentment at the remembrance of Uncle Joseph not getting to attend his own mother's funeral—lying in a military hospital trying to survive life-threatening combat wounds.

"Janet, how do I begin to find Uncle Joseph?"

"You start by eating a wholesome breakfast. Then we'll drive to town and check out the courthouse square. Some of the street-smart folk hang out there all day long."

"Yeah, like the winos," Sherri said snidely. "Oh, my, surely you don't think Uncle Joseph has stooped to drunkenness," she pondered.

"No. If there is one thing I am sure of, it is that he would never actually return to his former lifestyle. I know Joseph Short better than to suspect anything unrighteous of him. Sherri, you've got to lighten up a bit. You'll drive us both crazy."

Studying Janet frying bacon and eggs, she asked, "Have you ever given your heart to Jesus?"

Janet turned to stare out the sliding glass doors overlooking the lower hills. She seemed lost in thought.

She waited, hoping to hear an affirmative answer.

"I kind of lost the mood for Christianity when I caught James cheating on me." Janet's chin quivered and she returned her attention to the skillet.

"Janet, just because he proved to be unfaithful doesn't mean Jesus is unfaithful. We can't put our trust in *people*. They'll destroy what confidence we have in the Lord. I can assure you that God is not pleased with James' unfaithfulness toward Himself nor toward you."

"I know," Janet said shakily. "I just can't seem to activate that kind of faith. I know that it requires a full commitment to Christ. I'm just not ready for that."

"Maybe I can get you fixed up with Uncle Joseph when we get this mess straightened out." Sherri spoke jokingly but suddenly hoped for such a match.

"What about the unequally yoked thing I've heard preachers talk about?"

"Well, we will work on fixing that problem, before I play matchmaker."

"I know you are jesting, Sherri, but I have had a secret crush on Joseph since my high school years."

Sherri's mouth dropped open, and then formed an elfin grin. "I can't believe you have never told me this before." Possibilities raced through her mind.

Janet turned to face her. "What are you grinning so hard about?"

"I have been praying that God give me someone to help me in Uncle Joseph's behalf. Someone who would take up his cause as lovingly as I do."

"Don't be raising my hopes for romance. Joseph has never even slightly hinted that he had any interest in me. Only four years older than us and he always called me kid."

"Yeah, kid with a capitol 'K.'"

"What do you mean by that?"

"You have never noticed the affection in his calling you kid?"

"No. And I don't think it meant anything."

"Anyhow, I feel almost like I've been called by God to go to Uncle Joseph's aid. And I am sure glad that you are going to assist me."

"You are taking a bit for granted, aren't you?"

"Not at all," Sherri teased. "You said that you would do what you can to help me. And I happen to know that you can be taken at your word."

"Oh, you are good!" Janet shook the pancake turner toward Sherri and quipped, "Well, Sherlock, do I at least get an official investigator title?"

"Sure. Your title will be the same as mine—'called.'"

"Called? What kind of title is that?"

"Romans chapter eight and verse twenty eight promises that 'all things work together for good to them that love God, to them who are the called according to his purpose.'"

"I can hardly say that I am called of God to anything," Janet said hanging her head. "What does it really mean to love God, Sherri? I have heard people say that they love God but then I see them doing all kinds of sinful things. I couldn't do that. How *can* someone do that?"

"I don't know exactly who you are referring to, but some are just immature in their walk with the Lord. Others are just plain hypocrites. That's why we must follow Jesus and His Word, exclusively."

"I guess. Maybe someday I'll get saved. But not right now."

Sherri whispered, "Thank you, Lord. I'll wait for your leading to set the hook. Janet is so special to me. Help me win her for you."

"Do you think you are a special guest, young lady?" Janet teasingly snapped. "Set the table. The dishes are in the cabinet to the right and the glasses and cups are in the one on the left. The silverware you'll find in the drawer just to the right of the sink."

"I've never known you to be a mood-swinger before," said Janet. "You haven't said a word since we finished breakfast."

"More so now than before you called about Uncle Joseph's

problems," Sherri replied reflectively. "Janet, I'm really apprehensive about this whole thing. I haven't the slightest idea where to start or even how to start."

"You have already started. Just take one day at a time." She began singing "One Day at a Time".

Sherri joined in. She missed how they use to break into song to lift one another's spirits during their junior high and high school years. Janet seemed to know how to lighten her mood more than anyone she has ever known. She recalled how they sang their way through the anguish after learning of Uncle Joseph's critical wounding in a war neither of them understood.

Sherri's voice tapered off and Janet began another tune. "I've come too far to look back, my feet have walked through the valley, I've climbed mountains—crossed rivers; desert places I've known. But now I'm nearing the home shore. The redeemed are rejoicing…I've come too far to look back."

Sherri's heart floated like a fluffy breeze-borne down feather. "How do you know that song?"

"I only know the chorus. And I'm not sure I even have it right. I went to a homecoming service one afternoon, a few years ago, at Nicholson Chapel and heard a group sing it. I kind of felt strange when they sang it. I guess I wasn't the only one feeling the song. There were people throughout the church saying amen in emotion-choked voices. I've never seen so many crybabies in one place. I think *everyone* broke out the hankies and tissues."

"Well, it sure fits my life right now. I needed the reminder."

"I know. But I didn't know I stored it away like that," Janet exclaimed with eyes alight. "Just before they sang it, one of the women singers testified that she had lost her husband to another woman and a few months later, a teen-age son—killed by a drunk driver. She had subsequently suffered a nervous breakdown. She claimed the song as her resolve. Ah, Sherri! You should have heard her angelic voice. You would have surely thought it came right from Heaven."

"I suspect it did. Just when we think things are so terrible in our lives, God sends encouragement. Thanks, for listening to the Holy Spirit."

Janet sat motionless, dreamily staring out across the mountains.

Sherri dared not interrupt whatever might be happening between her and the Lord. A couple minutes passed before Janet announced that they better get busy or the day would be wasted on their chatter.

The courthouse square, with its old quaint floor of red brick rectangles, set in concrete, seemed too quiet to be a central open-air gathering place. The small trees and well-trimmed bushes offered an invitation to relax. The courthouse's old towering steeple housed a huge clock with a white face and long black hands that triggered the bell's toll. "How is that for punctuality?" Sherri asked. "You said we should get here about ten o'clock."

"True," Janet replied. "But I expected more people to be around here than these four. The problem is that they all appear to be waiting for the 10:15 buses. Hardly, the folks we need to talk to."

"Maybe they frequent the square enough to have seen Uncle Joseph, though."

"Maybe."

Janet approached an elderly man sitting on the front-most park bench.

Sherri admired her confidence.

"Excuse me sir." Janet pleaded, flashing her perfect gleaming smile. "My friend and I are looking for a man..."

"Well," the old gentleman teased, "You are in luck. I'm not only a man. I'm also widowed and available." He scooted over to make room for them. "Now who is this fortunate fellow you two beautiful flowers are searching for? Must be someone special."

"Sherri, you have Joseph's picture with you, don't you?"

"Yes." She pulled a small thin picture wallet from her jeans and flipped it open to the first photo. "Maybe you know this man. Have you seen him?"

"Is this Joey Short?" the man asked admiringly.

Sherri's heart leaped. "You know him? This is my uncle. We really need to find him."

"No offense intended, sweetheart, but you surely couldn't be a niece. You sure you aren't his sister? You look just like him."

"No. Most people think we are brother and sister. He is only four years older than Janet and me."

He searched Janet's face and replied, "Are you two sisters?"

"No, sir, better than sisters." Janet said. "How do you know Joseph?"

"By the way, my name is Clem Castleman," he said and reached to shake hands with Janet.

"I'm Janet Pixler. And this is Sherri Mosley."

"Joseph use to be my neighbor—until his ex-wife took him for everything and he moved out. I never did like that girl. I reckon you know Angela?"

"I'm afraid so," Sherri mumbled.

"So, you must live at Baker's Ridge," Janet inquired.

"Been there for forty years. And never had a better neighbor than Joey Short. How come you are looking for him? I mean, is he lost or something?" Clem smiled teasingly.

Sherri interjected, "Well, it seems our darling Angela has reentered his life and caused him more trouble and subsequently forced him into poverty and homelessness."

"I read in the newspaper that he had gotten in trouble again. But I figured it to be more unjustness being done him. I know this boy wouldn't hurt anyone unless provoked."

"You sound confident of that."

"Sure am." He stood and faced the girls. "One day, years ago—before Joey even started going to church—another neighbor threw a booze party. Several people were drinking and making a ruckus. One of the guys from Stanley's party came across the street and interrupted Joey from his grass cutting. My wife and I were weeding the flower garden in our front yard. Joey stopped the mower to see what the fella wanted. What a loud mouth jerk—this fella. Anyhow, he began deriding Joey, calling him a 'murdering menace to society' and 'a government-hired killer.'"

"Why do people have to be so evil?" Sherri asked through taut lips.

"Soon, two more drunken slobs from Stanley's crowd accompanied that jerk. Spike Cottrell, the big guy who started the trouble, told Joey that he should have been killed in Vietnam and that he didn't even deserve to breathe free air. Joey started his mower up and made an attempt to turn away. The big guy pushed Joey's back and then kicked his bad leg."

Sherri burned with vengeance. "I hope Uncle Joseph taught him a lesson."

"Well, he taught all of us a lesson that day."

"Really?" Janet piped with a look of anticipation.

"Sure did. He just caught his balance and proceeded to cut his grass. But the three of them kept shouting obscenities and insults at him. I called the state police and reported that a mob had gathered, assaulting an innocent neighbor. They sent a trooper to the scene. A sheriff's deputy came too."

"He should have kicked their butts before the law got there." Janet exclaimed.

"Well, he did. Joey started to go into his house to avoid any further confrontation, but one of the other young men ran to cut him off at the front door. I heard Joey order him to leave before things got ugly. The boy went to push Joey and Joey flipped him to the ground and had him in some kind of martial arts hold. Someone murdered Spike just a week later. I guess you know how they tried to frame Joey for the murder. Well, anyhow, while Joey held this first guy face down to the ground Spike charged at him.

"Joey spun around and kicked Spike in the chest and punched the third guy who had joined in on the attack. He knocked the third guy out with one punch. The first guy then, tried to tackle Joey but Joey kicked him in the head and put him to sleep for a while. Spike then had gotten up from the kick he received and pulled a big knife from his pocket. Joey ended up with the knife and held it at Spike's throat, warning him to get up and leave peacefully."

"So, then what happened?" Janet asked excitedly.

"Well, about that time the police got there. Not immediately recognizing Joey as the victim, they cuffed him and sat him in the back of the state police cruiser. When the smoke cleared I explained the whole event to the officers and they let Joey go. They asked if he wanted to press charges on these fellas. When I asked Joey why he took so much before whipping those guys he said that he needed to overcome a quick temper that had gotten him into too many fixes already."

Clem paused and glanced down at the bricks and dragged his right foot across them reflectively. "I think that is the only time I actually ever got peeved at Joey. I tried to get him to file charges on them. He refused, saying that sometimes you just have to allow people room to punish themselves with their own ignorance."

Janet proclaimed, "That's my… I mean; that's *our* Joseph."

Sherri's piercing rage nearly dissolved at Janet's forthrightness. How could she not have known that Janet had such strong feelings for Uncle Joseph?

A bus parked in front of the courthouse square and a couple of the other people got on. Clem announced that he had to go before he got left behind. "My number is in the phone directory. Clement Castleman. Call me if you learn of his whereabouts or if I can help in any way."

Janet looked around the square and then walked toward a man, who had lingered nearby, rapidly walking away at the north side of the square toward Walnut Street. "Hey, wait a minute, sir."

The tall skinny man, dressed in torn jeans and a gray wrinkled tee shirt, looked alarmed.

"Wait," Janet called again, picking up the pace.

Sherri followed, wondering what benefit she supposed there would be by talking with this man.

He slowly lowered his pillowcase of belongings to the ground and stood motionless and expressionless. A tattered brown leather belt looped through his worn jeans and hung half way down his thigh. Long knobby fingers stroked his several day-old beard as he croaked, "yes ma'am, can I help you?"

Sherri thrust the picture of Joseph toward the man. "We are trying to find this guy. Have you seen him?"

"I have to go. Sorry."

"No. Wait," Janet insisted. "You know him, *don't* you? Please, we are friends—not foes."

"Can't help you any, lady. Just leave me be." He grabbed his belongings and scurried off.

Sherri grasped Janet by the arm to stay her from following after him. "Don't scare the man, Janet. We'll probably see him again if we don't spook him."

"I guess you're right. I hate playing cat and mouse with people."

"Chill, girl."

"Now I know things are mixed up when *you* need to tell me to chill," Janet said with a slight giggle.

"At least we can assume that he is still around the area."

"I hope so, Sherri. Maybe this guy will let him know we're looking for him."

"Yeah. I think he heard every word of our conversation with Mr. Castleman. Maybe he'll pass the word."

"Let's walk around town and do some window shopping," Janet said. "Maybe I can unwind a bit. You have me as tense as a fishing line with a prize muskie refusing to be reeled in."

After spending the day in town, Sherri and Janet returned home to unload the rental car. Sherri marveled that she had been able to stuff so much into the car. She'd have to return to Youngstown to retrieve the rest of her belongings. Sometime. They dropped off the car and used the rest of the evening to plan their next steps to find Joseph and work on clearing his name.

"You've got my number at work," Janet said. "If you need me, call."

"Hopefully, I'll be able to handle most of this on my own. However, I may need your measure of confidence. I sure admire your nerve."

"Oh, quit. You are the bright and brave one."

"I always get too fired up instead of remaining calm but firm like you do. And I would never have approached that homeless guy as unreservedly as you did."

"I knew you were backing me," Janet teased.

"I think I'll take your copies of the *Scoop Weekly* to the bedroom and read the letters to the editor. Maybe something will stand out to give us some direction."

"Just don't lose them. I promised Jack I'd return them within a week or so. What reading that slop will do is get your blood boiling and you'll not get any sleep."

"Maybe so. I need to read them, sometime. I might as well get it over with."

"Good night then. See you in the morning."

Sherri bid Janet goodnight and grabbed the stack of newspapers from the floor. She gave thanks to Janet and to God that Janet had the mind to borrow them. Maybe she could get a better sense of the situation by reading the letters to the editor about Uncle Joseph's most recent legal battles. Perhaps she could find a supporter among the writers. Surely, there would be a sympathetic soul or two.

Janet's warning proved true. The more she read, the angrier she grew. Finally, she forced herself to lay aside the papers. "Well, Ellis Fenton," she threatened, "Maybe I'll deal with you first."

CHAPTER FIVE

Thursday, April 26, 1979

Sherri whipped Janet's robin-egg blue Oldsmobile into the packed-dirt parking space facing the building. The dingy red and brown brick building, housing the *Scoop Weekly* Publishing Company, pressed against the steep hillside. Except for the sign screwed onto the wall outside the shop, one would never expect the old former machine shop building to be occupied.

Wooden debris strewn about the property testified to the smutty weekly publication that focused on defaming area citizens. Piles of cardboard and other paper product waste assaulted the landscape surrounding the business, hidden at the rear of the industrial park. Its neighbor businesses, sitting respectfully throughout the main complex, shined with pride. The lawns were well groomed, the structures clean and inviting. They hinted not of the ruins beyond.

Sherri grumbled, "What a contrast! But how fitting. I should have guessed that if the base tabloid defamed Morgantown's hospitable disposition, its facilities would surely reflect their filthiness." She exited the two-door Olds' Cutlass guardedly. Shivers crept up her back. The place looked eerie at best. She approached the open doorway and asked nervously, "Is anyone home?"

"Come on in," echoed a shrill male voice from beyond the huge archway to her left. "Be with ya in just a minute. Have a seat."

She cautiously stepped inside but chose not to be seated, wondering who could sit in such clutter. Her skin crawled in apprehension.

"Now, what can I do for you, beautiful?" the short stubby man asked, wiping his hands on his soiled white dress shirt. His ink-smeared tie hung loosely over the shirt that stretched open wide below the neck.

"I'm looking for Mr. Ellis Fenton."

"That would be me, unless you're from the I…R…S," he squeaked.

"My name is Sherri Mosley. I have a crow to pick with you. If you have time I'd like to have a long talk with you. The sooner, the better." Her hands shook from ire toward the bald arrogant looking man wearing what seemed to be a permanent smirk.

"I'm a busy man, miss, uh…."

"Mosley. Not too busy to ruin an innocent man's life though," Sherri shot back at the man. "You can either talk to me face to face or our lawyers can talk to one another."

Ellis Fenton looked up and down Sherri's frame and laughed. "You threatening me, little miss?" His short fat neck swelled as he pointed a stump of an index finger at her. "You better know who you are dealing with when you go around making threats, young lady. Now get out of my shop before I throw you out."

"Are you threatening *me,* Mr. Fenton?" Sherri yelled. "We will meet again, slime."

She turned to leave and heard the man sneer, "It is apparent that what you need is a good man. Maybe we ought to connect sometime, sweetheart."

She gritted her teeth and pressed her lips tight to refrain from unleashing the rage that pushed so hard she thought her eyes would pop. Every muscle in her body tensed as she fought the urge to turn and slap him. She wanted to connect all right. She would like to have connected her fist to his trashy mouth.

Walking to the car, as if she hadn't heard him, she forced herself to act calm. The early spring sun's rays warmed the interior and unleashed the powder-fresh scent from an air freshener hanging from the rear-view mirror. The automobile's sterile atmosphere consoled her.

She cranked the engine, jerked the gearshift into reverse and immediately slammed on her brake. A gray, roughly patched van pulled to a halt crossways behind her. The driver jumped from the van and force-marched toward the shop. She quickly rolled her window down and called, "Excuse me, sir. Can you move your van to let me out?"

The squat figure with short choppy dark hair turned and snorted, in a feminine voice, "Say what?"

Sherri hadn't seen the womanly features pushing tight against the long sleeve plaid flannel shirt until the girl spun around combatively.

"Sorry, Miss."

"Shouldn't have parked in the way in the first place," the driver growled as she approached the van. The young woman snatched hold of the van's door handle with a vengeance, jerked the door open and leaped into the driver's seat. She pulled the vehicle forward, slowly, keeping her piercing green eyes squinted at Sherri.

"It isn't enough she has to look like Ellis Fenton; she has his attitude too," she muttered to herself. Her fury subsided as she reasoned that this would be a comical story to share with Janet at supper. She giggled to herself at the thought of how Janet would have handled this situation. She wished she were as cool-headed and quick-witted as Janet.

Coming to a stop at the top of Dupont Hill, she pointed the car down River Road toward Morgantown. She prayed, "Well, Lord, I guess I've got my work cut out for me. I sure need your direction and your grace. Thanks for letting me get out of there safely. Father, you know I wouldn't dare be so headstrong in this cause if I didn't think you called me to it. Please direct me all the way. In Jesus' name I pray. Amen."

She glanced through the rearview mirror. The gray banged-up van pulled onto the old River Road from Dupont Road at a high speed, running the stop sign. Her heart pounded, shaking her whole body. "Now what?" she squeezed through taut lips.

The van tailgated her, making it impossible to see the driver. At a left snaking turn she looked through the left side-view mirror and caught a glimpse of the driver. The young woman's eyes seemed stuck in that piercing squint. The left curve in the road gave way immediately to a right curve and Sherri could see from the right side-view mirror that Ellis Fenton road shotgun—his menacing grin still tattooed to his round unfriendly face.

The van followed close the entire mile, to the end of the Old River Road at the Westover end of the Morgantown Bridge. Sherri braked at the stop sign, pointing the Oldsmobile toward Morgantown. Descending traffic from Westover hemmed her in. Her heart resounded in her ears as she anxiously waited for a safe opportunity to turn onto the bridge.

Her heart leapt and she let out a short startled scream at the sudden realization that Ellis stood outside her driver's side window, snapping her picture. He turned and scurried like a fat rat to the waiting van, darting between it and the Olds. As he climbed into the van Sherri watched the woman writing on a notepad, apparently copying the license plate number.

She caught a break in the traffic and whipped right, on to Route 19 across the bridge just as the van made a U-turn and headed back toward Dupont industrial park. She felt a surge of reprieve but her insides still convulsed.

Sherri spent the next four hours at the courthouse square hoping to see Uncle Joseph or Mr. Castleman. Maybe the tall skinny homeless man would show himself. Surely, the man knew Uncle Joseph. She suspected that he, for whatever reason, wished not to reveal Uncle Joseph's whereabouts.

People came and went in leisurely regularity—some were there when she arrived and were still there when she left. She tried to get up the nerve to approach those who lingered, but just couldn't muster the resolve. What would she say to them? She couldn't handle it if someone put her off like that homeless man had done yesterday. She would probably blow up like she did with Fenton.

Earlier, Janet had tried to explain to her that she couldn't approach people with guns blazing. Why hadn't she heeded the advice? She reminded herself that she must get control of her emotion packed temper.

She politely responded to an occasional hello, but failed to strike up meaningful conversation. Finally she returned to her car.

After grocery shopping at the Kroger store in Sabraton she returned to the mountain and the refuge of Janet's scenic residence. How she loved the lofty perch of Janet's house! So serene! She stole glances across the lower mountains as she prepared supper and understood why so many Christian songs were about living on the mountain; symbolic of spiritual highs.

Sherri anxiously snatched up the phone on the second ring. She hoped for Frank to call. He should be home from work. "Hello."

"Hi, Miss Pixler?" The woman's voice sounded faintly familiar.

"No, this is her friend, Sherri. Can I take a message?"

"Well, actually, it is you I wish to speak with," the woman said sarcastically. "My dad wants to set a meeting with you, at your convenience."

Sherri's heart hammered with anticipation. Would she be better off declining the invitation? Pretending to not recognize the caller she replied, "Who is your dad? And why would he want to meet with me?"

"This is Ramona Fenton. My dad is Ellis Fenton. I think you two have already met."

She forced herself to act civil. "I don't know. Let me think about it and I'll call you if I decide to meet with him."

"It is you who wanted to talk," Ramona taunted. "Should I tell him that you have nothing to say, after all?"

"Oh, I have plenty to say to him." Sherri felt her face turn hot with rage at the challenge. "Put him on the phone."

"That's not how it works, missy. He has a business to run. If you want to talk with him we'll make you an appointment."

"Like I said, *missy,* I'll think about it. Maybe I'll just save my comments for the courts."

"Have it your way, lady. We like a good fight. Especially when it comes to Joseph Short."

Sherri slammed the phone's receiver onto its cradle. "How did they make the association between me and Uncle Joseph already?" she asked as she stared out the double glass sliding doors to the deck overlooking the Morgantown area. She heard Janet's Jeep pull into the driveway and wondered how she'd explain that she had provoked the Fentons.

Janet stepped through the front door and teased, "My goodness, girl. I got heartburn before getting to the house. You think you spiced the spaghetti enough?"

"It's chili-mac. Is it really that strong of a smell?"

"Just teasing. You seem awful tense. Bad day?"

"Nothing I can't handle. I am afraid I might have caused you a bit of headache to come. Not intentionally. You know I wouldn't do that on purpose."

"Do what on purpose?" Janet asked calmly.

"Well, I went to the *Scoop Weekly* cesspool today and kind of stirred things by confronting Ellis Fenton, the owner. He and his wacky daughter followed me to Westover and copied your license plate number."

"So? Big deal. What can they do with it, unless you committed a crime?"

"They evidently have already tracked you down. I just got off the phone with his daughter, Ramona. She called asking for you and when she learned who I am she tried to set a meeting between her dad and me."

"So, when are you meeting with him?"

"I don't know that I am. She got smart-mouthed—like that ought to surprise me—so I hung up on her."

Janet laughed. "You are so tactless. If you are going to be a detective, you've got to conceal the chip on the shoulder."

"How can you think this is funny? If you met those two freaks you'd understand why I'm so concerned. They chased me down and took my picture and then did a U-turn at the end of River Road and headed back to their bat cave."

Laughing even harder, Janet said, "Let's eat. That chili mac smells delicious and I'm hungry. I just hope your culinary talents aren't as sorry as your investigative skills."

The conversation at the dinner table centered on the day's events. Sherri described the Fentons and their headquarters in tones of shock and disgust. Her exasperation over Janet's amusement of the accounts evoked even more uncontrollable laughter. Janet's contagious giggling finally infected Sherri, who slowly saw the humor in it all.

"You are so hilarious!" Janet exclaimed.

"I'm just telling you what really happened. I'm not exaggerating. Those two are scary."

"Your spit-fire personality just makes it even funnier."

"Jerks like that are enough to fire anyone up."

"Maybe so. But your perception is so condensed and it makes you more contentious."

"How do you come to that analysis?" Sherri asked defensively.

"I don't mean to criticize, Sherri. But your quick temper gives you tunnel vision."

"Really? How so?"

"For example: your fury toward the Fentons clouded your powers of observation and discernment."

"Okay, what do you mean by that?"

"You said you couldn't imagine how they figured out that you were there on behalf of Joseph. You didn't even mention his name or anything about his case. You didn't give any indication whatsoever why you were there, except to pick a fight."

"I didn't go there to pick a fight."

"No, but you picked one, nevertheless."

Only Janet could get by with such forthrightness. Sherri hated to admit to the correctness of the accusation. But how could she deny what Janet said?

"Even though I want you to give it to me straight, I don't know if I can bear to hear anymore truth about my worthlessness or my stupidity."

"Hey, come on. I'm not trying to hurt you, Sherri. And I didn't call you stupid."

"I know. I hate myself so much. No wonder Frank hates my guts."

"That isn't fair. I won't allow anyone to talk so negatively about my best friend. Not even you, Sherri. You are worth a whole lot more than most people. We'll have to work on your self-esteem. Besides, Frank is the one with the problem. If he doesn't want someone as beautiful and loving and devoted as you, he obviously is not very smart."

Sherri wiped her eyes with her fingers and sniffled, "I'm sorry. Go ahead and finish your explanation about how the Fentons figured Uncle Joseph and I are related."

"You said that you knew almost immediately that Ramona Fenton must be related to Ellis Fenton. How did you come to that conclusion?"

Sherri grinned awkwardly and said, "How in the world could I have missed that? Why, I even look more like Uncle Joseph than what Ramona looks like her dad!"

"Bingo."

"See. I am so stupid. I hate being so ignorant."

"Easy, girl. You know what I think is your primary problem?"

"No. What?" Sherri asked searchingly.

"I think you let your temper control you until you are unable to think clearly. If you could just learn to slow your angry combative thought processes, you'd fair well."

Though peeved at the analysis, or at least the truth it revealed, she felt compelled to consider the advice. "Come to think of it, I remember Pastor Richards preaching from a scripture that instructs us to be quick to hear and slow to speak. Why is it that I hear the preaching but you are the one who knows and practices it better?"

"Don't forget that I grew up in a Christian home. I may not have made a profession of faith in Christ but I sure heard the Word while growing up."

Sherri longed to ask Janet to pray for her. How could she pray effectively if she doesn't even follow Christ?

"Didn't you say you were seeing a Christian counselor in the Youngstown area before Frank asked you to leave?" Janet asked with a look of enlightenment.

"Yeah, I got my hopes up for nothing. I think I could have gotten a lot from good biblical counseling. But I guess it wasn't to be."

"The reason I asked is that my Uncle Jake may know a preacher who does counseling. Do you remember Travis Riggs from high school?"

"Oh, my! I reckon my temper is well controlled compared to Travis'."

"I guess he has made some real changes in his life. Uncle Jake said he started seeing some preacher for counseling. But not until his wife left him because of his meanness. I don't know that he abused her but we all knew him to be terribly bitter and quick tempered. After he started getting counseling he got saved and learned to control his anger."

"Oh, Janet, I'd love to return to counseling. Reverend McCormick convinced me that I'd learn to control *my* temper, too. But I can't travel that far for counseling. And I can't afford to pay for counseling right now."

"We could ask Uncle Jake about it. I suspect we won't get an answer if we call him now. We'll call about dark when he is most likely back in the house. He works his farm about every daylight hour when he isn't working his construction job or doing something ministry related."

Janet spent the rest of the evening helping Sherri devise strategies for turning public opinion to Joseph's favor and planning how to search for him. "We forgot to call Uncle Jake," Janet gasped, glancing at her watch that read 11:30."

"No biggy," Sherri replied calmly. "We can do it sometime later."

Sherri's prayers at bedtime bathed her in hope. Her lungs filled with fresh confidence in what God would accomplish in her. The tension over her present calling vanished. She smiled contentedly as she marveled how God's peace descended, unannounced, baptizing her in tranquility. She concluded her prayer, "Thank you, Lord, for the assurance. Thank you in advance, Father, for the resolution you are going to bring about."

CHAPTER SIX

Friday, April 27, 1979

"Wow!" Janet exclaimed. "You must have slept with the angels last night."

Janet's compliment put icing on the cake. "I did have a heavenly sleep last night," Sherri replied with an easy smile.

"You haven't shined like that since I don't know when. It even makes *me* feel better."

"Thanks, Janet. You are such a great help. Your encouragement is a real boon. Just think how God will use you for His glory if you put your trust in Him as Lord and Savior. I really believe He is calling you, Janet."

Janet's cheeks turned light pink and then quickly paled. "Sherri, I didn't plan on sharing this with you. But I've got to tell someone."

Sherri's anticipation begged her to push forward to reel Janet in for Jesus. Uncle Joseph's earliest instruction to her and Frank just three years ago resounded clearly. "Be careful to not confuse your emotions with the moving of the Holy Spirit," he had warned. "However, be also cautious that you don't quench the Holy Spirit." How would she distinguish between the two? She reminded herself that she must wait on Him to let her know when to speak. She elected to just listen to what Janet had to share, without interrupting.

"I had a miserable night," Janet said with her eyes focused on the dining room table. Tears dripped softly into her cereal. "I know they are just dreams, but in my first dream, Mom and Dad were calling for me. Their utterances were indescribable but I recognized their voices just the same. I looked toward the beckoning tones. Their faces glowed so brightly. They looked nothing like they did when they were on earth. But I still knew who they were." She rose to her feet and stepped toward the sliding glass doors and stared over the hills toward Morgantown.

Sherri waited for her to regain her voice and gather her thoughts.

"You're going to think I'm crazy for letting a dream move me to such emotion."

Sherri stood beside her and laid her hand gently on her shoulder. "I don't think you're crazy. Sometimes God may use dreams to inspire us or to move us toward His will. I believe that our dreams are most often reflections of our subconscious thoughts, fears, and hopes."

"The first dream of Mom and Dad was comforting. It is the second dream that has kept me awake all night. The very thought of it tears at my insides."

Sherri whispered, "It's my turn to be here for you. Tell me about it and then we'll pray together."

Janet's shoulders shook violently as she tried to harness the sobbing. "I can't even bear to let myself revisit the second dream. But it won't leave me be."

"What is it, Janet? You must tell me. We'll turn it over to God. He'll take care of it."

"I dreamt about Joseph…Oh, Sherri! It can't happen… that way."

"Janet, keep in mind that we shouldn't confuse dreams with reality. I don't mean to make light of your concern over whatever you dreamed, but let's put things in perspective. Okay?"

Janet slowly regained her composure and continued, still weeping. "Joseph called me, too. In the same heavenly tones with which my parents called to me, he summoned. If I had the power to keep him here in this ole wicked world, I wouldn't. But I can't bear the thought of losing him right now. I wish I had let him know how I felt about him. Many times I attempted to. I feared rejection. Maybe I could have kept all this from happening to him."

"We are going to find him, Janet. You'll have a chance to tell him how you feel. We have to remain optimistic."

Janet broke into heaving as she exclaimed, "What if the dream contained some sort of message? What if he is dying? Worse yet, already dead? I couldn't survive that, Sherri."

"It would be tough, but God would give you the strength. But I really don't think God is telling you this. You know how our thoughts can get all jumbled up in our dreams."

"I know, but this seemed too real and it scares me."

Sherri gently laughed. "Now, who is the emotional one? You wore yourself out pulling me up from the mire of gloom. Come on, let's pray."

Janet rushed off to work and Sherri cleaned house and washed dishes before setting about her plan for the day. This time she felt more in control. Her first order of the day would be to go job searching. Then she must try to learn more about Uncle Joseph's most recent legal problems. What caused Angela to file charges that he made death threats against her? Why did no one come to his defense? Why would the community, as a whole, be so set against him?

After filling out a few job applications in the Morgantown area, Sherri visited the Monongalia County Magistrates' Office. The old dark-brick building, originally built as a funeral home, sat along a busy downtown section of University Avenue. Once inside, she saw no signs of its first use, except a couple small parlors that probably served as smoking rooms.

"Hi, may I help you?" the receptionist asked from behind her desk.

"Yes, ma'am. I would like to check on charges filed through your office on a Joseph Short." Sherri knew nothing of the court systems and silently prayed that she would not appear completely clueless.

The young blonde, wearing a mint green slack outfit with a white neck scarf, reached into a drawer and brought the information request form to Sherri. Leaning on the counter between them, the woman asked the pertinent questions and wrote Sherri's replies. "What is the name of the accused, again?"

"Joseph Short."

"His age and birth date?"

"Thirty four years old. His birth date is May 12, 1945."

"Well, it looks like someone has a birthday coming up in about two weeks," the tall slender woman said, smiling politely.

"Oh my! It slipped my mind until now," Sherri gasped. The thought of Uncle Joseph spending his birthday on the streets or under a bridge shot pangs of anxiety through her. Desperation towered over her with a vengeance.

"Who is the complainant in this case?" the woman asked.

"Um…Angela Hillman."

The receptionist grimaced. "Really? Why doesn't that surprise me?" She then apologized for the sarcasm.

"No need to apologize. I doubt that you could be as appalled at her as I am."

"You look faintly familiar," the woman said as she searched Sherri's face. "Have we met before?"

"I don't think so. But everyone says that Uncle Joseph and I look like twins. He is only four years older than me. When I call him *Uncle* people think I'm joking."

"Pleased to meet you, Miss Short. I'm Brenda Flowers."

"I'm Sherri Mosley. Mrs. Frank Mosley. Joseph is my mother's baby brother."

"I remember now," Brenda said, "Your uncle is a preacher, isn't he?"

"Yeah. And a fine preacher, at that."

"I'll see what we have on file, Mrs. Mosley. I'll be back in a minute."

Sherri pulled a note pad and pen from her purse and wrote down the receptionist's name. She might prove to be a big help navigating the legal system.

Brenda returned with a folder and asked, "What is it you need to know about the case?"

"I need to know what the actual charges are and what the disposition of the case is?"

Brenda hummed as she reviewed the file's contents. "Okay. It seems that Mrs. Hillman filed a charge against Reverend Short claiming that he threatened her life. Joseph Short failed to appear at a subsequent hearing. Magistrate Pagone issued a warrant for his arrest, dated October 1978. It appears that Joseph has not been arrested. The warrant is still outstanding."

"Is there any way we can get the warrant dropped?" Sherri asked.

"If the complainant drops the initial charge, the magistrate can then dispose of the case. I think Mr. Pagone is in his office. Would you like to speak with him?"

"Yes. Thank you so much."

Brenda dialed Mr. Pagone's extension and asked if he had time to speak to someone making inquiry on an outstanding case.

Sherri heard a door close from up the hall. She peered around the corner of the front office and saw a short chunky, well-dressed man with a thick dark mustache and well groomed curly dark hair. "Hi, I'm Pete Pagone. Can I help you?"

"Yes, sir," Sherri squeaked as she stepped into the hallway. "I'm Sherri Mosley, Joseph Short's niece. I wish to check on his case and see what we can do to resolve it."

"Well, we can resolve it by Mr. Short turning himself in and answering the charges on file, and paying fines for failure to appear—unless of course, he'd rather further aggravate the court."

"That's it?" Sherri spat with indignation. "No discussion of possibility of getting the charges dropped?"

"No offense to you personally, Mrs. Mosley, but this man is a menace to the community. But to answer your question—no charges will be dropped." His eyes widened with raised brows accentuating his bias.

Sherri's cheeks burned with fury. "So, you just issue warrants on any ole whim? I suppose you're another of Angela Hillman's pawns," she railed.

Pete Pagone gritted his teeth, wrinkled his forehead and threatened, "Maybe *you* would like to spend some time in jail, smart mouth."

"Maybe you better have a good reason to fulfill that threat, Mr. Magistrate. You big shots think you can just throw your weight around and expect everyone to bow to you. Well, let me give you fair warning, sir. I don't scare easily."

Mr. Pagone forced a grin. "Well, just like your precious uncle, aren't you?"

"Joseph Short is ten times the man you could ever hope to be. At least I'm not someone else's puppet. Obviously *you* are a Hillman puppet. But that's okay. Angela will cut your strings and leave you to pick up the broken pieces. You'll see."

"I think you better leave with your big mouth, young lady, before you get in deeper than you can manage." He turned and hastened to his office.

Sherri turned toward the front office. "Thanks for the assistance, Brenda."

Brenda whispered, "I like your spunk. But be careful with him. He can be a real bear."

Sherri returned the grin and winked. "I always wanted to go bear hunting. Thanks again. God bless."

Brenda looked behind her and then asked if anyone was in the hall.

"No. Why?"

"Give me a number where you can be reached. I'll call you if anything breaks in Reverend Short's case. Hurry before someone catches on."

Sherri wrote Janet's home phone and tore the page from her note pad. "I'll be there after five this evening and most evenings except Wednesdays."

"Okay… And good luck."

Sherri hurried to the Oldsmobile, anxious to distance herself from the magistrate's office. She hoped to catch Ellis Fenton at his shop before calling it a day. Anxiously waiting for a green light at the corner of Walnut Street and University Avenue she caught a glimpse of the homeless man she and Janet spoke to at the courthouse square. He sauntered toward the Monongahela River carrying his stuffed pillowcase. The signal light turned green but Sherri hesitated, trying to decide whether to pursue him or stick to her plan to visit Fenton.

Startled by a motorist blowing his horn behind her she whipped onto lower Walnut Street and slowed to observe the tall skinny stranger. A parking lot to her left appeared and she quickly darted into an empty space. Hurrying from the car she followed the man on foot.

He turned south along the riverbank as Sherri stepped onto the red brick road. He jerked his head toward Sherri and broke into a trot.

"Please wait," she begged. "Please? I need to talk to you. Come back. Please?"

She watched the man run with his pillowcase of belongings bouncing against his back with each stride. He disappeared around the bank of Decker's Creek. She whispered a prayer while returning to the parked vehicle. She had time yet to visit Ellis Fenton in hopes that his offer for a meeting still stood.

Cautiously, Sherri drove onto the dirt and gravel road. The eeriness of the abandoned rear section of the industrial park made her skin crawl.

Ellis Fenton, setting on the stoop outside the *Scoop Weekly,* puffed heavily on a fat cigar. He didn't seem to notice that she parked just ten feet from him. He stared straight forward. Clouds of cigar smoke swirled around his head fouling the air.

Should she bother him? She surmised that he seemed cantankerous enough when he is in a good mood—if there were good moods. She carefully studied his profile as she exited the vehicle. Drawing in a deep breath, she forced a cheerful "good day to you, sir."

"What's so good about it?" he groaned.

"You sound really down about something. I hope nothing is seriously wrong." Taken aback by her own genuine concern, she voicelessly prayed, "Wow! Thank you, Lord, for letting me feel for this man. Let me be a good witness for you."

He glanced at Sherri and bowed his head in submission. "Hi, Miss Short. I guess you've come to finish me off, huh?" he said in resignation.

"May I sit with you?" Sherri asked politely.

He scooted to the left side of the stoop and leaned against the open door's facing. He bent forward and dashed his cigar out in the dirt.

"Mr. Fenton, I came to see if your offer for a meeting still stands. But I can call later or come to see you at a better time, if you like."

"You know what, Miss Short?" he humbly asked.

"That's Mrs. Mosley. But I prefer you call me Sherri."

"Sorry...Sherri. You know what? I am tired of the life I'm leading and the hassles it brings about." He paused reflectively and then asked, "What is your relationship to Reverend Short? I forget. If I even knew."

"I'm his niece. He and my mother are siblings."

"I thought you were his sister. Can't be too many years between the two of you."

"Just four. So, what is this about you being tired of your life?" Sherri had never actually tried the one-on-one evangelism techniques that Pastor Richards had taught his congregation. The lessons seemed to speak more confidence to her now than when she sat in the classroom.

"It's a long story." His gaze fixed on Sherri and his eyes relaxed. "I guess you don't know much about me, but you probably know that I'm a mean and hateful soul. I can't take anymore. I reckon I've lost the last relationship that ever mattered to me. The last two days have been especially miserable and void for me."

Sherri asked softly, "What is the last relationship you think you've lost?"

Ellis' brow furrowed. He interlocked his fingers and squeezed until his hands shook. "I have hated the whole world for so long that I have poisoned my daughter. I saw it coming for some time, but just ignored it. But she has turned out meaner than me." His voice choked and his chest heaved. "She even hates *me*. She made that quite clear the other day when she left with that dope pushing Bobby Stafford. I suppose I shouldn't be surprised she turned out this way. After all, *I* raised her."

"How about Ramona's mother? How does *she* get along with Ramona?"

"She died three months after Ramona's sixth birthday. Alma was a good woman. She trusted in Jesus to the end." A faint reluctant smile crept across his lips. "You would have liked her. I still harbor a grudge against Christ for letting her suffer with cancer for eighteen months and then taking her from us." He lowered his stare to the dirt and gravel beneath his feet.

She touched his shoulder to assure him that he could speak without being judged or ridiculed. "Go ahead. Speak your heart's pain. It's okay. There is just us two—and God to hear."

"God. I hadn't given Him much thought since my early childhood, until Alma got saved. I reckon that is when I first hated Him—for coming between us." His voice crackled as he visibly fought back tears of confusion and sorrow.

"Oh, Mr. Fenton," Sherri gasped, "don't let yourself hate God. He loves you." She sympathetically rubbed Ellis' back as he began to sob. His body quaked as he rocked back and forth with his arms folded across his round abdomen.

Sherri listened attentively as he recounted his life since his youth.

His mother had been killed in an automobile accident shortly after Ellis turned eight years old. His alcoholic father routinely beat Ellis and his older sister, Glenda. Glenda ran away from home at the age of fifteen. She hadn't been heard from since. His only aunts, uncles, and cousins all lived out west and never associated with his father. His mother, an only child, became an orphan at age twelve. His father, Elton Fenton, an illegitimate child of a barroom queen from Cleveland, claimed that she kicked him out of the home before he turned fifteen.

"I know this may sound cheap, but I say it sincerely," Sherri politely interjected, "It appears that you have done well for yourself in light of all your unprivileged past."

"How do you get that idea?"

"You are apparently a learned man. I've read some of your articles in the *Scoop Weekly.* I don't care much for the story lines but your writing is superb."

"Superb junk," he blurted with a hint of self-disgust.

"Regardless, it is talented writing."

His sobbing eased and his body steadied. "How gracious of you to say that! I haven't had a compliment for so long it makes a fellow a bit suspicious of such kindness."

Sherri silently reproved herself for wanting to tell him that if he'd not print such hateful trash he might receive an occasional compliment. She glanced at her watch and jumped to her feet. "Oh, my! It's later that I realized."

“I’m sorry, Sherri.” Ellis said. “I rambled on and ignored your purpose for visiting me.”

“That’s all right, Mr. Fenton. I think what we talked about fit into God’s immediate will anyhow. May I come to visit you another time?”

“On one condition, if you do so very soon. And you pick the topic the next time.” The smirk that distorted his smile at their first meeting had vanished.

“I wish I could stay longer today, but I’m to meet my friend after work. She’s dropping off her Jeep at the garage and I have her car.”

They both rose and Ellis reached to shake hands with Sherri and thanked her for being the angel he desperately needed. “Please, come again. I need to make some apologies and it might take more than a minute or two.”

“God bless you, Mr. Fenton. I’ll be back. I promise.” Sherri left with a new mission in her heart and mind. She thought of how Jesus often ministered to those whom He met along His way to specific places and purposes. What an opportunity for her to emulate Him!

Sherri prayed while she waited in the parking lot outside the garage.

“Well, how many fights did you get into today?” Janet teased as she climbed into the passenger’s seat.

“Only one—not really a fight, per se.”

“Yeah, right.”

“That magistrate, Pete Pagone, proved to be a real treat.”

“How so?”

Sherri shared the details of the confrontation with Magistrate Pagone. “Good for you. That guy has a reputation for being a real jerk to everyone except the rich and influential of the community. You should have told him that you have a friend who also doesn’t scare easily. I wonder what his angle is?”

“What angle?”

“Well, he apparently is another Hillman pawn, like you said.”

“I suspect we will find out soon enough.”

“So? How did the job search go?”

“I filled out a few applications, but then I got sidetracked.”

"Doing what?" Janet asked accusingly.

"Arguing with Pete Pagone, trying to follow that skinny homeless guy we talked with at the courthouse square, and witnessing to Ellis Fenton."

"Witnessing to Ellis Fenton? What—are you suicidal? What's wrong with you?"

Janet's agitated tone flabbergasted Sherri. "He isn't the monster we all perceived him to be."

"You didn't go back there to his place, did you?"

"Yes, *Mother,* I did."

"I thought we agreed that you wouldn't go there without me. Stuck out there away from all the other businesses he could hurt you and probably nobody would even hear your cry for help. You said, yourself, how weird he and his loony daughter are."

"Calm down, Janet. We didn't agree that I'd not go there alone in the first place. You ordered me not to go there alone. We made no such agreement."

"I can't believe you are that stubborn." Janet shouted. "No wonder you fight with everyone around you."

Janet's charge rendered Sherri speechless.

"Oh, now I guess you are going to pout," Janet moaned.

Neither of them spoke on the way home.

CHAPTER SEVEN

Saturday, April 28, 1979

Saturday morning came too soon for Sherri. She wanted to accomplish much more during the week than she had. Her body cried for more rest but her mind rebelled. She peeked at the alarm clock on the antique Regency side table and moaned, "6:30 is much too early to rise and shine on Saturday." She lay facing the side table, admiring its design. The realistic looking eagle spread its majestic wings to assist the pillars of the stand, supporting the rectangular white marble top.

Her mind wondered to Youngstown. Had Frank missed her as much as she missed him? Does he really want to dissolve the marriage? Maybe she ought to call him and suggest they still make a try at their marriage. No. He'd insist that she drop the idea of finding Uncle Joseph. Besides, she'd not subject herself to his abusive behavior like she had early in their marriage. She wouldn't know if he is willing or not until she at least tried to reconcile. The barrage of what-ifs wearied her.

She drifted off into petitioning the Lord until 7:15 a.m. By the time she finished praying, her heart had recovered its normal rhythm.

"Hey, you gonna sleep your life away or what?" Janet yelled from the living room. "Let's get moving. I am hungry and I am not in the mood to fix breakfast."

Sherri scrambled to the hallway. "I'll fix breakfast this morning."

"Oh no you won't. I want to survive the experience."

"Do you have any plans beyond breakfast?" Sherri asked.

"Yeah. But if there is something you would rather do..."

Sherri rushed to find a way to suggest they go to town and search for Uncle Joseph. The urge to submit to Janet's wish won out. "Why? What did you have in mind? I can forgo my plans for one day. After all, I haven't exactly been good company."

"Good. I thought we'd go Joseph hunting today."

Sherri's heart floated to her throat. "That is what *I* had in mind."

"Sherri, I want to apologize for the verbal attack yesterday."

"Well, it may have been warranted."

"Nevertheless, I need to apologize."

"Conditionally accepted."

"Conditionally?"

"Only if you'll accept my apology for pouting."

"Done. Now get dressed."

"Do you think we can take time to call Frank before we leave. I want to talk with him before he gets out and about."

"I think you should. I'll try to keep my nose out of that part of your life."

"I may need you to stick your nose into that part of my life anyhow. So don't be too resolute about it."

"I know. I know," Frank cheerfully squawked into the phone. "I'll be there in about half an hour. I just got up."

"Really," Sherri teased, "are you flying down this morning?"

"Oh. It's you," he snarled. "What do you want?"

"Well, good morning to you, too."

"I'm running late, Sher. What is it?"

"What it is, my sweet adorable husband, is I thought we ought to talk and try to work things out." Sherri's resolve to remain calm and objective quickly eroded.

"What's there to work out? I am where I ought to be. And you are where you should be. So, what's the mystery?"

"I guess you think you are doing the right thing. Let me tell you something, Frank Mosley. When you decide to grow up and be a man, call me." She slammed the receiver down and said, through gritted teeth, "Sometimes I'd like to just belt him right in the mouth."

"Maybe you got his ear instead," Janet giggled.

"I can certainly relate to what the Apostle Paul meant when he wrote to the Corinthian church that it is better for a person to remain single."

"That is in the Bible?"

"Actually," Sherri corrected, "he addressed a question about the distractions from Christian service to please a mate. Earlier, in the same chapter, he wrote that marriage is honorable. It isn't that he spoke against marriage."

"You had me worried there for a minute."

Janet and Sherri planned tentatively during breakfast at Gran's Home Style Restaurant. Surely, they would find out something of Joseph's whereabouts. How elusive can a homeless person be?

Sherri parked the blue Oldsmobile in the lot behind the old Gabriel Brothers' store. At the halfway point between the red brick road leading to the boat ramp and where Decker's Creek emptied into the Monongahela River, they stopped to speak to a lone fisherman.

"Excuse me sir," said Janet. "Do you fish here often?"

"Most Saturdays," the long slim middle-aged stranger replied. "But you need a fishing pole and bait to do any good at it," he said, smiling up at them with his feet resting over the bank.

"Well, there is no use wasting good money on equipment if the fishing is no good. Now is there?" Janet rebutted jokingly.

"I guess you're right, young lady," he said looking back at his fishing line. "Woe!" he yelled. The line tightened and the pole bent and jerked. He grabbed the pole, yanked it upward and to the side, and reeled frantically.

Sherri and Janet stared anxiously at the water anticipating the appearance of the catch. The taut line moved left to right and right to left repeatedly until the huge channel cat flopped ferociously on the surface of the water trying to free itself.

Janet rushed over the riverbank and reached for the end of the line and tugged the catfish to shore. She held the line with her right hand and slipped her left hand skillfully over the dark gray creature, placing her middle finger behind the needle of its back and her index finger in front of the needle. She blocked the needled fins with her thumb and ring finger.

"That's quite a grip you have there, young lady," the man said.

"I grew up on catfish, groundhog, squirrel, and other game," she replied proudly.

"I suppose you must have. Do you want him?"

"No thanks," Janet said, as she removed the hook. She handed the fish toward the man.

"I just fish for fun, miss. If you two don't want him, just throw him back in. Some homeless fellow usually hangs out here and takes whatever I catch. But I haven't seen him this morning."

Janet tossed the fish back into the river, wiped her hands on the legs of her jeans, and climbed to the top of the bank.

Sherri excitedly asked, "You wouldn't happen to know the man's name, would you?"

"Sure. Everybody knows ole Lanky Lang. I've seen him haul off as much as eight fish at a time from fishers along this bank," he said, lifting his ball cap and repositioning it. "I never bothered to ask him what he does with them all. I guess he eats 'em right away."

Sherri immediately recalled the homeless man from the courthouse square. "This Lanky Lang; does he carry a pillow case of things with him?"

"See, I told you everybody knows him. I've never seen you girls here before. But you know him too, huh?"

"Not exactly," Janet said. "Sherri and I are trying to find another homeless man—our Joseph. We briefly met Mr. Lang recently."

"By the way," Sherri announced, "I'm Sherri Mosley and this is my dear friend, Janet Pixler."

He gripped his cap bill and tipped it. "I'm Milo Polchec. Everyone just calls me Stick."

"Mind if we sit with you and chat a bit?" Janet asked.

"Not at all. Dust your britches off and have a seat," he jested as he patted the ground with his right hand.

Sherri reached for the man's plastic cottage cheese container and drew out a night crawler.

Stick reached for the worm and said, "Thanks."

"I can put it on the hook, if you'll just lean the pole toward me."

Stick lowered the line and hook as Sherri sat down on his left side.

She baited the hook and wiped her hands on the grass. "Let's see if you can do any better than the last catch."

Stick cast his line and gave the reel a couple turns. He carefully laid the pole on the ground and placed a large stone atop the handgrip, and grunted. "You two are fishing for something other than what is in the river, huh? Ole Lanky didn't do you any harm, did he?"

"No, no," Sherri responded, "Why would he do us any harm?"

"He is a strange sort, you know. He's pretty harmless except when he takes a serious spell of paranoia. I've seen him become alarmingly defensive when he imagines someone is out to get him."

"He is very avoidant. He acts nervous and uneasy," Sherri said.

Janet added, "We tried questioning him about the man we are searching for and he cut the conversation short and rushed off. Sherri tried to catch up with him along here yesterday and he took off running from her."

"That's Lanky for you," Stick replied with a short huff.

"What's he scared of?" Sherri asked innocently.

Janet snickered. "You are so uninitiated!"

"About what?" Sherri replied defensively.

"Hey, if you two are going to squabble let me get out from between you," Stick barked.

"Sorry," Sherri said as she felt her cheeks flush with embarrassment.

"Yeah, me too," Janet added.

Looking fatherly at Sherri, Stick explained that Arthur (Lanky) Lang had been homeless at various times in the past ten years. "I hear that when he is absent from the area he is being treated at Weston State Hospital for paranoid schizophrenia."

"How sad!" Janet sighed. "We thought he just avoided us to keep from getting involved with our search for Sherri's uncle."

"Even on his best days he isn't talkative. Don't take it personally when he avoids you," he explained.

"Have you ever met a man named Joseph Short while fishing along this stretch of riverbank?" Sherri asked hopefully.

"Well, I'm not sure. I don't think so. Now, I have heard some talk of a homeless fellow they call Joe the Baptist. That's about as close to any Joseph I can think of that might occasionally hang out around here. But I don't think I've ever seen him."

Sherri's heart hammered with excitement. Her eyes caught Janet's widened gaze and they simultaneously exclaimed, "Uncle Joseph!"

"Hey, ladies. I didn't say that this Joe the Baptist is your Uncle Joseph," insisted the fisherman.

Sherri grabbed Stick's wrist and pleaded, "Why do they call this man Joe the Baptist?"

"The rumor is that he is a former preacher and he still preaches to the other homeless people and even others who recreate along the river."

"Uncle Joseph is a preacher. We heard that he had become homeless. It has to be him."

Janet latched onto the man's right elbow. "Please, tell us where we can find him?"

"My goodness, you two are intense! I don't know him or where he hides out. I have never met the man; as far as I know."

"Can you think of any other homeless people or fishermen who might know where we can find him?" Janet asked excitedly. "Joseph Short has red curly hair. It is now about shoulder length. He might be sporting a ragged red beard."

"Well, I did see a man that fits that description, somewhat. Only this fellow has an exaggerated limp. But he isn't debilitated."

Sherri rose quickly to her feet and began nervously prancing. "Have you seen him recently? Where did you see him? Did you get to talk with him at all? Where is he sleeping?"

"Give the man time to answer one question, Sherri, before exploding with others," Janet yelled.

"Oh, my. Oh, my," Sherri said as she pressed her temples with rigid fingers. "We've found him, Janet." Her eyes flooded with sweet salty joy.

Janet jumped up and grabbed Sherri's biceps. "Settle down. We haven't found him yet. Stop getting hysterical."

Sherri heard Janet's instruction but seemed helpless in controlling her emotions.

"Listen to me," Janet shouted.

Sherri broke Janet's hold and clutched her chest. She dropped to her knees, bowing her face to the grass beneath her. "Oh, Father, please keep Uncle Joseph and help us find him. Lord Jesus, give us wisdom and grace in our search for him." She'd prayed without thought of Stick's or Janet's presence. When she ended her prayer she rose to her feet feeling a little embarrassed over her rash unreserved reactions.

Janet's face blushed with obvious chagrin. Stick Polchec stood about fifty feet upstream puffing rapidly on a cigarette. He averted his stare when she looked at him.

"I wish you wouldn't act like some religious maniac," Janet scolded. "Can't you wait until you at least get to the car? This is so embarrassing!"

"I'm sorry you feel that way, Janet," she replied with a shaky voice. "There is nothing wrong with spontaneous prayer. I didn't do it for anyone else's benefit, anyhow. Excuse *me,* if I offend you by talking to God. But I am not ashamed of my Lord."

"I don't expect you to be ashamed of Him, Sherri. Just don't act like you are ready for the funny farm. Okay?"

"Hey, you have another bite, Mr. Polchec," Sherri yelled.

He darted for the pole and stumbled over a small tree stump along the edge of the bank. Splashing into the river, five feet below, he bellowed from the cold water.

Sherri burst into laughter, immediately joined by Janet and Stick.

Stick staggered to the top of the bank and stood smiling like a young mischievous boy. "I figured that if you could pray so impulsively I should be able to go swimming just as uninhibitedly. Whoa, is that water cold!"

Sherri stepped toward the fishing pole and realized that the line had relaxed. "Uh, oh. The fish got away."

"Well, I think I'm finished for the day. It's probably not worth reeling in anyhow." Stick reeled in his line and removed the lifeless, half eaten worm from the hook. He looped the hook around an eye of the pole and tightened the line until the pole slightly bent. Bending to grab his tackle box, he said, "I can't say that it has been an uneventful day."

"I suppose you'll have some explaining to do when you get home," Sherri joked.

"I think this makes for a good fish story. It isn't often that a man hooks a fish so big that it not only gets away, but it pulls the fisherman into the water before slipping the hook."

"Yeah," Janet added, "you can tell your wife that the two young women you *fell* for, witnessed the whole thing."

"I just might leave that part out. She wouldn't believe the truth anyhow," Stick said as he squished away.

"Don't look now," Janet whispered to Sherri as she rolled her eyes toward Decker's Creek, "but we are being watched."

Sherri jerked her head around to see who it might be.

"I said, 'don't look now,' knot head."

"I don't see anyone," Sherri said lowly.

"Of course not. You scared him away again."

"You mean Lanky?"

"Yeah. I still think he knows something about Joseph. Something he isn't wanting to reveal, for some reason." Janet gazed thoughtfully southward and started walking slowly toward the point where Decker's Creek spilled into the Monongahela.

Sherri turned to join her. "Where are we going?"

"I don't know. Let's see if we can determine where Lanky wanders off to."

They followed a narrow footpath along the steep edge of the bank of Decker's Creek and caught a glimpse of Lanky walking the railroad tracks above them. They climbed up to the tracks and intended to follow him. But he disappeared.

"Okay," Sherri sighed, "where did he go? He couldn't just vanish."

"He must have left the tracks just after crossing over the creek. Hurry, maybe we can catch him on Clay Street."

They briskly walked across the railroad trestle, to the south bank of Decker's Creek, and scrambled onto the brick parking lot beside an old three-story brick warehouse. The old brick Clay Street appeared deserted. Even the few existing businesses in the area appeared quiet. Sherri and Janet looked about, stepping softly southward, hoping not to be heard in case Lanky hid nearby.

They visually searched the area as they strolled the length of Clay Street. "He could have doubled back northward to the creek again," Janet suggested.

"Well, he is long gone by now," Sherri whined.

"Maybe he dodged into one of the buildings along here?"

"I doubt it. But let's check."

A young woman exited the nearby West Virginia Paper Company with arms full of bagged supplies. "Excuse me, Miss," Janet said, "did you happen to see a long skinny man carrying a pillowcase of personal belongings along here?"

"Yeah. As a matter of fact, I did," the woman said, searching Janet's face quizzically. "What did he do, steal something?"

"No. We think he has some valuable information he is unwilling to share."

"That sounds interesting."

"I guess I ought to explain," Janet said with a smile. "We are trying to find her uncle. We think this guy knows of his whereabouts, but he always eludes us."

"My uncle has become homeless," Sherri interjected. "We are trying to locate him so he'll know we have come to his aid."

"Well, if you look behind that old building," the woman said, winging her left elbow toward an old vacated single story block structure along the creek bank, "you may find the skinny man."

"Oh, is that where you saw the pillowcase-carrying man?"

"Yes. He dodged behind there just as I parked my car in the lot across the road."

"Thank you. We really appreciate your help. God bless you."

They quickly discerned that the area behind the building offered no hiding place. Once more, Lanky gave them the slip.

"If I get hold of that nut I'm going to give him something to fear," Sherri snarled.

"Yeah, giving him a good old thrashing would solve a lot, now wouldn't it? See what I mean? You can't resist the urge to fight. You don't care who it is, just as long as you can feud with someone. Oh, you frustrate me!"

"Really? Remember that statement you made, when we first saw ole Lanky? I believe it went something like, 'I hate playing cat and mouse games with people.'"

"At least I didn't want to beat the man up."

"Well," Sherri said, rolling her eyes, "don't deny that you are as disgusted as I am with Lanky's behavior."

"Come on. We might as well stroll the railroad tracks for a while. Maybe we can happen by some sort of lead or idea."

CHAPTER EIGHT

Sunday, April 29, 1979

"Janet, are you ready yet?" Sherri yelled from outside Janet's bedroom.

"Almost. What is the hurry? It only takes five minutes to get to Nicholson Chapel."

"Well, I would like to make a slight change in our plans," Sherri said as she silently prayed that Janet would be receptive.

"I'll be out in a minute."

Sherri anxiously waited on the deck overlooking Morgantown. She marveled at the ability to see various landmarks that Janet once identified to her from nearby Marion County and from Harrison County, even farther south. No wonder, someone coined the phrase, "Almost Heaven, West Virginia".

Janet pulled the sliding screen door open and pranced out onto the deck. "What is this change of plans you mentioned? I hope you aren't going to tell me I got all slicked up for nothing?"

Sherri whistled teasingly. She hadn't seen Janet in a dress since their high school prom night. The shin length flowered garment complimented her fashion-model shape.

"Don't make a fuss. I dress up like this every week day for work."

"Hardly. If you dressed that attractively during the week you'd be swamped with marriage proposals."

"Maybe I ought to wear something else to church," Janet said as she turned to go back into the house.

"Oh, quit. You are supposed to look nice for church. Besides, you don't have time to change. What do you think about going to Grace Chapel, at Tennant Valley, instead of attending Nicholson Chapel this morning?"

"Why would we want to worship with those hypocrites? Oh, never mind. Don't answer that. I know what you're up to."

"I'm not going to stir up anything," Sherri assured her.

"Who are you trying to kid? I know how you fight at the drop of a hat."

"I promise. I won't make a scene. I remember Uncle Joseph mentioning a deacon by the name of Bill Drake whom he highly praised. Maybe he'll be there. I'm sure he wouldn't mind talking with us about Uncle Joseph's situation."

"How could he benefit our undertaking?"

"Maybe Uncle Joseph has been in touch with him. He could have some ideas about how to accomplish our goals. We can use all the help we can get."

"Now, you are using your head for something besides a hat rack. Let's get going, then."

Deep red exterior double doors accented the salmon-pink brick structure. Inside, the light blue carpet, with crimson crosses woven into it, quickened the sanctuary. The light bounced off the brilliant white walls illuminating the long sturdy oak pews. Three gray stone walls sporting golden candlesticks embraced the pulpit area.

"Good morning, ladies," the elderly gentleman said, reaching his right hand toward Sherri. "Welcome to Grace Chapel. I'm Deacon Drake."

Sherri shook his hand and introduced herself and Janet.

"Wow! What a beautiful sanctuary," Janet exclaimed as she shook his hand.

"Thank you. Is this your first visit to Grace Chapel?"

"Yes, sir," Sherri answered. "Did you say your name is Drake?"

"Yes, ma'am. I'm the senior deacon. You look familiar. Have we met before?"

Sherri replied, "No, but I look a lot like a friend of yours—Reverend Short."

Deacon Drake's eyes sparkled and a wide smile erupted across his thin wrinkled face. "You must be his niece. I would know you anywhere. How Reverend Short bragged about you!"

Sherri felt the glow of her heart as it reached her cheeks. "Janet and I are pretty fond of *him,* too."

"Have you seen Joseph?" the deacon asked eagerly.

"No. That is what we were hoping to discuss with you, after church. That is, if you have time."

"Are you kidding?" Deacon Drake asked. "I will *make* time for such lovely creatures. Especially the kin of Joseph Short."

A young couple entered the sanctuary and Deacon Drake excused himself to welcome them. "Make yourselves at home," he said, motioning Janet and Sherri toward the front of the sanctuary. "Introduce yourselves to my darling wife. She is the blue-haired doll on the left side; second pew from the altar."

The worship service opened with a hymn followed by a prayer. The song leader then welcomed visitors. He asked that each of the four visitors stand to be recognized when their names were called. A teenage boy and his younger sister stood while the congregation sang a chorus welcoming them to Grace Chapel.

When introduced, Sherri and Janet realized, from the lower volume, only about half the assembly sang. Even in the Adult Sunday school class Sherri felt the tense stares, unsettling her. The atmosphere during morning worship so thickened that she heard little of the preacher's sermon. She just couldn't shake the irritation building over the coldness of some of the folks. Why couldn't she have been introduced without revealing her relationship to Uncle Joseph? How dare these hypocrites judge Uncle Joseph, or her!

Sherri and Janet waited outside for Deacon Drake while he said goodbye to others who attended services. A few people spoke to them and asked them to come again. Most passed by without saying a word. Some pretended not to notice them.

Sherri couldn't resist the urge to speak wryly to those who seemed to avoid them. "It was nice to see you," she said to many of them. To others she said, "What a joy to worship with such friendly people. God bless you." She delighted in their awkward responses.

An elderly plump woman waited for her husband to drive under the carport at the front entrance. Her lower lip pressed hard against the upper and her eyes fixed straight ahead in an angry glare.

Janet leaned close to Sherri and snickered. "You are so sly. That poor ole pompous lady is about to come undone. I guess she didn't appreciate the remark about what a pleasant smile she wore."

The new shiny black Cadillac hadn't come to a complete stop when the old woman reached for the door. "Take all day, why don't you?" she barked at the distinguished looking gray-haired gentleman in the driver's seat.

Sherri heard her mumble as she stumbled into the front seat, "The nerve of some people!" The door closed and Sherri could see the woman unleashing her annoyance.

"Poor man," Sherri whispered to Janet, "he'll probably get lectured all the way home."

"Now, you know why I can't see any sense in attending church and making a profession of faith in Jesus," Janet griped. "I haven't seen it fail yet. Every church I've ever been in has hypocrites in it. At least I know not to expect anything more from sinners like myself."

Before Sherri could respond to Janet's excuse, a young woman with a fair unblemished complexion approached them. Her long lustrous brown hair bounced with each step. "Hi. I'm Tammy Stewart. I'm so glad I caught up with you."

Sherri tried desperately to recall from where she knew the lively Ms. Stewart.

"I don't know if you remember me, but I attended Morgantown High with you two."

Janet said, "I thought you looked familiar. You were a Brice. Right?"

"Yes."

"You were the head cheerleader, and every boy's dream."

Blushing, she replied, "I don't know about that. But I do know that I envied you two. I worked at gaining only a portion of the admiration either of you unintentionally attracted." Quickly changing the subject, she asked, "Would you like to go to lunch with my husband and me? We'd like to talk with you about some things of mutual interest."

Sherri looked at Janet and asked, "What do you think? Do we need to get back home right away?"

"No. But we *are* waiting to talk to Deacon Drake, aren't we?"

Tammy said, "Steve and I can wait for you in the parking lot. He'll be out in a minute."

Janet shrugged and promised, "We'll try to be brief. But we really do need to speak with Deacon Drake."

"Oh, here's Steve, now," Tammy announced as she reached her hand to the tall blonde exiting the church.

"Hi," he said with a wide grin. "Sorry we didn't get a chance to say hello before church took up. We were a few minutes late." He then asked Tammy if she had thought to invite Sherri and Janet to dine with them.

"How about Ruby's and Ketchy's, over Cheat?" Tammy asked.

"Ladies?" Steve asked smiling down at them. "My treat."

"I hear their meals are outstanding," Sherri said. "But we couldn't allow you to pay for our lunch."

"Don't argue with him," Tammy said, gazing admiringly into his deep blue eyes. "He can contend with the best." She slipped her arm around his elbow and led him off as she declared, "We'll wait for you. We're in the White Buick Electra at the end of the parking lot. Take your time."

Janet finally located a parking space in the family style restaurant's recently paved lot. Inside, pictures of local Cheat Race Track heroes and their stock cars hung proudly on lacquered oak walls. On a wall at one end of the dining room a hubcap clock completed the theme. Tammy chose a table near the wide window facing the large field that had once been home to the Cheat Race Track, a popular attraction during their youth.

Though the place stirred and few seats were vacant, the waitress promptly appeared with glasses of ice water and took their orders.

"While we are waiting for our meals," Tammy said, "let me explain what it is I wish to talk to you about. Steve and I have joined with Deacon Drake to make serious inquiry with the Regional Headquarters of the Independent Pastor's Group about Reverend Short's dismissal and license revocation."

"Uncle Joseph had once declared Deacon Drake his closest friend at the church," Sherri said. "That is why we needed to talk to him."

Janet added, "We were unaware of anyone else's efforts on his behalf, so we decided to take on the task of getting Joseph back into his rightful place in society."

"Well, I'm glad you are in allegiance with us," Tammy said cheerfully. "The Pastors' Group agreed to rehear Reverend Short's case, but we have been unable to locate him to relay the message."

"That is what we are working on now," Sherri said. "But we haven't found him yet. We are certain that he is living as a homeless person in the area."

Janet interrupted, "We expect stiff opposition from Angela Hillman and some of her cohorts as we try to clear Joseph's name. I guess you know some of the details in his situation. We are convinced that the recent charges against Joseph are just as trumped up as the false charge of murder had been eleven years ago."

"Yeah," Sherri said excitedly, "but what puzzles us is, why Angela would, after so many years, renew her hostilities against him."

"I'll tell you why," Steve exploded. "Because Reverend Short received an anonymous tip that implicated Angela as a participant in the 1968 murder of Spike Cottrell. The caller also claimed that Angela spearheaded the attempt to frame Reverend Short. He wouldn't tell us who the alleged murderer is. He would only say that he wished not to believe the information, at least without absolute proof. We intend to get to the bottom of it all. I, for one, am sick and tired of people like Angela Hillman who exercise their privileges of power for evil, going unchallenged."

Tammy reached across the table and gently touched Steve's hand.

"Sweetheart, don't get so wound up. We will eventually succeed, but you need to learn to approach the subject more calmly."

The redness of Steve's cheeks and neck responded to Tammy's tenderness. His face regained its fair complexion as he lowly remarked, "I know. I just get so irritated with people. If the general public knew Reverend Short as we know him, the powers-that- be would not have driven him into isolation. Instead, they would embrace him and his Christian ideals."

"I sure am relieved to learn that I'm not the only one who expresses fiery indignation," Sherri said with a slight grin.

"It is difficult enough for me with one quick-tempered partner in this quest," Janet said. "No offence intended, Steve. But if you knew how combative Sherri is you'd understand. She is very loving, but she flares up much too quickly."

"I'm learning to be more tactful," Sherri replied defensively.

"I think you are trying very hard, but you have a long way to go."

Tammy looked quizzically at Sherri. "You said something about Reverend Short still being in the area. If he is homeless, how do you know he is still around here?"

"Janet recently saw him walking near the courthouse square, but she lost him when she circled the block looking for a parking place. Then we talked with another homeless man who avoided our questions about Uncle Joseph. We are sure he knew of Uncle Joseph's whereabouts."

Janet added, "Yesterday, we talked with a fisherman along the river near where Walnut Street ends at the boat-launching ramp. He had seen Joseph in the area, under the Morgantown-Westover Bridge. The other homeless people refer to him as Joe the Baptist."

"Steve and I have already agreed that if he needs a place to stay, we will let him live in one of our rental apartments," Tammy said. "Free of charge for as long as he wishes to stay."

Steve's eyes moistened. "I can't begin to tell you all he has done for us and our families." His chin quivered and his face wrinkled under the apparent emotional pressure he struggled to contain. "You tell them, Tammy."

Tammy clasped his hand between hers and gently squeezed. "I bore

Steven a son with serious respiratory problems and a partially formed heart. He lived on life support for two and a half weeks after delivery." She paused to wipe the blackened tears streaming down her face.

Steve laid his left hand atop Tammy's. "Reverend Short spent a lot of hours with us at the hospital. He would even sit with little Steven while we slept in recliner chairs in the room. He knew just what to say and when to say it."

"He even knew when to say nothing," Tammy sniffled. "He would just hold us and cry with us. I have never known such a gentle man. His strength seemed all the more enhanced by his ability to genuinely love."

"Evidently, you know the same Joseph Short we know," said Sherri. "I guess that is why it frustrates me so much when others assail him."

"Oh, that isn't the half of what this man means to us," Steve quipped. "My dad, Jesse Stewart, took sides with those who sought Reverend Short's dismissal from the pastorate. Dad and I argued heatedly over the issues surrounding Pastor Short. Dad even confronted Pastor Short openly before the congregation a week before Reverend Short left the church. Even then, the pastor kept his cool and simply said that he regretted that some of the congregation believed the false indictments against him, and affirmed his love for all of us."

"Yeah," Tammy said enthusiastically, "then, when Steve's dad suffered his heart attack, Reverend Short, unperturbed by their unfounded hostilities, still visited him and prayed with him. My father-in-law now attends another church because of my and Steve's support of Reverend Short."

Steve shook his head in disbelief. "Then, when Mom fell and broke her hip, Reverend Short visited her, too. He led my mother to the Lord when she returned home from the hospital. She had attended church for as long as I can recall but never got saved until then. She attends church with Dad, as she should. But she's torn between her appreciation of Pastor Short and Dad's firm, albeit ignorant, stand against him."

"Wow!" Sherri exclaimed. "Deacon Drake said that you two would be more informative than himself. I see why he insisted that he not say too much until we've talked with you. He seemed thrilled that we were going to lunch together."

Steve wiped his eyes. "Brother Drake is working with a few law enforcement connections trying to get Reverend Short's case properly investigated. He's a retired police detective and still has a few connections he hopes to employ for our purposes."

They shared strategies during lunch and promised to keep one another informed.

Just as Sherri opened the door, the phone rang. She rushed across the living room and answered, "Hello."

"This is a warning," a muffled male voice proclaimed. "If you are smart you'll go back to Ohio and mind your own business."

"Who is this?" she shouted.

"Never mind who I am. Just do what I tell you."

She could faintly discern familiarity in the man's speech, but not enough to identify him. Maybe she could keep him talking until she fitted a face or a name to the voice. "I know the trick with the mouth filled with a balled up hanky or something. What's the matter, you too cowardly to speak in your own natural tone? Or do you always run around with a mouth full of manure?"

"Leave and never return to Morgantown, again," he ordered.

"Why should I leave? Maybe you called the wrong number."

"I have the right number, Sherri Mosley. If you care for your friends' and your own safety, you'll leave immediately."

Janet stood in the doorway with a puzzled look on her face.

Sherri motioned for her to come and listen to the caller. Tipping the earpiece so they both could hear, she said, "You might just as well know that I am not afraid of cowards like you. If you were a real man you'd not have to speak anonymously."

"Don't be a fool," he growled. "You're sticking your nose into something that will get you killed, ya numb-noggin."

Sherri slammed the phone into its cradle and exclaimed, "That Frank is so stupid. He thinks he is really slick. What a moron!"

"Why do you think it's him? I couldn't make out his voice."

"Neither could I, at first. As he talked I detected some of his families mid-western accent. Then, when he called me 'numb-noggin' it definitely gave him away. I have never heard anyone use the term 'numb-noggin' besides Frank. He used to get mad when I teased him about it."

CHAPTER NINE

Monday, April 30, 1979

A soft drizzle floated in occasional wind-driven sheets. Sherri's bed beckoned her to stay, promising to keep her warm and cozy. "When looking for a job, always visit the prospective employer early in the week and early in the morning," her father had often reminded her. His advice rang out clearly, but not loud enough to drag her from the bed.

"Sherri," Janet called, "I'm going to be late for work. Come on." The mechanic promised to have Janet's Jeep repaired and ready for pick up, after noon.

"Oh, I'm coming." She yawned and stretched like an unconcerned feline. "I have a notion to let you just take the car and I'll sleep all day."

"I don't think so. Now get dressed and let's go."

Sherri hurried to shower, brush her teeth, and dress. Her thoughts turned to Uncle Joseph. She wondered how his predicament could possibly be working to his good. She knew, without a doubt, that the Reverend Short loved the Lord. Moreover, she found consolation in Christ's love for Uncle Joseph. But she just couldn't make sense of his ostracism and homelessness, nor her own marital woes.

Driving up Murray Road, her mind wandered in slow swirling contemplation. "I wonder what Frank is doing right now," she said, not realizing she had uttered it aloud.

"Probably moping like you are," Janet snarled. "Only *his* blahs are likely from a hangover."

"You don't know that. He might not be drinking at all."

"You think that he quit drinking after you left?" Janet scolded.

"I don't know what to think about him, anymore. I just know that it is not God's will that we end our marriage."

"Well," Janet said, "it takes two to make a relationship work. You've done all that you can do. It is up to him now. You can't be responsible for his misbehavior. Nor can you take the blame for his wanting to end the marriage."

"I guess you're *half* right."

"I guess I'm one hundred percent right. He doesn't deserve you, Sherri. I don't know what you ever saw in him, anyhow."

"If you felt that strongly toward him, why didn't you say all this before I married him?"

Janet slapped the top of the dash and yelled, "Are you going to sit there and tell me that I didn't protest your engagement? That is, if you want to call a two weeks notice of intent to marry an engagement."

"You only complained about my rushing into a lifetime commitment with my head up my behind," Sherri snapped back.

"I beg your pardon. I distinctly remember a certain young redhead storming out of the bowling alley one night and walking all the way from Chestnut Ridge Road to Granville because her *friend* told her that the redhead should listen to her mother about this matter. You always heard only what you wanted to hear. Everything else you immediately trash-canned. You were determined to marry that loudmouthed boozer in spite of the advice."

"Frank behaved no wilder than the rest of us back then," Sherri said with a hint of remorse. "How I wish we had all become Christians before that time in our lives!"

Janet placed her hand gently on Sherri's shoulder. "Sorry, I didn't intend to hurt you."

"I know. I'm just so confused. I hate this helpless feeling."

Janet snickered softly. "You know what's really scary? I am getting as testy as you."

"Testy? You are down right combative," Sherri said with a chuckle.

"So, where are you planning to apply for work this morning?" Janet asked.

"First, I'm going to the West Virginia University employment office. Then I think I'll go to the Job Services office and register with them. I thought I'd stop by the Kennedy Youth Center and see if I can get an application to fill out for a secretary position or something of that nature."

"That would be a good job, if you like working with young convicts. Sherri, don't forget to pick me up at four o'clock. We need to pick up my Jeep and then go to Bowlby's to have the Oldsmobile registered in your name. They'll send in the paper work for us and call when the title returns with the proper license transfer."

Sherri job-hunted the entire morning. At 12:15 p.m. she decided to get a couple of Yan's hot dogs. Yan's had the hottest hot dog chili in the area. The bell, hanging on the doorknob, jingled as she stepped inside and the old hardwood floor creaked, prompting all five patrons to turn as to see who encroached their domain.

As teenagers, she and Janet often stopped by Yan's, before going home after extracurricular school activities. Back then, the place swarmed with hurried teens that wanted a couple hot dogs to eat on the way home. This day, five older strangers greeted her. The young woman behind the counter said, "Hi. What will you have?"

"Two hot-hot dogs with onions and mustard and a cola, please."

She pulled herself onto a stool near the end of the counter. The elderly gentleman next to her, reading an article from the *Scoop Weekly* said, "Wonder what got into ole Fenton?" He spoke to no one in particular, apparently fishing for conversation.

"What do you mean, what got into him?" another grandfatherly white-haired man replied. "Why, he's a heathen. A devil—that's what got into him," he growled.

"Have you guys read his paper lately?" the first man asked. "He seems to have lost his fire for hammering people. Why this stuff isn't even worth reading. No bite to it."

Sherri listened intently, pretending to pay no mind to the conversation.

A third man spoke in a strained voice as though he had laryngitis. "I heard his daughter ran off with an older boy and threatened never to return. You know, that ole coot has nobody but the girl."

"Well, I certainly don't feel sorry for him," piped the first man.

"That is one fellow that everybody loves to hate," the whispering man said.

"Read this article," the first man said throwing the paper toward the second man. "He sounds like he is considering closing shop. Why, he almost apologizes for his style of journalism in that article. What is wrong with that nut? Doesn't he know that is what kept him afloat all these years? If he doesn't expose the garbage around us, who will?"

"Listen to this," the second man bellowed, "he even says that he is going to be reporting more on the Reverend Joseph Short case." He then read aloud from the *Scoop Weekly*, "'Unreported and mishandled information about Reverend Short will present to the public a different man than what has been previously published. Hold on to your hats. Shocking revelations are forthcoming. Once the air is cleared I intend to discontinue the smutty journalism that for too long made up the *Scoop Weekly*.'"

Sherri choked on a bite of hot dog. Swallowing hard and rinsing it down with a drink of cola, she felt an ecstatic rush of blood to her face.

"You all right, dear?" asked the elderly gentleman sitting next to her.

"Just a little embarrassed."

"No need to be embarrassed, sweetheart," he said. "If you aren't used to those fiery hot dogs, they can kill you."

"I guess," she said smiling. She didn't particularly want them to know what really caused her to choke. "May I see that paper, sir?"

"Certainly," the man said as he passed it down to her.

Sherri read the article and laid the paper on the counter. Imagining how that took guts, she just had to visit him. She finished her lunch and told the others to have a good day as she stepped out onto the cracked sidewalk.

Sherri barely avoided collision with the oncoming black mud-splattered Ford Bronco that sped around the graveled corner as she negotiated the turn toward the *Scoop Weekly*. She dismissed it as another angry victim of Fenton's, leaving a typical argument with him.

The building seemed as dreary as ever. Dark clouds and drizzle added to its mystique. She thought that Fenton would have kept the front door closed on such a damp day. She stepped inside and startled at the ransacked appearance of the front office. File cabinets were overturned, files of paper were strewn about the floor, and a couple wooden chairs lay around in pieces.

Sherri called, "Mr. Fenton. Mr. Fenton, are you here?"

A faint groan crept from the large drab room to her left. She cautiously entered the massive chamber where an old printing press and a couple other machines stood with plenty of space between them. The room seemed much too dark for a printing shop. Dimly lit, it would hardly pass for a warehouse. She scanned the huge high-ceilinged room looking for Mr. Fenton. Along each side, stacks of boxes and other supplies piled high against the brick walls, evinced that indeed it doubled as warehouse and print shop. In the right rear corner she detected a slight movement beneath several toppled boxes.

"Mr. Fenton, are you okay?" she asked almost whispering.

Another faint grunt and a small stir under the boxes revealed someone in trouble.

Sherri visually searched the room before rushing to Mr. Fenton's aid. She grabbed heavy boxes and rolled them from atop the plump little man and gasped at the sight of his bleeding head and torn clothes.

"Lie still," Sherri said, "I'll call for an ambulance."

Ellis Fenton reached weakly toward her. "No," the barely audible voice beckoned. "Please, no. They. They. Uh." His reaching arm plopped to his side.

"Okay. Let me at least treat your wounds. Do you have a first aid kit handy?"

He raised the other arm slowly and pointed toward the huge printing press. A white metal box with a large red cross hung on the side of the machine.

She rushed to the restroom at the far side of the office and wet several paper towels and grabbed the first aid kit on her return. She washed the blood from his bald head and his bruised swollen face.

"You need to go to the emergency room and get this gash sewn up." She gently wiped at the long gaping wound. "Let me call an ambulance. I would take you to the hospital but there may be internal injuries to consider. We can't take any chances."

"Please, just let me get my strength. I'll be all right in a minute or two."

She bandaged his head wound and treated the lacerations on his face. He weakly pulled himself up from the floor and stumbled toward the office. She grabbed his left arm and insisted on steadying him.

Ellis stopped and leaned against the doorframe before entering the office. Among the clutter of file folders and papers on the floor laid a note on a large piece of cardboard, written with red paint: "It is time for you to close down." He tottered to the sign and leaned to pick it up. "I beg your pardon, sirs. It is time I become busier than I've ever been," he said in his usual squeaky voice. Glancing back at Sherri in the doorway, he grinned. "They only made me more determined to print the truth. What they don't know is that I have promised God and myself that I am going to make things right. With His help I'll do just that."

"You promised God to make what right?" Sherri asked as if she didn't already know. She wanted to hear it straight from the source.

"Of all the cases I have reported on and of all the people I have ever slandered, none ever received the measure of dishonest and slanted publicity as that of Joseph Short."

He limped to a metal folding chair along the front wall of the office and sat down. Pointing to an old black leather swivel chair across the room, he softly said, "Take a seat young lady. I have something to tell you."

Sherri obeyed his request and looked him in the eye. In spite of his badgered puffy face he looked serene and composed.

"After you left the other day I made an important decision. I had been thinking all that morning that I needed to surrender my life to Christ. I just couldn't see how I would balance such a commitment with my determination to continue my business. I am not exactly marketable to mainline newspaper and publishing companies." He took a deep breath and raised his right hand toward heaven and declared, with moistened eyes, "I had convinced myself that I had become unforgivable. I had half-heartedly prayed before you came that day. I asked God to somehow show me that His love is still available to me."

Sherri's heart leaped within her. She thought of going to his side and hugging him, but resisted. She didn't want to spoil this moment by even the slightest interruption.

"You were a Godsend that day," he said in a throat-stricken high pitch. "You had every reason to tell me that I am reaping what I have sown. You'd have been justified in saying so. But you showed a kind of compassion of which I have known little."

The telephone on his old worn and faded wooden desk rang. "Do you want me to get it, since I'm closer?" Sherri asked.

"No. Let it ring. If it's important they'll call again." He shuffled in his chair and continued, "I made a promise to God that I would go to church Sunday. I vowed that there, I would repent of my sins and commit my life fully to Him."

"Ah, Mr. Fenton, that is such good news. So, tell me about your experience."

"Well, I attended the morning worship services at Blair Ridge Community Church. That's where my wife worshipped. I suspected I'd not receive much of a welcome. But that didn't matter too much to me. The congregation's genuinely warm reception flabbergasted me."

"See, God's people love you and are glad to see His hand at work in any sinner's life."

"I always thought that a person could only get saved in response to hellfire and brimstone preaching. That little old preacher delivered the most comforting message I have ever heard. He preached about eternal judgment for those who reject salvation through Christ. But he also explained how the Lord loves us. How He died for us while we were yet sinners. And by the time he gave an invitation for those who would be saved to come to the altar, God's Spirit had me under undeniable conviction. I could hardly wait to go to the altar and receive Jesus."

"Amen," Sherri cheered. "I could tell something happened to you. Your countenance shines, even through that banged up face."

Ellis bashfully glanced downward. "Thanks for noticing." He

looked back at Sherri and sincerely added, "And thanks for being God's messenger. I had my heart set on getting saved before ever going to church yesterday. You had a lot to do with that. My wife would have appreciated your efforts to console me in Jesus' name."

"She must have been very special."

"Yes. If only I had realized that... back then! She often begged me to close down the *Scoop Weekly.* How she bore the embarrassment I caused her is truly amazing." He dropped his head into his palms and wept. "How I wish I could hold her now and tell her that I have finally accepted her Jesus."

Sherri leaned forward and spoke reflectively, "Well, I recall reading where Jesus said that 'joy shall be *in heaven* over one sinner that repenteth, more than over ninety and nine just persons, which need no repentance.'"

While Ellis explained that his behind-the-scenes colleagues had read last week's *Scoop Weekly* and decided to silence him, she scurried about the office helping him pick up the scattered files and setting the salvageable furniture aright.

She looked at her watch. "Well, I better get going. Are you going to be okay?"

"Sure, I'm leaving too. We need to get together and share information. I'll need your help to amend my terrible injustice against your uncle."

"I'll be back tomorrow," Sherri answered.

Ellis' eyes widened with alarm. "Oh, no. You can't come here anymore. I'm closing shop as of this evening."

"You can't do that. You just said that you were going to make things right, first."

He flashed a disarming grin. "I have it worked out. I have property these punks know nothing about. I'll contact you within a few days and let you know what I'm up to. Meanwhile, you just stay on your toes. The guys who visited me today were asking about you."

"What did they want to know about me?" Sherri angrily asked. "They don't scare me." Her body trembled with fury.

"Just don't be getting too geared up, young lady. We don't need to fight their fight. We will get the best of them in due time. Be patient. I've got a plan. They wanted to know where you are staying while in Morgantown. I didn't tell them anything."

Sherri promised she'd not return to the old printing shop. She spent the rest of the afternoon contemplating Ellis' complete change of heart and mind. She couldn't wait to share the news with Janet. Of course, she could expect a lecture about the possible dangers of associating with him.

Janet climbed into the Oldsmobile and whispered, "Don't look now, but I think you are being watched."

Sherri instinctively jerked her head from one side to the other. Seeing nothing suspicious she replied, "Don't do that. Ellis Fenton just told me that some thugs were asking about where I'm staying while in Morgantown."

"First off, I told you not to look," Janet snarled. "Keep your head on straight. For the past fifteen minutes I have watched two guys in a black Ford Bronco keeping you in view. They're parked three rows behind you. One of our patients got the license plate number and called it back in to me from a pay phone."

"What do we do now?" Sherri asked.

"Just drive to the Star City Police station. It's only a couple miles away. If they follow us, they will probably decide against pursuing us any further. My cousin is on duty this afternoon. We'll talk with him about what to do."

Sherri's hands trembled, as much from anger as from fear. She cranked the engine and jerked the gearshift into drive. Glancing through her rearview mirror, she said, "Those are the scoundrels who beat up Ellis Fenton today. They nearly ran me over, getting out of there, just as I pulled onto the short road to Fenton's shop."

"Why would they beat Fenton? Isn't he in cahoots with them?"

"He printed an article in last weeks issue of the *Scoop Weekly* declaring that he is going to print some unreported truths that will benefit Uncle Joseph. Whoever is behind this conspiracy sent these thugs to convince Fenton to abort his plans and close up shop for good."

"Are they still behind us?" Janet asked nervously.

"Yeah, but they're keeping their distance."

The Bronco followed Sherri and Janet from Van Voorhis Road to the Star City municipal building. Sherri pulled the Oldsmobile into the parking lot of the Star City Fire Hall, behind the police station. The Bronco continued on Congress Avenue and turned right at the next intersection, onto Stafford.

Janet hurried from the car and yelled, "Hey, Officer. Stop right there."

Sherri looked over her shoulder as she exited the vehicle and saw a tall handsome man dressed in a well-pressed uniform and wearing a dark blue Smokey the Bear hat.

"What are you doing here, Jumping Janet?" the young officer yelled back. He walked briskly toward them and added, "I almost missed you. I just came back to the station to exchange portable radios."

Janet informed the officer that a couple men, who had just beaten up a man over in the Westover area, were following them. Janet described the Bronco and pointed to the street where it had last been seen.

"Stay here at the station while I make a few rounds to see if they're in the area."

The policeman returned about half an hour later. "They must have kept going. I radioed the Sheriff's office and asked them to also notify the Morgantown police department to keep a look out for the Bronco and its two male occupants. Westover Police hasn't received a report of an assault. Neither have the Counties nor the..."

"I doubt that Fenton will notify the authorities or press charges," Sherri said.

"Oh. Thad Ashbury, this is Sherri Mosley," Janet exclaimed. "She is the niece of Joseph Short that I told you about last week."

"It is a pleasure to meet you, Sherri. Janet has told me a lot about you."

Sherri felt blood rush to her cheeks as she turned to face Janet. "You didn't say anything about contacting the police about my…or Uncle Joseph's case."

"You aren't the only one who can take initiative, you know," Janet retorted.

"Ladies," Officer Ashbury said, "let's go inside and argue." His teasing grin evoked embarrassed smiles from Sherri *and* Janet.

"You started it," Janet said teasingly.

"Did not."

"Did too."

"If you two start fighting I'm calling for backup," Thad said. He led them to the conference room. Janet gave him the Pennsylvania license plate number of the Bronco.

He informed them that a detective friend from another department recently launched an unofficial reinvestigation of the charges against Joseph Short, both new and old. He assured them that they would find out who is behind the conspiracies and cover-ups in the eleven-year-old unsolved murder of Spike Cottrell.

"We need to get going, Sherri," Janet announced.

"What's the hurry?" Thad asked. Ogling Sherri, he added, "I'm enjoying the scenery."

Janet playfully grabbed Sherri by the arm and exclaimed, "We have to pick up my Jeep before the shop closes…and she isn't available—at least, not yet."

CHAPTER TEN

Tuesday, May 1, 1979

"Hello. Mrs. Mosley?" the man on the phone asked. Passing traffic in the background nearly drowned out the caller's voice.

Sherri hesitated to answer affirmatively, fearing it may be her pursuers. "Who are you trying to call?" she asked cautiously.

"This is Ellis Fenton. I am trying to reach Sherri Mosley. Do I have the wrong number?"

Sherri recognized the shrillness in Ellis' voice. "I can barely make out what you are saying, Mr. Fenton. The background noise is terrible."

"I'm calling from a pay phone. Can we meet somewhere and discuss business?"

"Sure. When and where?"

"How about the courthouse square? It will be in an open public place. That way you needn't fear that I am up to anything strange or mean."

"Mr. Fenton, the Holy Spirit bore witness that you are now the Lord's. I don't need to be reassured."

"Well, praise the Lord," Ellis shrieked.

"The courthouse square would be a suitable meeting place. When?"

"Right away, if you can make it," he said with a certain urgency.

"I can meet you there in about an hour," Sherri said. Anticipation accelerated her pulse, impelling her to offer a quick, but fervent, silent prayer.

"Good, I'll see you then. But make sure you aren't being followed."

"Okay. Bye." Her hope did an abrupt about-face. Paranoia surged through her like an unforeseen hurricane. She rushed through her housecleaning. Driving to town she continuously checked her rearview mirror. What if those thugs do find out where she lives? She couldn't risk putting Janet in harms way. She could move out, but her savings wouldn't last much longer—especially if she had to pay rent and utilities. At least she would pay only a portion of the utilities at Janet's—against Janet's protests.

She pulled into the parking lot at the corner of Pleasant and Spruce Streets, scanning the entire lot to be sure nobody spied her. She drove through the lot and out onto Spruce Street and back into the lot before feeling safe enough to park. She stared into each passing car on her walk to the courthouse square. She studied every face on the sidewalks and through store windows.

The courthouse square bustled with people like she and Janet had expected when they first visited it, in hopes of finding Uncle Joseph or someone who might know where he is. No familiar faces appeared. Too nervous to sit, she searched for a vantage point and then stood at the southwest corner of the square.

A bus parked along the front of the square to let off passengers and waited about five minutes before departing with new riders. She spotted Clem Castleman and started to yell his name, but gave it a second thought and straightaway dropped the idea, fearing that Mr. Fenton may be alarmed if he saw her talking with someone he didn't know.

"Ma'am," an unexpected male voice called. It sent porcupine quills all over her body.

Sherri stood so close to the courthouse she didn't see Lanky Lang approach from Chancery Row. "Oh, hi. You startled me. Sorry about the squeal."

"That's okay, ma'am. I thought you were expecting me."

"I'm meeting someone here, but he said nothing about anyone else meeting with us. Why do you think I would expect you?"

"Mr. Fenton said to meet him and a beautiful redheaded lady here."

Lanky let down his soiled pillowcase. His eyes raced back and forth from side to side. He asked slowly, "Where is Mr. Fenton? Isn't he coming?" He reached for his pillowcase and started to leave.

"Don't leave. Please wait. Mr. Fenton will be here. He promised."

Lanky paused as he studied Sherri's face. "Okay. But I won't wait long. There are bad people around here. You have to be careful around here, ma'am. Sometimes these bad people pretend to be nice and then they entrap you. Are you nice?"

Sherri shuddered at the thought of how terrible it would be to live in constant paranoia. "Yes, I'm nice. I won't harm you, Lanky. I think *you* are a nice person, too." Her heart lifted as she saw a bashful grin creep across his slender face.

He dropped his head in humility and said, "Thanks, ma'am."

"You're welcome. Would you like to sit down on one of the benches?"

"Maybe over there on the flower garden wall."

"Okay. That way we can still see Mr. Fenton when he arrives."

They sat atop the concrete-capped brick wall. "Are you Joe the Baptist's sister?" Lanky asked in his slow unpretentious manner.

Sherri's eyes welled up. She had to force a reply. "I'm his niece. Do you know him well?"

"I don't know if I should say any more. Sorry, ma'am."

"It's okay. You can talk to me about Joe the Baptist."

"I can't say anything else."

Silence fell upon them both. Finally, Lanky asked, "Did I hurt your feelings, ma'am? I'm sorry. Please don't cry."

Sherri looked into his face. Through the weathered features a childlike innocence shined. "No, you didn't make me cry or hurt my feelings, Lanky. I just get so emotional about Uncle Joseph. He and I were very close at one time. The world has been so cruel to him. I want so desperately to find him and make sure that all is well with him. But I feel helpless."

"Is your name Sherri, ma'am?" Lanky asked.

"Yes. I'm sorry. I should have at least introduced myself."

"I just remembered—Joe the Baptist talks a lot about you. He said that you are special. He cried one time, like you're doing, when he told us about you. He thought you might be ashamed of him. He is a nice man. He loves everybody… Hey, here comes Mr. Fenton."

Sherri got so caught up in conversation with Lanky that her unnerving caution had vanished.

"I see you two have already met," Ellis said. "Have you introduced yourselves?"

"This is Sherri, Mr. Fenton. She is Joe the Baptist's niece."

"I know. Looks like him too, doesn't she?"

"Only a lot prettier," Lanky said blushing. "Nice like him too."

"Well, let's get down to business," Ellis said rubbing his hands. "Two things. Sherri, I need help at the *Scoop Weekly.* I'll pay you well…"

"I don't…."

"Don't answer yet. Let me finish. The pay is good and what you don't already know I'll teach you. I need someone who is going to put her heart and soul into this work. And we have a lot of work to do. You and I will have to share duties. Some parts of the job will be taxing and unpleasant. You'll be investigating, writing, and even manual labor to get out the weekly paper, early every Saturday morning, to the various vendors."

Sherri could think of no good reason to decline his offer. In fact, she could only think of the possibilities it afforded in her mission. "Well, I certainly need a job. And I can't think of a better opportunity. Can I speak honestly with you?"

"I suspect you are capable of nothing less," Ellis answered with a knowing grin.

"I need to think on this a day or two. I don't mean to sound unappreciative, but the *Scoop Weekly* doesn't have a good reputation. I am very particular about my witness for Jesus."

"That is all the more reason I want you, and nobody else, to be my partner in this new direction for the paper. We can rename the paper if need be." He reached out his hand and said, "How about it, partner."

"Tentatively," Sherri said as she shook his hand.

"I mean partner in the truest sense of the word. Sherri, I want to make you full partner. You'll have the same amount of decision-making power I have. We will do nothing without mutual agreement. I have my lawyer working on the contract even as we speak. That's why I'm late."

"I don't have anything to invest. Not even collateral."

"I didn't say anything about selling you a partnership. I just need you and your determination and commitment. We will turn this paper into a Christian oriented weekly."

"You're serious, aren't you?"

"Yes, I'm serious. I don't know how to explain it to you except to say that I am convinced that God laid this idea upon my heart and I can't rest from the thought of it. You *must* say yes."

She spontaneously hugged Ellis and said, "It's a deal." Releasing him she added, "But you know how hotheaded I can be. Of course, I'm working on that. With God's grace I'll improve."

"I understand what you're saying. But retain some of the spunk. You'll need it. We'll make a great team." He looked at Lanky and announced, "Now for the second business item at hand. Lanky is going to take us to Joseph, or at least where he sometimes stays while in the area."

"He might not be there, Miss Sherri," Lanky said. "But if he isn't there he'll be back, sometime. He travels a lot, preaching to other people who don't have homes."

Sherri reached up and hugged Lanky's neck. "God bless, you." Looking Lanky in the eyes and then looking back at Ellis, she proclaimed, "I don't know if I can stand any more blessings." Lifting her right hand toward heaven, she said, "Thank you, Lord. Thank you. I don't deserve such grace, but thank you, Jesus."

Ellis motioned toward Lanky and said, "Take us to your leader."

Lanky led them upstream, along the riverbank, southward toward Fairmont. They walked the railroad tracks along the east bank of the Monongahela until they crossed the railroad trestle that spanned Decker's Creek just before it empties into the river. Lanky stopped behind an old four-story brick warehouse and told Sherri and Ellis to wait.

Sherri watched excitedly as Lanky removed a half-rotted piece of plywood from a crawl space opening and crawled under the massive structure. "Surely, they don't live in there!" she said to Ellis while staring at the entrance.

A moment later, a small battered wooden rowboat appeared at the opening, being pushed from behind.

Ellis said, "Let me give you a hand," and grabbed the heavily soiled rope attached to the front of the boat, and pulled. The rope broke, sending Ellis to the ground.

Sherri slipped out a snicker as she hopped from the tracks to assist him. "We don't have time for a break. Now get up," she teased.

He released a short squeaky laugh. "I guess that rope is about as old and rotten as I am."

Lanky took the rope from Ellis and began retying it to the other piece of rope that showed signs of previous repairs. The two men lifted the boat and carried it to the river's steep bank.

Sherri carried the only oar. She examined it in dismay. The splintered paddle had several cracks and chips from age and use.

Crossing one quarter mile downstream of the Morgantown Lock and Dam, Lanky rowed vigorously, skillfully stroking along one side then the other, as the rushing waters pounded the left side of the boat. Once on shore they pulled the boat to the top of the bank and across the railroad tracks and slid it into a huge culvert that passed under Old River Road. Sherri marveled how they were only yards downstream of their starting point. Lanky interrupted her pondering with a motion for them to follow him.

"I could have driven over here, Lanky," Ellis scolded. "You said it wasn't very far."

"It ain't far, Mr. Fenton," Lanky answered apologetically.

"I could have at least driven across the Westover Bridge and parked on this side of the river. We wouldn't have had to cross over in that ragged old death trap."

Sherri interceded for Lanky. "Well, he probably has a good reason for approaching this side of the river that way."

"Yes, ma'am," Lanky said. "Joe the Baptist told me I shouldn't walk along the River Road. He said to always walk the tracks along here."

Sherri grinned toward Ellis. "See, there *is* a good reason? You're very wise to listen to Uncle Joseph, Lanky."

They walked nearly two miles before climbing up into the steep wooded terrain. Ellis insisted on resting for a few minutes. "Why are you guys living so far up the hill? Wouldn't it be much easier to make camp closer to the river or a roadway of some sort?"

"It isn't much farther," Lanky said.

Sherri turned toward the river and sat on the hillside. "Now I know how you stay so thin, Lanky. My legs feel like rubber."

Ellis plopped beside her.

"Wait here, while I go see if Joe the Baptist is back yet," Lanky said. "He might get mad if I bring you to our hideout."

"Why do you think we came *this* far?" Ellis growled. "Just wait a minute and we'll go with you." As Ellis struggled to his feet, Lanky broke into a run, bounding up the hillside.

"Come back here, you simpleton," Ellis shouted. "I'm going to tie a leash to him next time we go anywhere with him."

Sherri watched as Lanky bounced up the steep grade like a frolicking deer. Busting through the briars and the weeds and darting between the trees like a scared rabbit, he soon disappeared into the thick growth.

"Well, I guess we'll have to wait for him to return," Sherri sighed as she gazed down the hill to the rustling water. "Wow! I didn't realize we had climbed so far, already."

"We could try to follow him," Ellis said as he looked up into the spring foliage. "We ought to be able to find their hideout if we ascend the hill a little farther."

"Better not spook him now. He may never trust us again. If Uncle Joseph hasn't returned we need him to let us know when he *does* get back."

"I suppose," Ellis moaned. "I told that nut that we wouldn't let anyone else know where the hideout is."

"We were fortunate to get him to bring us this far. Let's count our blessings and wait for him to return."

Ellis sat down, then reclined against the hill and folded his hands under his head. "I hope he doesn't see his shadow before coming back. We may never see him again. He'll think someone is following him."

Sherri studied the landscape then remarked, "You know what? We can't be too far from your print shop."

"Yeah," Ellis said excitedly. "I hadn't given it much thought since we passed the coal barges below the Borg-Warner plant. But, you're right. I wonder how close to the shop they are staying. They must be somewhere behind or above the shop. I have never ventured into the woods behind my business. There is a lot of undeveloped acreage up there."

"Think we should climb a little while we wait?" Sherri asked, rising to her feet.

"No. Like you said, if Lanky sees us moving about he may misinterpret our motives and disappear. Better stay put."

While they awaited Lanky's return Ellis explained that he is ready to set up shop at a remote location near an old abandoned logging camp in Preston County. He had already placed a rush order for new equipment to arrive in a few days. "Even the Hillmans don't know where it is. Angela will have a hard time finding us there. You'll just have to be alert when coming in and out of the place."

Sherri glanced at her wristwatch and exclaimed, "My goodness, he has been gone for forty-five minutes. What in the world could be keeping him?"

Rising to his feet, Ellis replied, "I don't know. But I am sure that if he was going to return, he would have done so by now. Come on, let's go."

Sherri quickly bounded to his side and insisted that they not leave yet. "Better yet, let's go find him."

"There is no telling where he went. You'll learn that you can't always depend on Lanky. He is about as skittish as they come. He knows how to contact me. Believe me, I'll hear from him soon."

"What if Uncle Joseph is there? We'll miss him if we leave now."

"If he were there, either Lanky or Joseph would have come back by now. Relax and just be patient."

"Be patient?" Sherri snapped. "We are too close to finding Uncle

Joseph to be nonchalant." The anticipation of finding Joseph and having him come home with her gnawed relentlessly as they descended toward the railroad tracks. She kept looking back in hopes of seeing Uncle Joseph and Lanky.

Ellis gave her the directions to the new printing shop and insisted that she disclose its location to no one. "And be absolutely certain that nobody follows you," he demanded. "Report to work at seven in the morning, ready to read over old files and take notes. We'll resume our search for Joseph when the time is right. Trust me, Sherri, it will all come together in due time."

When they drew near to the Morgantown-Westover Bridge they climbed the upper bank to Old River Road and walked across the bridge into Morgantown. Sherri got to her parked car and decided to drive around town, passing the courthouse square several times. She kept reminding herself that she must be patient—a virtue heretofore she could not claim as her own.

Sherri whipped her Oldsmobile onto Summers' School Road and looked through her rearview mirror to see if the black Bronco still followed. She sighed, "Whew. Maybe it wasn't *them*, after all."

Just before the Summers' Elementary School the menacing Ford reappeared in her mirror. It seemed to keep just enough distance to make it difficult to determine if she should be alarmed. She tried to convince herself that it must be someone from the mountain.

She jerked her wheels sharply to the right, into the school's graveled parking lot and let the Bronco pass by. She exited the upper end of the lot and quickly drove back toward the bottom of the mountain—just in case.

Along a short, straight, flat stretch of the narrow two-lane road the Bronco pulled up beside her and tried to force her over the mountainside to her right. Daring not to lose concentration on spoiling their purpose, she had no opportunity to view the culprits. She slammed on her brakes, causing the Bronco to rush past her. Its brakes lights lit up and she tromped her gas pedal to the floor, barely passing them without colliding. She managed to lose them long enough to dodge into a hidden driveway just beyond a quick turn in the road.

Seconds later, the Bronco sped by. Her split-second maneuver worked. She jerked the gearshift into reverse and backed onto the road and raced back up the mountain.

Not until she safely reached Janet's house did her hands start shaking in rhythm with her accelerated heartbeat.

She spent the entire evening on-guard. Nothing Janet said or did calmed her. Only after Janet gave her a loaded 12-gauge shotgun would she agree to try sleeping.

She checked the safety and said, "I'll sleep out here on the couch." She laid the gun on the floor—perpendicular to the couch—and sat on the middle cushion.

"Now, you're carrying this too far, Sherri."

"No, I'm *not*."

"Think about it, Sherri. If you sleep out here you would be more easily overcome. At least in your bedroom you'd have a few seconds to get oriented if someone breaks in."

"There's no way I'll sleep so sound that someone could drive up here or even walk onto the deck without me hearing them. The bedroom is too far away with walls to insulate such sounds."

Janet grumbled, "You are so hard-headed," and force-marched to her room and slammed the door behind her.

CHAPTER ELEVEN

Wednesday, May 2, 1979

Sherri's body jerked at the sounding of the alarm. She grabbed the clock from the stand, flipped the alarm button, and growled, "Goodness! I just got to sleep." She had wrestled her pillow most of the night, gaining only occasional catnaps.

"Hey, Janet," she yelled down the hall, "you up yet? It's five-thirty already."

Hearing no answer, she walked to Janet's closed bedroom door and repeated her wake-up call. Still no answer. "Janet, are you going to sleep your life away?" she called again as she opened the door. The bed had been made up. She searched the house for Janet and soon became alarmed. Surely, she hadn't left early without telling her. She turned on the kitchen light and began preparing breakfast. The sliding glass door, leading to the deck overlooking Morgantown, slid open, causing Sherri to draw back her egg turner in self-defense as she shrieked. Adrenalin rushed through her like a bolt of lightning. "What are you doing out there? You nearly scared me out of my skin."

"I couldn't sleep. I love sitting out there on the deck covered up with a warm blanket and staring off over the hills. It helps me deal with troubling thoughts and everyday problems."

"Must be something in the air," Sherri said. "I couldn't sleep either. I tossed and turned all night. I'm anxious to get to the investigative reading and other duties at *Scoop Weekly*. However, I wish we could have found Uncle Joseph before I get swamped with the research for his case."

"Sherri," Janet said reflectively, "do you really believe that Ellis Fenton is on the straight and narrow after all these years of misdeeds?"

"Oh, yes. Janet, you ought to see his countenance now. It is apparent in his face *and* his mannerisms."

"I just think you ought to be very cautious," Janet warned. "Give me the directions to the printing shop in case I need to check on your safety."

"Actually, it's just a large cabin. You can't be coming out there. The fewer people who frequent the place the less chance we'll be found out by Angela and her cohorts."

"Sherri, I am not going to frequent the place. It only makes sense that I know how to get there in case there is ever reason for concern. Don't be so foolhardy."

"How many eggs do you want?" she asked, wanting to divert the conversation to avoid Janet's lecture.

"Two eggs, two toast, three strips of bacon, and the directions to your hideaway."

Sherri turned to reply and laughed at the sight of Janet poised to take notes at the kitchen table. "Okay, Dick Tracey, I'll give you the directions. But, I will do so with conditions."

Janet penned the directions down. "How are you supposed to find this place without more specific instructions? I don't think you'll find it on your own the first time."

"Well, Ellis planned for that. He is going to place a florescent green ribbon around a locust tree at the beginning of a barely distinguishable road leading to the old farm. Then I am to walk back to it, after parking out of sight from the dirt road, and retrieve it."

"Florescent green? You sure he didn't say florescent orange or pink? I have never seen a florescent green surveyor's ribbon."

"He said that if he used the common orange or pink, it would be his luck that someone would have survey stakes nearby. This way I can't be confused about which one is his marker."

"Maybe this guy isn't so dumb," Janet teased. "He has already figured you out, hasn't he?"

"What do you mean by that?" Sherri asked.

"Well, you aren't the most cautious person I've ever known. After all, you tend to jump into danger without taking necessary precautions. One of you needs to exercise some measure of watchfulness."

"Oh, go get ready for work while I finish preparing breakfast," Sherri demanded. "Save the preaching for someone else."

The narrow rutted dirt road climbed gradually along the edge of the mountain to Gobbler's Peak. The blue Oldsmobile scraped bottom several times before reaching the turn onto Coon Lick Run. The rugged terrain certainly proved to be all that Ellis described. "Finally," she exclaimed, "I thought I'd never get to the old Franklin farm." The old two-story farmhouse bowed toward the rocky hillside behind it. The massive structure showed only a hint of its once white exterior. Weeds and briars surrounded the homestead, overtaking what used to be a yard.

Just beyond the yard's bent and twisted metal fence, Sherri turned right, onto the barely noticeable road, carved into the landscape by farm equipment. Just as Ellis had said, the mountaintop meadow appeared at its end, giving way to a spectacular view of the lower hills and valleys. A barely discernible house roof, several ridges north of the Franklin farm, presented the only sign of human life. She got out of the car and surveyed the vast expanse of meadowland. An old faded green International Harvester pick-up truck bounced and limped slowly toward her, adding to the early spring-day chill. "Great," she griped. "Now, who is this?" She had no way to get past the unfamiliar vehicle if she chose to rush back down the mountain. She quickly scanned beyond the meadow hoping to find an escape route, but found none. Returning her gaze into the truck's cab she recognized Ellis, repeatedly bouncing from the driver's seat. She chuckled a little more each time Ellis nearly disappeared back onto the seat from whence only the top of his bald head could be seen.

"Well, I see you made it," Ellis chirped as he hopped from the cab.

"I just didn't imagine one could drive so far without a hint of civilization. Not even in West Virginia. This place is so beautiful and serene!"

"Yeah. Let's just pray we aren't working up here come late fall or winter."

"Oh, my, there is no way I'd try to drive up here in bad weather. I barely made it this morning."

"All the more reason to rush to our tasks," Ellis cheerfully announced. "Park your car off to the side and ride with me the rest of the way. We're almost there."

She parked her car along the narrow patch of woods between the meadow and the old farm, and then climbed into Ellis's truck.

He pointed toward the far corner of the meadow. "About fifty feet to the right of that lone deer you can faintly make out a narrow opening in the woods just as the hill starts to decline."

She squinted laboriously. "I can? What deer?"

Ellis laughed, "Anyhow, the cabin is about one half mile over the crest of the meadow."

"I am sure I locked that door yesterday," Ellis said as if to reassure himself.

Trailing slightly behind, Sherri cautiously peered into the majestic log structure before entering. The few furnishings in view appeared undamaged. She and Ellis briefly searched the dwelling, but nothing seemed amiss.

"Well, let's see," said Ellis as he rubbed his hands together, "we'll begin by systematically going through those file boxes," nodding toward several white file boxes in the right rear corner of the front room. "I put all the files relating directly to Reverend Short's case and other pertinent files first, left to right. The other twenty or so boxes are not likely to be needed for his case."

"Three whole boxes?" Sherri exclaimed. "All concerning Uncle Joseph?" she continued, trying to not sound overly protective.

"Four," Ellis corrected. "If you count the one containing information on the Hillman's and their pawns, thugs, and cohorts," he explained, as he closed the door against the biting mountain air.

"Then shouldn't we place it with these other three boxes?"

"I…I…" His face hardened as he looked around the room. "Can't be! They couldn't have known about this place." With increasing agitation he threatened, "I'll get them. One way or another these scum are going down."

Stunned by Ellis' ranting, Sherri stood motionless and nearly thoughtless as he scurried to the truck.

Returning with two brown leather rifle cases and a large blue gym bag, he kicked the door shut behind him.

"Mr. Fenton, are you all right?" Sherri asked, hoping to calm him.

He tossed everything onto the sunken cushions of the faded red couch sitting against the front wall beneath the room's only window. He turned quickly and bolted the door. Looking pleadingly at her, he said, in a deliberate low tone, "I'm so sorry. I honestly thought this would be a safe haven for us."

"It will all work out, Mr. Fenton. But, you've got to chill out."

"Doesn't this alarm you, girl?"

"What? That the cabin has been broken into? Or, that a box of important files has been apparently stolen? *And* the 'safe place' has been compromised?"

Her lighthearted sarcasm seemed to disarm him of his fierce anger. With a boyish grin he squeaked, "What a stupid question! Huh?"

"Seems odd to me that nothing appears to have been vandalized."

He cocked his head to the right and rubbed his round chin between his right index finger and thumb. "Yeah, it does seem a little odd," he mused. "Only one box missing. And it's the one with all the files on the Hillman's and company…" He walked searchingly through the three spacious rooms and stopped precisely where he started. "Not a bit of damage to the place, no evidence of ransacking."

Briskly, he turned an about face and unlocked the door. After visually examining the door, its jam, and its frame, he announced, "Whoever got in here either picked the lock… or… but no one has a key besides me."

"Well, lets see," Sherri quizzed. "Who installed the lock?"

"I did it myself."

"Didn't it come with two keys?"

"Yeah, but I have never given anyone the other key. I keep it in my office desk drawer. Even if someone found it, they wouldn't know what it fits."

"Your daughter?"

"Ramona? Yeah, but she'd have no reason to…"

"Maybe. Maybe not."

He shut the door and locked it, then dropped onto the couch and nervously unzipped one of the brown rifle cases. "Ever shot a gun, Mrs. Mosley?"

"Sure. I used to hunt with Uncle Joseph up until he went into the Marines. Surely, you don't think we really need this weaponry."

"I hope not. But, I think the Hillman band are capable of unlimited viciousness."

"So, what's in here?" Sherri teased while unzipping the gym bag. "Hand grenades?"

"That one is yours," he said, when Sherri retrieved a small-frame Rossi .38 caliber revolver from a perfectly fitted brown holster.

"I don't want this thing," she insisted.

"Apparently you don't understand the potential peril you are apt to encounter. You think these thugs wouldn't knock you off, too, if it seemed advantageous to them?"

"Knock me off, *too*?" Sherri probed. "Who have they already killed?"

He tilted his head slightly downward, raised his eyebrows as if peering over eyeglass frames.

"So, you do know Uncle Joseph didn't kill Spike, after all. You little weasel," she fumed, "and you knew even back then that he didn't do it!" Her voice grew more threatening. "Still, you publicly made a case against him," she grimaced.

"Please, try to understand that I truly am sorry," he pleaded. "Why do you think I'm willing to take serious risks to make it right? I could have just closed up shop and maybe gone into hiding until all this blows over. But…"

She spun around and stomped to the door. Hurriedly unlocking the door, she bolted onto the porch and kicked the center 4" by 4" porch roof support. She fought back the stinging tears, uncertain if they were tears of anger or if they were evoked by deep hurt.

"Uh!" she gasped. Her body tightened as she tried to determine if she had actually seen someone move among the trees. Her heart thumped tempestuously. Cautiously studying the woods she slowly backed into the cabin. Once inside she slammed the door shut and locked it with her trembling right hand.

Ellis clutched the Westernfield 30-30 rifle he had removed from its leather case and leaped from the couch. "What? What?" he urged while peeking out the lower left corner of the window.

Breathlessly, she entreated him to watch the woods slightly to the right and about fifty yards from them.

After scanning for several seconds he said, "I don't see anything."

Sherri cautiously hunkered down at the lower right corner of the window and pointed. "I'm sure I saw someone dart behind one of those big oaks. Just barely caught him through my peripheral vision."

"Are you sure it was a person? Could have been an animal startled by your sudden appearance on the porch."

"Maybe. But I really don't think it was wildlife. I could even feel their presence."

"Are you sure you aren't just unnerved by all my talk of danger?" Before she could answer he continued, "I'm probably unduly alarming you."

"Are these people really that dangerous?" she asked, hoping the answer would be "not really."

"Listen...if you want to step aside from this it would be all right. In fact, it might be best that you do."

Sherri's face flushed with hot anger.

"Now, wait a minute. Hear me out before you attack me. I am the one who created this mess or at least I willingly partook of the shenanigans that brought us to this point... I'll keep you informed all the way to the end."

"I certainly am not about to declare you faultless. But, neither can I, nor anyone else, lay all the blame on you."

"I made some choices—stupid and utterly wrong choices. I wrote some pretty mean and blatantly false things about the Reverend Short. You shouldn't be risking your life to undo the damage of my evil deeds."

"I believe you sincerely repented, Mr. Fenton. And that is good enough for me. Now, about my deserting this battle—forget it…I'm in it for the long-haul."

"If you ever change your mind…"

"Don't even suggest it again. You are stuck with me to the end."

"Have it your way," Ellis surrendered. Inhaling deeply he sighed, "Let's get to studying these files and making notes."

"Okay, I'll see you back here at 7 a.m." Ellis yawned as he pulled his truck alongside Sherri's parked Olds.

"I'll be here," she promised.

Ellis waited courteously in the truck to be sure Sherri got going before returning to the cabin.

She tried starting her car a few times before she and Ellis simultaneously hopped from their vehicles to check under the hood.

He lifted the hood and proclaimed, in angry alarm, "Your ignition coil wire is missing."

"You have got to be kidding!" Sherri acknowledged, staring at the ignition coil. She searched the surroundings looking for whoever might be still in the area. Even the early spring birds were undisturbed as they chirped merrily from the encompassing woods.

"Well," he interrupted, "come with me and we'll search the shed and hopefully we'll find something to use temporarily to get you going."

Sherri felt overwhelmed by the possibilities during the eerily silent ride to and from the cabin.

Ellis wound the ends of the fourteen gauge multi-strand wire around the nipples of the coil and distributor cap. "Now try to start it," he commanded.

She cranked the engine and nearly shouted, "Thank God."

"Change of plans," he announced as he lowered the hood and pushed down on it to be sure it latched. He walked quickly around to Sherri's door and finished in a lower tone, "Meet me at the bottom of the mountain at the old company store instead of coming all the way up here in the morning."

"Why don't I just drive all the way to the cabin?"

"First of all, you probably would get hung up in the soft soil on the other side. You saw how my four-wheel-drive truck barely makes it in and out. Later, when the heat of summer does its work, you can drive all the way. Secondly, we must be sure you aren't intercepted along the way up the mountain. Once you get on the narrow deserted ascent you have no place to retreat if anyone tries to ambush you."

Sherri opened her car door, eased out and suggested they pray before they part ways.

After praying, Ellis said, "I'll follow you off the mountain to be sure all is well. Then, I'll head on back to the cabin."

"Surely, you don't plan on staying there tonight."

"It'll be all right. I think it's necessary… at least for now."

All the way home Sherri grappled with the creepiness of the mysterious prowler at Gobbler's Peak. Of all the imaginable suspects, Ramona kept resounding as the likely scoundrel. "But why, Lord," she whispered following her third vision of Ramona, "if it is her… what is her angle?"

"Sherri," Janet demanded as Sherri entered through the front door, "where on God's green earth have you been? Do you realize what time it is?"

"Yes, Mother Janet," Sherri retaliated, "it is *time* that you quit treating me like a little child."

"Somebody has to worry about you since you don't have the sense to worry for yourself."

Sherri dropped into the overstuffed recliner and sighed in submission, "Ah, Janet, lighten up. I'm much too tired to argue. Besides, you are the last person I wish to alienate."

"You aren't alienating me—you are infuriating me. Don't you think it's time we both agree on some strategies and some ground rules for one another's sanity sake?"

"I'm sorry. I guess I just get too engulfed in what I'm doing and lose track of time. I promise to be more attuned to your sensibilities. I know I should have come home earlier. Mr. Fenton and I were gathering some really good notes for his first printing of the new, and improved, *Scoop Weekly.*"

"Are you saying that Fenton had honest and correct information available to him before and still published all that evil against Joseph?"

"I'm afraid so. He even has incriminating notes on Angela Hillman and her gang. That is, he *did* have."

Janet and Sherri talked for several hours.

"Goodness, Sherri! I forgot to tell you that Frank called just after I got home from work…"

"Maybe I better…"

"Wait. Let me finish."

Sherri sucked her lower lip between her teeth, determined to not interrupt.

Janet continued, "You are going to love this. He only called to get my mailing address so his lawyer could send you a certified 'notice of intent to sue for divorce' or whatever it's called."

Sherri strained to dam up the river of heartbreak that blurred her vision. "Oh, God," she sobbed, "what have I done? Please, Lord, help me do the right thing." She paused several seconds then wiped her tear-soaked face with her hands. "I better call him," she sniffled. "Maybe, I can get him to at least let me come home while we try to patch things up between us."

Janet perched herself on the arm of the chair, patted Sherri's hand, and promised, "Whatever you decide to do—or not to do—I'll stand behind you."

A lone tear splashed onto Sherri's hand sealing Janet's words—a payment of earnest. "Thanks, Janet," she whispered.

"Sherri, don't call him tonight. He sounded a little tipsy."

"I think your advice is worth heeding. Drinking or not he'd probably get mad over my calling so late."

"I'm a little reluctant to tell you who else called. I guess I must."

"Let me guess," Sherri said irritably. "Dear ole Mom."

"Why, yes. Were you expecting her to call?"

"No. It's just that any time Frank and I ever disagreed or fought, Mom always took his side."

"Well, apparently she called Frank when she learned you were staying awhile with me."

"I guess she called to give me another one of her famous tongue lashings."

"It pains me to even relay her message."

"Janet, I already know that if it is a message from Alice Lance, it is something hateful or hurtful. She is capable of nothing better. So, what species of venom did she send me?"

Janet looked slightly away. "She said that until you grow up and make things right with Frank, you are not to write, call, or visit her nor your dad."

"Did you know that when I told her about Frank beating me about a year after we married, she blamed me and accused me of being melodramatic?"

"That is so unfair!"

"That is Mom."

CHAPTER TWELVE

Thursday, May 3, 1979

"Come on, Mr. Fenton," Sherri said in anxious anticipation. "We have a lot to do today. Where are you?" She felt no safer sitting in her car alongside Adam Town's old abandoned company store than she had at Gobbler's Peak. Ellis Fenton promised to meet her at 7 a.m. and her watch read 7:35.

A few minutes later she thought she heard a bang of some sort. She shut off her engine and quickly cranked open her window. She jumped at the sound of rifle fire and breaking glass. Realizing that someone had just shot out a storefront window just twenty feet from her, she restarted her car and raced back to Morgantown.

"Hi, this is Janet. How can I help you?"

"Janet," Sherri said in a trembling voice, "I'm calling from a pay phone along Route 7 in Sabraton. Can you get off work right away—it's urgent."

"Probably. What's wrong, Sherri? Are you okay?"

"Physically, yes. I just had the scare of my life. I must hurry and get off the phone. I feel like a sitting duck. Where can you meet me? We need to contact your cousin, Thad. Is he on duty today?"

"Why? What is going on?" Janet probed.

"Meet me at the Star City police station right away and I'll fill you in." Sherri slapped the phone in its cradle and rushed to her car.

Janet pulled her Jeep alongside Sherri's Oldsmobile. When Sherri approached her car, she asked nervously, "So, what is going on?"

Sherri explained what had happened at Adam Town and that she didn't know what to do about it.

"Come into the police station. Let's see if whoever is on duty can advise us."

Sergeant James stopped his typing when Sherri and Janet entered the room. "Can I be of assistance, ladies?"

"I don't know if you remember me," Janet said, reaching to shake his hand. "I'm Thad Ashbury's cousin."

"Sure, I do. It's Janet, isn't it?"

"Yes, sir, it is."

"We met at Thad's birthday party last year."

Janet introduced Sherri and inquired of Thad's schedule.

"Sherri," Sergeant James repeated. "Oh, yeah. So, you are the little redhead that Thad declares he is going to marry someday."

"I'd only met Thad once, and even then we briefly spoke to one another. What a bold and presumptuous thing for him to have said. Tell me, is that *dreamer* on duty?"

"He isn't officially on duty today. However, he is out and about working on something about an old unsolved murder case from several years ago."

"Can he be reached by radio or phone right now?"

"If you head on over to the Holiday Inn dining room you'll probably find him there drinking coffee and talking shop with a retired detective friend."

"Over here," a slightly familiar voice echoed.

Sherri looked toward the southeast corner of the restaurant. One of the two figures, silhouetted by the sunshine through the large glass windows, waved them over.

"What a small world!" Janet exclaimed as they approached the men.

Bill Drake stood to hug Janet and then Sherri. "Indeed it is a small world. Please have a seat."

Sherri sat in the chair next to Deacon Drake and Janet took the one beside Thad.

"Well," said Thad, "I guess I needn't make any introductions."

Sherri felt reassured by the thought of these two men working on Uncle Joseph's behalf, in conjunction with her own efforts. "Please, forgive our intrusion. We urgently need to speak to you... both of you, actually."

Deacon Drake informed the girls that Thad and he were discussing Reverend Short's case. "This young man is one of the police connections assisting me. Sort of unofficially."

"You said something about urgency," Thad inquired.

"Yes," Janet interjected. "Sherri had a very serious encounter this morning. Go ahead, Sherri. You're the one they shot at."

Thad's eyes widened, "What? Who shot at you? When?"

It flattered her that he took it so personally. "I think I'm the one who is suppose to get worked up about it," she teased. "Thanks for the concern."

Thad grinned and then insisted she tell them what happened.

She recounted the incident and assured them that she saw no one. "I didn't hang around long enough to find them either. I really don't think they intended to do more than scare me."

"Well, did they?" Thad joked, in an apparent attempt to put Sherri, Janet, and himself at ease.

"Let's just say I saw no need to stick around to challenge them."

"So, Fenton didn't show at all?" Bill Drake asked.

"Oh, no! Oh, no!" Sherri cried as she jumped to her feet and started pacing around the table. "Oh, no! We have got to go check on him. Oh, my! Hurry, let's go."

Janet hurried to her side and growled through clinched teeth, "Stop it. Stop it. You are acting like a maniac. You're embarrassing us."

Mr. Drake rose from his chair and put his arms around Sherri. "We'll check it out, sweetheart. You did the right thing; getting out of there when you did."

Thad added, "You girls follow us back to the station. We'll contact the Preston County Sheriff's office and ask them to check on Mr. Fenton.

"Okay," Thad said as he turned around to Sherri and Janet, "Deputy Burk is going to drive up to Gobbler's Peak and check on Mr. Fenton."

Handing the phone to Sherri he said, "You need to give him precise directions from Adam Town to the cabin."

She detailed the directions to Burk, word for word, as Fenton had given them to her. She replaced the phone's receiver and breathed a sigh of relief. "Now what do we do?"

"I'll take one of the spare portable radios with me so they can contact me when Deputy Burk reports back," Thad offered. "Where can I reach you two, later?"

Janet and Sherri looked quizzically at one another and shrugged.

"Well," Janet suggested, "we could hang around the courthouse square and hope to get a lucky lead on Joseph's whereabouts."

"Excellent idea," Sherri quickly agreed. "We'll call you later, Thad. Where can we reach you?"

"Call here first. If I'm not here, call the house. I'll phone your house, Janet, if I don't hear from you, first."

"It has been two hours, Sherri. I think we are wasting our time sitting here. Let's go walk the Westover riverbank and railroad tracks awhile."

"Janet, do you get the impression that Uncle Joseph doesn't want to be rescued?"

"What kind of a crazy conclusion is that?"

"I don't know." Sherri felt embarrassed but the thought haunted her.

"Think we ought to see if we can find out where Lanky darted off to that day he evaded you and Mr. Fenton?" asked Janet.

She and Sherri surveyed the steep brushy hillside before them. "I don't know what to do, Janet. We need to contact Thad and see if he heard anything on Fenton. I need to call Frank, too."

"Sherri, I'm not trying to play matchmaker, but you can't help but notice that Thad has eyes for you."

"How can you even suggest such a thing? I'm married, remember?"

"Yeah, but for how long? You don't know that Frank will even give you a chance. I personally think you are placing your bets on a dead horse."

"That's enough, Janet. Let's change the subject." She wished she could deny the secret feelings she dared not entertain or speak. As long as she could suppress any related notions, she could stay on course with her Christian convictions.

"I suppose we should head on home."

Sherri barely heard Janet's suggestion.

"Hello," sang the unfamiliar female voice.

"Oh, I'm sorry," said Sherri. "I must have dialed the wrong number."

"Who are you calling, dear?"

"The Mosley residence at…"

"Frank is right here, Honey. Hold on for a second and I'll get him."

Sherri quickly sorted through the possible explanations for a female answering the phone as if she had the right. He has no sisters. His cousins are all out west. She can rule out his mother. Could she be a girlfriend or wife of one of his friends? She certainly sounded nothing like either of his brothers' wives.

"This is Frank."

Sherri stammered, "Uh…Uh…Frank? Um…uh…who answered the phone?"

"Sherri," he growled, "what do you want?"

She replied with mock confidence, "*You*, darling. I'm coming home." She could faintly hear the young woman asking if she caused a problem. "Frank, are you still there?" She reveled in his apparent discomfort. "Hey, sweetheart, I'll be home in about four hours. I am leaving Morgantown as soon as we hang up."

"Sherri…"

She playfully hung up the phone before Frank could say more. "Maybe I enjoyed that too much."

Janet asked, "Who answered the phone?"

"His new woman, I guess."

Janet's phone rang just seconds after Sherri hung up.

"Let it ring, Janet. It is surely Frank. Let him sweat a while. By sun-up, he'll realize I'm not really coming."

Janet grinned in agreement. "You are so rotten. I thought you were seriously considering going home, though."

"I thought so too. Now that he already has a plaything, I guess not."

"There may be a logical explanation, you know."

"Yeah, right. That girl answered the phone like she owned the place. I choose not to let him tromp on my heart anymore. If he comes to his senses, before I wax cold and hard, I may still try to salvage this marriage. In the meantime, I'm going to focus on more pressing and more hopeful matters."

After several rings, the phone fell silent.

"What do you say we call Thad and see if Mr. Fenton is okay, Janet?"

"Look his number up in the phone book, there beside you. Thaddeus Ashbury, Route 10."

She leafed through the front of the phonebook and then quickly dialed his number.

"Hello."

"Hi. Thad. This is Sherri. Any news from Deputy Burk?"

"Are you calling from Janet's?" he asked solemnly.

"Yes. She is right here. Hold on a second." Sherri handed the receiver to Janet fearing the news would prove too terrible to hear straight out.

"Bad news? How bad?"

Sherri pressed her hands against her ears. Her spine tingled. Her trembling hands emitted hot sweat, soaking her ears.,

Janet replaced the receiver and motioned for Sherri to sit back down in the recliner. With deliberate clarity, she said, "I want you to focus on remaining calm. Promise me, and yourself, that whatever Thad tells us when he gets here, you will absorb it without your typical hysteria."

Sherri bent forward and fitted her face between her knees hoping to slow the spinning that nearly forced her to vomit. She mumbled, "I promise. It's really bad news, isn't it?"

"Let's just sit here quietly until Thad arrives," Janet caringly instructed.

Moments later, Sherri sat up and composed herself, determined to be exceptionally cognizant for Thad…for Janet…for her own self. She silently prayed, "Calm the storm, Lord. Please, calm the storm."

"My goodness, Thad." Janet griped. "It took you long enough to get here."

"Sorry, I received a phone call I couldn't cut short." Thad lacked his usual cheerfulness. He said, "hello," to Sherri, avoiding eye contact. "Can you excuse Janet and me for a few minutes?" He head gestured for Janet to follow him outside.

Janet rendered a look of puzzlement and trailed behind him.

Sherri offered a weak, "Sure." But she deplored being excluded. After all, he came on business concerning her close associate, Mr. Fenton—not Janet's. How bad could the news be?

After what seemed to her an unreasonable amount of time, Janet and Thad returned.

Janet slid an ottoman across the living room and positioned herself on it, directly in front of Sherri.

"Sherri, Thad has some difficult news to share. I want you to hear him—really *hear* him."

Sherri scowled at Thad. "I'm not a little baby, Thad. Anything you can tell Janet, you can tell me."

Thad rolled his eyes dependently at Janet.

"Stop being so contentious," Janet said. "He is going to tell you what he told me. He sought my advice about how to approach you... Is it any wonder he thought it best to get my input first?" Janet softened her tone. "Thad wishes to make things as easy as possible for you. You need to give him a chance. He is on *our* side. Remember?"

Sherri dropped her head in shame. "Please, forgive me, Thad. I offer no excuse for my misbehavior—it's inexcusable."

"Forgiven. Let's forget it. You've been through a lot lately. This morning's incident alone is enough to rattle anybody."

Janet interrupted, "Remember what the Bible says—something like, 'let every man be swift to hear, slow to speak, slow to wrath.'"

Almost grinning, Sherri shot back, "It's truly amazing how you can recall scripture when it fits your fancy."

"Well, that seems to be the only reasoning you'll listen to."

Sherri sheepishly looked at Thad and said, "You must think I am awful."

"Absolutely not."

"Anyhow, I'm ready to listen to what you have to say."

"Sherri, just so I don't have to pad everything I tell you, let me assure you that Janet and I have your best interest at heart. No matter what the days ahead hold for you, be mindful that I'm on your side."

"Sounds like things are about to be a bit weighty."

He approached the recliner and knelt on one knee beside her. Tenderly taking her hands in his own he spoke softly, "I wish you could drop your guard enough to see that I have confidence in your genuineness and integrity. Then, you wouldn't need to defend yourself with me."

His sincerity lifted her spirit. How she longed to again trust another human! Dare she open herself to vulnerability? "Thad," she said timidly, "I want very much to trust you. It's just that I have had only two people in my whole life who have not hurt me, betrayed me, or otherwise terribly disappointed me." She raised her eyes to read *his* and felt as though she could see his very soul. "I think I *can* trust you."

He looked into her big sky-blue eyes and said, barely beyond a whisper, "I hold you in highest regard, Sherri. I honestly admire you." He paused. "If I… If I may be so bold—I adore you."

Sherri lowered her eyes and bashfully bowed her head.

As if on cue, Thad withdrew his left hand. Reaching to Janet he said, "Let us pray."

Janet and Sherri joined their free hands as Thad began praying.

Sherri prayed along with him, thanking God that he is a man of unashamed faith.

Having ended the prayer, Thad stood, walked across the room, and sat on the couch.

Janet likewise rose from the ottoman and sat at the opposite end of the couch from him.

He stroked his neatly trimmed brown mustache and mumbled, "Where do I start?"

"With a report on Mr. Fenton," Sherri said, politely.

He blew air. "Okay, this is going to be tough; for you to hear and for me to tell." He squirmed in his seat as though he couldn't get comfortable. Then, matter-of-factly, he said, "Deputy Burk didn't locate Fenton. I personally searched his old print shop beyond the Borg-Warner industrial park. I even went to his residence. Judging from the mail filling his letter box on the outside of the house and after speaking to his nearest neighbor, I gather that he hasn't been home in at least a couple days."

"So, now what do we do?"

"Well, we remind ourselves to be strong and patient while working toward our goals. We mentally, emotionally, and spiritually brace ourselves to meet whatever challenges are ahead."

"Sounds to me that you are sensing stormy times."

"I'm afraid so, Sherri. From this moment onward we three must remain focused. I am certain we will encounter obstacles that would otherwise derail us. We must have faith that whatever besetting circumstances arise they will not prevail. It is also imperative that we remain undivided."

Sherri flashed a bright smile. "You really *are* on board, aren't you?"

"I am," he replied confidently. "Are you up to a potentially long and arduous fight?"

Sherri discerned a new and unfamiliar strength for which she could not claim credit. "By God's grace, and by His might, I am ready for battle."

"Are you sure?"

"Absolutely. Positively. Indubitably."

"Good. Brace yourself for the rest of the story," Thad said with pretend lightheartedness. "Tomorrow morning, we are to meet with Deputy Burk at nine o'clock. He must, by police protocol, interview you regarding your relationship with Ellis Fenton. Also, concerning this morning's shooting incident at Adam Town."

"That shouldn't be so difficult."

"Hopefully not, but be aware of the possibility you could become a suspect if they think Fenton met with foul play. Especially, if it is determined you are the last known person to have seen him."

"You have *got* to be kidding. That is ludicrous."

"You, Janet, and I know how absurd such a suggestion would be. What you must consider is, whoever investigates this case—if that is actually called for—will not know you. Even if they *would* happen to know you they would be compelled by professional standards to follow proper procedure. They'd have to apply the same investigative practices as would be employed in any other case. In such cases, seldom is only one source or just one suspect immediately ruled in *or* out."

Sherri leaped to her feet and started pacing the floor. "If you weren't so serious this would be laughable."

Janet interjected, "Think about it, Sherri. They will want to know who had motive to harm Fenton. Plenty of people, I'm sure. Including you, as far as the authorities will be concerned."

"Well, aren't you encouraging?"

"Do you realize how easy it would be to make a case that you have motive? For example, how about Magistrate Pagone? He knows of your ire toward anyone who had a part in Joseph's woes. Or, how about Ramona Fenton? She is privy to your initial squabble with her dad. You are likely to be scrutinized—if for no other reason than to be ruled out as a suspect in the event there has been foul play."

Sherri paced even faster, waving her hands as if to extinguish an invisible fire. "This is crazy talk," she growled. "You two have flipped your lids." She rushed to the front door and halted suddenly. Knowing not whether to stay and debate or run away, she froze. She spun around and said, "How can you even entertain the suggestion I had anything to do with Mr. Fenton's disappearance? We don't really know that he has come up missing. If he has *vanished*, it may be that he had second thoughts about his crusade for the truth and went into hiding. It isn't as if he had never considered that option."

"Sherri," Thad pleaded, "please, sit back down. There is more."

"You rather mean it gets worse," she said lowly, not sure if she posed the statement to Thad or to herself.

"Maybe worse. I just don't want you walking into this thing blindly… Come on, have a seat. Please?"

Letting herself slowly into the recliner, Sherri sighed, "All *this* because Uncle Joseph got mixed up with Angela *'Jezebel'* Dermont."

Thad reasoned, "If nothing in the investigation points to foul play there will be no need for concern, after all. Maybe Fenton *did* go into hiding. In light of all the nasty things he has done over the years to folks around here, it's a wonder he hadn't run long before now. And the shooting at Adam Town will probably be hard to follow up. There's little chance anyone witnessed it. Damage to the old dilapidated store probably won't invite much attention. I'm sure Deputy Burk will do his best. He has a good reputation as a thorough and skillful investigator."

"I did understand you to say *we* have an appointment with Deputy Burk, didn't I?"

"Right. I will go with you. In fact, if you'll allow me, I'll pick you up around seven in the morning and treat you to breakfast before we meet with Burk."

She rose from the chair, stretched, and sauntered to the door. Looking out at nothing in particular, she said, "Uncle Joseph use to say, 'never pass up a free meal.'" She remained facing the outside, trying to hide her quivering chin. "I sure pray he isn't going hungry."

Thad said genuinely, "I can't wait to meet your uncle. He must be quite a man to have two beautiful and lovely ladies admiring him so."

The hardwood floor creaked just behind Sherri. She turned around and met Thad's gaze. Stumbling into his inviting arms, she set free the pressing stream of emotion.

Thad tenderly held her. "It's all going to work out. You'll see."

After several seconds, she composed herself, stepped back, then half-stepped toward him and delicately thanked him with a kiss on the cheek.

"Well," he said awkwardly, "I best be going. You two get some rest tonight."

Sherri stepped aside to let him pass and watched after him until his vehicle went out of sight. "I bet Uncle Joseph is going to really like him," she muttered.

"I suspect it will be mutual," she heard Janet softly say.

Sherri twirled about just in time to catch her wiping a telling tear from her cheek. Pretending not to have noticed, she yawned, "I'm ready to hit the hay."

"Yeah… me too. Before we turn in I need to tell you something."

"Is it too important to put off until morning?"

"I think so. I may forget to tell you before Thad gets here."

Sherri turned to lock the front door as she said, "I hope this is short. I'm really tired." She turned back to face Janet who had already walked to the kitchen. She followed after her inquiring, "So, what is so important?"

Janet slunk into the nearest chair. Playfully kicking an adjacent chair, she said, "Have a seat, lady."

Sherri obliged, but suspiciously.

"I took the liberty of telling Thad about what happened at Fenton's cabin, so he would have a heads up."

"What did you tell him?"

"Well, how someone stalked you and removed the ignition coil wire from your car."

"What did he think of that?"

"Like you, he figured it could have been anyone of many people. I also told him about Fenton thinking danger to be so imminent as to bring along firearms."

"And he is still pledged to our cause?"

"Yeah, but remember, he had already been recruited by Deacon Drake long before *we* vowed to seek justice."

"True. What makes a man like Thad tick? I mean, who would take on a cause that could cost him dearly? And for someone he doesn't even know?"

"Maybe," Janet said, "he is driven by righteous indignation."

"Probably. Does he realize he may be up against fortified alliances of some of the most influential people in the county… or maybe even the tri-state area?"

"He says he knows. It seems that he had a run-in with some of Angela and Marcus Hillman's cohorts. Marcus threw his weight around and got one of Thad's more serious cases dismissed—a case that Thad had overwhelming evidence to support two or three felony convictions."

"I suspect things like that happen often. Why would Thad take it so personal?"

"Well, to add insult to injury, *Scoop Weekly* ran a series of articles, in reference to that case, accusing Thad of entrapment and proclaiming him to be unprofessional. One article even called him Barney Fife."

"So, Thad has a vendetta against the Hillmans?"

"I think that Fenton's publication promoting the long standing fable that West Virginians are ignorant backwoodsmen angered him more than anything else. They really capitalized on the fact that Don Knotts, who played Barney Fife on the *Andy Griffith Show,* is from Morgantown."

"Oh, Janet, I hope he isn't too prejudiced against Mr. Fenton to be objective. I truly believe Mr. Fenton has repented."

"I think he is every bit the professional policeman… Of course, he has you to help him remain unbiased. If any *human* can steer Thad right now, it is you."

"Oh, quit. He hardly knows me. Besides, there is nothing romantic or unbecoming between us that he would be *steered* by me."

"Who are you trying to kid? Even a casual observer would recognize the mutual fondness between you and Thad."

"Hey, Janet," Sherri said timidly, "You have got to quit that."

"Quit what? Telling it as I see it?"

"Trying to fix me up. Even if I were available I couldn't let a romantic relationship evolve right now. I need to apply my energies to finding Uncle Joseph and clearing his name. You know that."

"Goodness, girl! There is no reason you can't live your life and pursue such a worthy cause at the same time."

"You're absolutely right. For now, living my life requires some shut-eye… I get the bathroom first."

"Maybe," Janet said, jumping from her seat and racing to the bathroom.

"Cheater," Sherri yelled after her. Sherri moseyed off to her room and dropped to her knees at bedside. She petitioned, praised, and pondered until she nearly dozed off, finding it difficult to keep her head from the soft down-filled mattress. Finally, apologizing to God for her weariness she forced herself from the floor. After rushing through an invigorating shower she returned to the bedroom for her bedtime scripture reading. Her eyes fell hard upon Matthew's gospel account of Jesus instructing the disciples to give no thought of what to say when they were taken before authorities for doing His will. "Heavenly

Father," she prayed, "am I to take verses nineteen and twenty of this tenth chapter as personally speaking to me? Are you warning me of pending persecution or difficulties from the judicial system? If it comes to that, Lord, please help me to remember to not worry about what to say. I claim this promise—that your Spirit will speak in me…"

Soon, she drifted off to sleep, waking only briefly three times during the night. Each time she woke she repeated His promises and fell fast asleep.

CHAPTER THIRTEEN

Friday, May 4, 1979

"Good morning," the fatherly looking deputy said, matter-of-factly. Extending his right hand to Thad he said, "I'm Deputy Burk. You must be Officer Ashbury."

"Thad. Glad to meet you, sir. I've heard good things about you and your distinguished career."

"Thanks for saying so." Burk then shook Sherri's hand, smiling warmly. "I'm sorry, Honey, I forgot your name."

"Sherri Mosley."

"I shouldn't have forgotten that name. I have a daughter named Sherri. She's about your age. Pretty as you are, too." He gestured toward a room at the end of the hall. "We'll meet in the last room on the left." He ushered them to the room where a small worn conference table and four solid wooden chairs crowded out any hint of comfort. Atop the table sat an old oversized tape recorder and two battered microphones.

The lifeless second-story cubbyhole had only one redeeming feature—the large unadorned window magnifying otherwise weak rays of sunlight.

"Ms. Mosley, if you will sit here," Burk said, pulling out a chair immediately in front of one of the imposing microphones.

Once they were seated—Thad beside her and Burk across from her—Burk grabbed a black briefcase from the fourth chair and plopped it on the table. Folding his hands on the table, he said, "Thad, there has been some interesting developments since I talked to you yesterday afternoon."

"I hope you are going to tell us Fenton has been located and that he is well."

"I'm afraid not. The blood we found just inside the cabin entrance..."

Before he could finish, Sherri turned quickly to Thad and yelled, "What blood? You didn't tell me they found blood at the cabin."

Defensively, Thad replied, "It could have been from anything. A self-inflicted accidental wound, a cut, or anything."

"Anyhow," Burk growled, cutting short what would have been a senseless argument. "It tested as type 'O-negative' human blood. We were able to contact Fenton's physician who verified that Ellis Fenton has 'O-negative' blood type. That would have been of little consequence had it not been for a couple other things."

Thad asked anxiously, "What other things?"

"Shortly after talking to you, yesterday, I received a phone call here at the station, from Fenton's daughter."...He paused to retrieve an official looking document from the briefcase. "Ramona Fenton," he read.

The very mention of Ramona shot needles of anticipation up and down Sherri's spine. Looking to Thad in alarm, she exclaimed, "Oh, this ought to be interesting!"

Thad pointed to the paper and scorned, "A Missing Person Report? You actually had her to complete this, already? Isn't that a bit premature?"

Deputy Burk's face hardened. "It would not have, under normal circumstances, been a matter of urgency." Sternly he continued, "When Miss Fenton explained to me, on the phone, that she had reason to believe her dad met with foul play, the matter demanded exigency."

Sherri glanced at the report and then turned her gaze upon Deputy Burk. "Do you realize Ramona Fenton is at great odds with her dad? Why, anything she says should be treated with suspicion."

"She reports that she and her dad get along exceptionally well."

Sherri argued, "That is such a crock! She could care less if Ellis Fenton lives or dies."

"Before we go any further, let me warn you, young lady, that you need to be more concerned for your own defense and less worried about Miss Fenton."

Thad laid his right hand on Sherri's left hand. "Let me handle this conversation from here on, Sherri."

Sherri threw up her hands and slumped back in her chair.

Thad leaned forward engaging Burk. "Before you jump to conclusions, Deputy, it would be fitting that you listen to this girls' story as it relates to the Fentons instead of going off half-cocked."

Grimacing, Burk retorted, "Don't tell me how to do my job, officer."

Sherri sprang to her feet, sending her chair slamming against the wall behind her. "Hey," she yelled, "I came here to find out if Mr. Fenton is okay." She leaned across the table, and with aching fury, squared off with Burk. She slapped her palm over the report and scolded, "I didn't come here to hear a bunch of garbage spewed out by Ramona Fenton. She is an evil crackpot."

Burk cracked a slight 'bring-it-on' grin. "Feisty young lady, aren't you?"

She reached back and pulled her chair under her and sat erect and poised. With moderate tone she asked, "What is in this report or in your conversation with Ramona that makes you think I need to defend myself?"

"Well, Ramona Fenton swears, *in writing*, that you and Ellis were keeping steady exclusive company."

Sherri blurted out an awe-filled snicker.

"Huh!" Burk said, "That is just the tip of the iceberg. She claims that Fenton told her that if anything happens to him during his rendezvous with you at Gobbler's Peak she is to seek justice for him."

"If it weren't for the seriousness of this matter, this would be downright amusing."

"You're right about one thing. This may be *very* serious. Especially in light of our finding a possible murder weapon."

Thad exchanged shocked glances with Sherri. Then, quickly turning his attention to Burk, he said, "Let's not put the cart before the horse. First of all, Fenton resides in Morgantown. How is it that Ramona rushes to Preston County to file a missing person report?"

Burk's face and neck reddened. "Still wet behind the ears, aren't you, son? Fenton was last known to be in Preston County. It appears that he owns the cabin and several hundred acres of woodland surrounding it. Therefore, at least in part, this case is in Preston County's jurisdiction. If you must know, *Ashbury*, I have made copies available to Monongalia County authorities.

Sherri strained to calm the emotional turbulence threatening to incapacitate her. "Um..." she weakly mumbled, "I'm feeling..."

Sherri jerked her face away from the powerful smell of ammonia. She rose to a sitting position on the old rugged oak bench. Searching her surroundings and recognizing the hallway outside the interview room, she asked, "What happened?"

Thad rose to his feet and tossed the smelling salts capsule into a nearby waste paper basket. "Are you okay?"

"I think so. How did I get out here?"

Teasingly, Thad said, "You suddenly decided to take a nap so we carried you here to a more suitable place to sleep."

Looking apologetic, Deputy Burk sat down beside her. "I'm sorry, Ms. Mosley. I guess I came on too strong. We can resume our meeting later. Maybe tomorrow, huh?"

Feeling surprisingly revived, Sherri replied, "No. I'm okay. Please, let's get this over with."

Deputy Burk looked to Thad as if to get a second opinion.

"Are you sure, Sherri?" Thad asked.

"Yeah. I really do feel much better."

Deputy Burk offered to finish the interview in the well-lighted and more spacious hallway. "Let me get my briefcase. I'll be right back."

Thad sat beside her and held her right hand, releasing her when Burk returned.

Positioning himself across the hall from Sherri and Thad, on a matching oak bench, Burk reopened his briefcase. After drawing a deep breath, he said, "Let's see if I can do this without overwhelming you."

She braced herself for the anticipated tumult, inaudibly quoting, "I can do all things through Christ which strengtheneth me."

Deputy Burk explained that he would summarize his investigation to date, reminding Sherri that everything thus far is only preliminary.

"I understand," Sherri said assuredly. "Will I have an opportunity to address or rebut Ramona's statements or offer other information I think useful in your investigation?"

"Yes, ma'am. In fact, I will be requesting such, especially as the investigation progresses. There may be others who need to talk to you, such as Monongalia County and State Police investigators."

"Whatever it takes," Sherri promised.

"Ramona Fenton implicates you as a threat to Ellis Fenton's physical well being. She charges that you are involved with him in a volatile romantic relationship."

Sherri repressed the laughter evoked by the absurdity of Ramona's accusations. "Absolutely and entirely untrue," she said confidently. "Go on… I'm listening."

"Miss Fenton further contends that Ellis had informed her that he and you were to rendezvous at the secluded cabin near Gobbler's Peak, though he had reservations concerning your real intentions."

"That girl has a serious leak in the attic!"

Burk continued as if he were afraid he'd be distracted or sidetracked. "Ramona said she called us because Ellis didn't show for their scheduled father-daughter breakfast."

Sherri let out an uncontrollable snigger.

"I'm trying to be patient with you, young lady. I fail to see how this could be amusing to you."

"I think it is ironic that a trained and experienced law enforcement officer of your caliber can be hoodwinked by this conniving hooligan. Did you honestly not detect any fabrication when you talked with her?"

Burk leaned forward, resting his elbows on his knees, and pressed his palms together, pointing all ten fingers at Sherri. Looking her squarely in the eyes he said, "I advise you to say nothing more until I have completely finished. Although you are not under arrest it would be wise of you to say as little as possible until you either consult with Officer Ashbury privately or have an attorney present. At the appropriate time I may ask you to either give me a written statement addressing these allegations or an audio recording of the same."

Sherri turned to Thad and asked, "Do I have to make an official statement?"

"Not at this time. But it may be helpful to the investigation in the event there has actually been a crime committed. I'll assist you if you decide to do that." Thad then asked Burk, "It sounds to me like she is being considered a suspect if a crime relating to Fenton has been committed. Is that a correct assumption?"

"She could be a suspect. But that is not the focus of *this* interview. Right now, I'm simply on a fact finding mission."

"Okay," Thad said authoritatively, "Sherri, say nothing more." Then, to Burk he said, "Go ahead. We're listening."

"After receiving Ramona's statements I returned to Gobbler's Peak. Based on her information we deemed it prudent to search inside and outside the cabin. We found more type 'O-negative' blood droplets where, judging from the tire indentations, a vehicle had been parked."

Sherri's skin crawled at the prospect of Mr. Fenton being beaten, maybe worse than he had experienced at the old print shop.

"Our search produced a fully-loaded, five-shot, .38 caliber revolver with two spent cartridges. We are sending it to the State Police Lab in Charleston for tests and finger print retrieval."

Sherri blurted, "a Rossi?"

"Sherri," Thad scolded, "be quiet. Did he not tell you to say nothing?" He stared sternly at her and commanded, "Just listen."

Deputy Burk stood and stretched. "I have *got* to dump some coffee. Now would be a good time for you two to have a serious, albeit, short talk. I'll be back in a couple minutes."

They watched him until he disappeared into the men's room at the opposite end of the hall.

"Thad, I can explain my finger prints on a Rossi .38 small-frame revolver. They are bound to find my prints on it. But I have never fired it. I picked it up and then placed it back in a gym bag where Mr. Fenton had it."

"For now, just keep your lips sealed. We'll discuss it later—out of earshot of Burk, or anyone else for that matter. I'm serious, Sherri. Bite your tongue—literally, if that's what it takes."

"But..."

Quickly cupping her mouth with his left hand and gesturing with his right index finger for her to wait a minute, Thad said, "But, nothing." He removed his hand and rolled his eyes to warn her of Burk's approaching.

Burk spryly dropped onto the bench and asked, "Now, where were we?"

Thad replied, "You were saying you found a fired revolver."

"Yes. We also found an old International Harvester pick-up truck registered to Ellis Fenton, hugging a tree about a mile down the other side of the mountain from Gobbler's Peak. It appears the driver had misjudged the soft bank of an old lumber company's tram road."

"But no sign of Fenton?" Thad inquired.

"Not yet. If he doesn't turn up in the next few days we will form search parties to scour a several mile radius from Gobbler's Peak."

Sherri couldn't resist declaring, "You can be sure Ramona knows of his whereabouts." Thad's soul piercing stare prompted her to mime her lips zipped and locked.

"We shall know in due time," Burk answered. "Right now, all I have is you. Do you know where Ellis Fenton is?"

She shook her head 'no' while looking to Thad for the okay to answer audibly. But he said nothing as though he neither heard the question nor comprehended her entreaty. "I can make a pretty accurate guess," she answered. "Wherever Ramona or her associates have taken him."

Thad asserted, "She'll not be saying any more, at this time."

She gritted her teeth. "Let me tell you something, Thad Ashbury. I'm not your little puppet—you overbearing boob." Immediately, her conscience chastised her for the insulting outburst. Leaping from the bench, she scurried down the hall to the women's restroom. Through thick blurring tears she beheld the hazy figure in the mirror. She studied the image, and then blinked away the dams gathered in the corners of her eyes. Then, studied her some more. "If I could get hold of you, I'd knock the snot out of you." She lectured her reflection and finally renewed her resolve to be less explosive.

When she returned, Burk tenderly asked, "Are you okay?"

She hung her head, too ashamed to face either man. Focusing on the floor at Thad's feet, she said, "Thad, please forgive me. You didn't deserve that."

Thad rose from the bench and hugged her. "Maybe I did deserve it. I mean well. Maybe I *am* too bossy."

Fighting back another surge of liquid sorrow, Sherri eased from his caress and started to sit.

"Don't sit down," Thad said, tapering the rest of the sentence, "we are taking a break…that is, if you agree, of course."

Sherri blushed from embarrassment for causing him to speak so cautiously *and* at his flattering benevolence.

"Go on, you two," Burk insisted. "If we need to talk more, I'll contact you."

Thad cranked the engine, and then shut it off. Turning to Sherri, he said reflectively, "I have something to share with you."

"Oh, Thad, don't," she interrupted. "Not now—in fairness to us both—maybe you should never say it."

Thad smiled and teasingly asked, "Aren't *you* a little presumptuous?"

"Ah, you don't think I know what you were going to say?"

"You *don't* know. You may think I was going to say what I wish I dared, but you couldn't even *guess* what it is."

"Really?"

"Really."

"Okay, Smarty. Say on."

Thad's countenance dulled. "Sherri, I must ask you something that you could totally misconstrue. Before I ask it, you must give your word that you will not prejudge it. You must be completely honest and forthright with me—not that I suspect you could be otherwise."

Twisting toward him, she pledged, "First, I would never lie to you. Of all my faults, lying is not one of them. Secondly, I sometimes am much *too* forthright. I've been told that I need to tame that part of my character. I promise to hear you out before judging what you have to say." Holding herself to limited flirtation, she coyly said, "Of course, I must admit that I have already judged you, somewhat."

"Is that so?" he asked playfully.

"It is, sir. I've judged you to be one of the most caring and kindest men ever I have met. Why, at this moment, I would proclaim your character second only to my Uncle Joseph."

"You give me shoes much too big to fill. And, that concerns me, for I'm afraid I'll disappoint you—not intentionally, of course."

"Okay, before we get too mushy, let's hear your question."

His visage again turned solemn. "When I believe in something—or someone—I give my all. I don't know how to pad this, so here it goes... If you are in any way—directly or indirectly—involved in any scheme or unlawful dealings where the Fenton's are concerned... I don't even think it possible but, I need to hear it from your own lips."

She beamed with appreciation at his polite candidness. "I am free of such. All that Ramona charges—all of it—is false and altogether unfounded."

"Good. Forgive me for having asked?"

"There is nothing to forgive. I couldn't put much confidence in anyone who exhibits careless abandon of wisdom. God knows I am gullible enough for the two of us."

"You want to hear something odd? At least, something I have never before experienced."

"I suppose I do. Maybe then, I'll not have to keep you on a pedestal."

He chuckled with delight. "I have this unexplainable confidence that Ellis Fenton is going to be found alive."

"That's interesting, Thad. Just after leaving the Sheriff's office I sensed the same assurance."

"Maybe this is just what I need to revive the passion I once had in my Christian walk. It seems that I have lacked spiritual purpose these last few years. When Deacon Drake asked for my assistance in reinvestigating Joseph Short's case, I immediately regained a spiritual aspect to my law enforcement career. I really believe the Holy Spirit is drawing me into this as a way of increasing my love for *God's* work."

Sherri answered, "It makes sense to me. After all, one could not attain more perfect justice than that effectuated by the Lord."

"Now that I have your ear," Thad said cheerfully, "let me tell you of a related incident. You may laugh at this, but it really happened."

"Why would I laugh at something so precious as the Holy Spirit's dealings with a man so humble and earnest?"

Thad grinned shamefacedly. "Deacon Drake's request for my assistance in solving Spike Cottrell's murder came at a very peculiar time. I had been interrupted from sleep two or three times a night for more than a week with a particular scripture running through my mind. Finally, around three o'clock one morning, I bounced out of bed, stumbled to the living room and grabbed my Bible. I hunted diligently until I found it. It read, word for word just as it had run through my head like a ticker tape." He paused to clear his throat.

Sherri's lungs swelled with excitement and anticipation of the story's climax. "Tell me what verse," she pleaded.

"Romans 8:28."

Sherri quoted it with him in perfect cadence. "And we know that all things work together for good to them that love God, to them who are the called according to his purpose."

She read the same wonder in his eyes that *she felt* in her heart. She shot across the front seat and hugged his neck and exclaimed, "God bless, you, Thad Ashbury. You are truly a blessing from Heaven."

"Really?" He asked, as to invite her exegesis.

"I had a very similar encounter with this verse. I claimed it as a call to specifically come to Uncle Joseph's aid because of the circumstances at the time. Until this very moment I wrestled with the idea that I may have been forcing it to be interpreted too specifically."

"Well," Thad said with comparable excitement, "I had the same problem at first. When Deacon Drake first confronted me with the prospect of the case, I shared my experience with him. He convinced me that although that verse normally is not interpreted so specifically, in this case it very well could be."

Pressing her crossed arms against her bosom, Sherri proclaimed, "I'm so blessed I can't contain it! I'm about to explode with elation!"

Thad cut short her savoring of the moment. "What are your plans for the rest of the day?"

"Nothing in particular."

"I thought we could go in search of Joseph. We could start by visiting the Salvation Army's soup kitchen. There also is a chance he may have, at some time, stayed at the Bartlett House. Bartlett House is a temporary shelter for the homeless, passing through vagabonds, and others who need it. We will decide, after those visits, what to do next."

"You are too wonderful, Thad." She turned solemn and said, "I have the most nagging suspicion that Uncle Joseph is, for whatever reason, reluctant to return to society."

CHAPTER FOURTEEN

Friday, May 4, 1979

Thad knocked on the open door. "Excuse me, ma'am."

The elderly woman at the desk, who had been reading, raised her head slightly and peered over her stylish glasses. "I suppose I can excuse you," she said teasingly. "It depends on what you did that needs excusing."

"Yeah, right. Like I'm going to confess my misdeeds to a stranger," he quipped.

With a big smile, she said, "Well, come on in and have a seat." Meeting Thad and Sherri halfway, she extended her hand and said, "I'm Ethel Ford."

Thad shook hands with her and introduced Sherri.

"I'm pleased to meet you both. What can I do for such a good looking couple?"

Sherri's uneasiness at the suggestion impelled her to politely correct Mrs. Ford. She flushed as much from the temptation of the idea as over the statement itself. "Oh… We aren't a couple… I mean, not romantically… We aren't… you know…"

Ethel's smile broadened as she motioned for them to have a seat, while returning to her chair. "It's okay, Honey. You needn't explain. I should not have been so assuming."

Thad, also blushing, replied, "We are trying to locate Sherri's uncle who may have visited you or maybe some other workers of the Salvation Army. He's been homeless for several months and reportedly is in the Morgantown area."

"Have you inquired upstairs at the soup kitchen?"

"Not yet."

Looking to Sherri, Ethel asked, "What's your uncle's name, honey?"

"Joseph Short. Some of the other homeless people in the area call him Joe the Baptist."

Ethel leaned back in her large black leather office chair and removed her glasses. "Well, there seems to be quite an interest in finding this mysterious Reverend Short."

"Yes, ma'am," said Thad. "We are aware the police are looking for him. I'm a Star City Police officer, but my interest is not in his arrest. In fact, we believe he is innocent of all charges alleged against him."

Ethel leaned forward and caringly asked, "Did you know there are others, besides the police, who are trying to find him?"

Thad asked, "Have others been *here* inquiring of Reverend Short?"

"Yes. Helena Johnson, our soup kitchen supervisor, reported that a couple men came in one day, threateningly asking some of our diners about Reverend Short. Helena asked them to leave after they refused to show identification. They didn't leave right away so she called the Morgantown police. By the time the police arrived the men had gone. Helena said they were very rude."

"Were the diners any help to those men?"

"I don't think. Some of these folks are very loyal to him. Others just don't like anyone nosing around in the business of fellow street folks."

Sherri scooted to the edge of her seat. Wishing Ethel could offer some hope, she asked, "Have you any information about Uncle Joseph? Like, where he sleeps? Or if he is well? Anything at all?" she pleaded.

"I'm sorry, honey. I really don't. It is rumored that Reverend Short seldom shows himself around town. Even the other homeless people out there seem to know little of him. They do know him as a godly man and they have utmost respect for him. Even the mean amongst them speak respectfully of him."

"You mentioned Ms. Johnson. Would she have such information about Uncle Joseph?"

Ethel chirped, "According to Helena, that man walks on water. Now, there is where you will find a true devotee to Reverend Short and all that he stands for. Let me call her to see if she can talk with you."

"That would be great," Thad replied.

Ethel slid her glasses back on and dialed the phone. "Hi Tom. You must have had your hand on the phone already. This is Ethel. Is Helena near by? No, no, Tom. Just tell her I am sending a young man and his lady friend to see her. Thank you, Tom." She gently replaced the receiver and gave them directions to the kitchen.

"Hi. I'm Helena Johnson." Her strong, yet delicate, features and coal-black hair were as telling as her Sicilian accent.

"Nice to meet you, ma'am. I'm Sherri and this is Thad."

"Please follow me. We can speak more privately in the office." She led them to a small rear-corner office with few modern furnishings, but neat and clean. "Please be seated and tell me your troubles," she said, pointing to a small-upholstered desk chair and a nearby tall wooden stool.

Thad insisted, "You ladies have a seat, I sit too many hours a day as it is."

Helena patted Thad's cheek and exclaimed, "What a gentleman. I would demand that you sit, but there are too few gentlemen nowadays. I will not discourage you, young handsome man." She pulled the office chair from the desk and spun it around. "Okay. I sit. Now, you sit, young lady. Tell me what it is you desire of me."

"Well," Sherri said, "Mrs. Ford suggested we speak with you regarding my uncle, Reverend Joseph Short."

"I saw him only once. What a peculiarly wonderful man! I think somebody tells lies about him. I don't like liars."

"Was it recently, that you saw him, Mrs. Johnson?"

"Call me Helena. Please? About four or five months ago, your uncle graced this place with his presence. It must have been just a couple weeks before Christmas."

"How do you know it was Uncle Joseph?"

"After he left, I asked some of our regular diners, 'who is this holy man?' They called him Joe the Baptist. One man spoke up and explained his real name is Joseph Short."

"Can you tell us how to find him?"

"Not even if I knew, would I tell anyone unless I knew he so wished."

Sherri pleaded, "Helena, we wish him only good. We want to help him. We love him very much. Please, if you can help us, he will thank you."

Helena's eyes glazed. She quickly rose from her chair and nervously wiped her hands with her apron. "I have much to do. You should leave now."

Thad asked, "Don't you want to help Reverend Short?"

"Why can't people let the man live in peace? Is it not enough he has been shamed and financially destroyed? He is God's anointed. I will not be the devil's tool. If you two kids love him, let him be."

"Helena," Thad begged, "we must find him before the police do. Mrs. Ford said that you knew of others besides the police who are trying to find Reverend Short. If these people find him first there is no telling what evil they will inflict on him."

Helena opened the office door and sternly ordered, "Leave now."

Sherri walked numbly to the doorway. Stopping to face Helena, she asked, "If you can get a message to him, will you tell him that his niece, Sherri, loves him? Tell him we've come to his aid. He must hear that I need his cooperation to defeat his foes." She then left, barely aware of Thad's arm gently wrapped around her as they walked through the dining room and outside.

"Sherri," Thad said, as he halted on the sidewalk to behold her face, "wait a minute."

"For what?" she asked lifelessly.

"Let's go back inside and ask Helena one more question."

"I don't know if that is wise, Thad. She may need time to think things over. I think she really cares for Uncle Joseph's welfare. What puzzles me is, why? She saw him only once."

"Exactly!" Thad said enthusiastically.

Thad's exclamation pumped new life into her. "Of course," she said gleefully. "Neither of us gave her the opportunity to explain how she concluded Uncle Joseph is a 'holy' man, having seen him only once."

"That is precisely what I want to ask her about."

They turned about and marched as one. As soon as they stepped through the doorway, Thad motioned for Sherri to be still. He quietly closed the door, turning the knob to keep the bolt from clicking, then releasing it slowly. The words Helena uttered beyond the closed office door were muffled, but unmistakably expressed in fervent prayer.

Sherri and Thad sat in reverence at the table nearest the entrance; each silently praying, also.

About one half hour later, Helena entered the dining area and gasped at the sight of unexpected company.

Thad said, "It is just us, Helena. We didn't mean to startle you."

"Oh, all is well. I have coffee. May I pour you each a cup?"

"Yes. Thank you, Helena." Sherri cheerfully replied.

Thad rushed to assist Helena. "Mmm, what rich aroma."

Helena grinned, but spoke not a word.

"Mrs. Johnson," Thad said, and then halted at her hand gesture to stop.

"I told you, young handsome man, to call me Helena. Now, sit and we will talk."

"Helena," he continued, "Sherri and I failed to ask one very significant question. May I ask it now?"

"Of course. First you must forgive my behavior—asking you to leave like that. I am a stubborn fool sometimes."

"Forgiven."

"And you too, must forgive me, beautiful girl."

Sherri leaned to the right and hugged her. "I forgive you."

"Thank you, beautiful people."

Thad reached across the table and laid his hand atop Helena's. "You told us you have a very high opinion of Reverend Short. Having only seen him once, there must be a very special reason you so quickly formed such a sentiment."

"Yes. For good reason, I feel obliged to stand up for him. Would you like to hear what happened that day?"

"Yes, ma'am," Thad and Sherri chimed in unison.

"I may not be able to tell it without tears. It is very precious—that day."

"That is quite all right, Helena," Sherri said.

Helena's face glowed as she began telling her encounter with Joseph. "It happened on a blistery cold Thursday afternoon. A light coating of fresh snow had accumulated outside. The wind whipped, and swirled the snow in hypnotic dance. Only a third of the usual number of people came for lunch. It is not rare for some of our diners to be more cheerless around Christmastime. Something about that day overburdened everyone. Even the volunteers seemed heavy-laden—including me.

"One lone middle-aged man, a stranger to us all, sat at the table in the far left front corner by himself, clothed much better than our typical visitors. In fact, he dressed in rather upper-class suit and tie. Even his winter coat looked expensive. He didn't come for something to eat. I offered him coffee, but he grunted and shook his head, no. He sat there very sullen, staring blankly for a long time. At first, I paid him no mind. I supposed he came in to escape the bitter cold awhile, before walking to wherever he was headed."

"Nobody knew him?" Sherri asked.

"No one here, that day, knew him. He wouldn't even look directly at anyone. I had thought to call the police, but he did nothing wrong. He just worried me. I could even feel something was not right about him. He kept his hands in his coat pockets. That made me wonder, since it was nice and warm in here."

Thad said, "You're pretty observant. I would have wondered, too. That kind of thing probably *should* make a person a little apprehensive or suspicious."

Helena's eyes widened. "Finally overcome by apprehension I decided to call the police. Before I reached the office, I had this strange feeling that I should delay that decision. At that very moment, another man, unknown to me, came in. Right away, he announced, 'I have come to offer you new life in Jesus Christ.' At first, I thought he must be deranged. His voice commanded everyone's attention. His speech possessed an enthralling quality."

"Yep," said Sherri, "that had to have been Uncle Joseph."

"Love radiated from his clear blue eyes," Helena continued. "He searched all our faces as he preached the most inspiring Christmas sermon I had ever heard. What little conversation had been going on ceased as he held us captive with his message. I have been saved for twenty years and yet responded to his invitation to let Jesus give unto me a new life. I needed revived and his message hit the spot.

"One of our homeless regulars got saved and vowed to return to Cincinnati to beg his wife's and two daughters' forgiveness for deserting them. He had turned to drugs and alcohol and, through a series of bad choices and misbehavior, found himself living a lowly street sot's life—if you dare call that a life."

Sherri asked, "Did the man return home? Or would you know if he did?"

"Yes. He and his family stay in touch with me. They always ask about Reverend Short. Billy now works in an industrial woodworking factory in the Cincinnati area. His family reconciled and they attend church regularly."

Sherri proclaimed, "That's my Jesus. Way to go Uncle Joseph."

"Oh, my dear girl," Helena sighed, "that is not the whole story."

Thad joined in, "Reverend Short just stepped inside and started preaching—unannounced or without introducing himself?"

"Sure did. I prefer to think he didn't want introduced. He came to introduce Jesus Christ. He sought no self-recognition. What an extraordinary, selfless man."

"Yeah, that makes sense to me. I don't know him personally, but those who love him would agree with you. You must have a measure of spiritual discernment, Helena."

"Thank, you. It isn't hard to see Reverend Short as a godly man. What happened next can only be described as absolutely wonderful."

Thad and Sherri joined hands in anxious anticipation.

"After preaching his sermon and then praying with Billy, Reverend

Short instructed us all about the tenets of the Christian faith. He advised us to all attend worship services, pray often, read the Bible faithfully, and find a way to serve Jesus until He calls us home.

"He opened the door to leave and suddenly slammed it closed and yelled, 'No, put it down. In the name of Jesus, hear His Spirit speak to your heart.' We all looked in surprise to see the wealthy man in the corner holding a handgun to his own temple. The man spoke in a very shaky voice and told Reverend Short to stay away or he would shoot him, too."

Sherri's heart sank as she mentally pictured the scene. "Please, don't tell me any more, if the man shot himself."

"Oh, my dear, he would have. Reverend Short fixed his eyes piercingly on the stranger and said, 'God has sent me on this very special mission. I am just now realizing that you were the one the Holy Spirit wanted to save today.' The man slowly lowered the gun from his head as Reverend Short approached him all the while assuring him that Jesus loves him. The man sobbed heavily as he handed the gun to Reverend Short, who emptied the shells from it and asked for permission to throw them in the Monongahela River."

Sherri excitedly said, "I bet you were sweating bullets that day." The words no more than cleared her lips than she burned with embarrassment over the unintended pun.

Helena rendered a forgiving smile and then continued, "After consoling the man, Reverend Short gained a promise from him that he would commit himself for emotional and psychiatric help. The man didn't promise to get saved right then, but said he would give serious consideration to becoming a follower of Jesus. He had difficulty believing that Jesus would forgive *all* his sins."

"Did he follow through with his promise?" Sherri asked with sincere interest.

"Oh, yes. Reverend Short told me who to call and how to get the process started. The man, whose name we learned is Steve Conrad, from New York City, agreed to the whole thing. The man at the Sheriff's office said a deputy would soon be here to transport Mr. Conrad to the hospital for an emergency evaluation and subsequent admission. Reverend Short told me that he must leave before the police get here since a warrant had been issued for his arrest. A fellow by the name of Lanky told me the story of Reverend Short's troubles with his ex-wife. I had read a little of it in the paper, but paid it no mind."

"It's a shame, how some people can cause so much havoc for an innocent man." Thad said angrily.

Helena lifted the corner of her apron to wipe her eyes. "God gave witness that day of the reverend's righteousness. Others may say lies about him, but I know Reverend Short is truly a man of God. God's Spirit filled this place when your uncle ministered here and even after his departure."

"Wow!" Sherri said. "I'm so glad you told us of that event. It confirms my expectations of Uncle Joseph—faithful to God, no matter his circumstances."

Thad concurred, "Yeah. It reminds me of the Old Testament Joseph, son of Jacob… Let's all pray that *our* Joseph is rewarded by God in like manner."

They joined hands and hearts in ardent supplication and praise to God for what He would do for Joseph.

Thad's glad-hearted pessimistic chatter fell flat. All the way back to the mountain Sherri felt compassed about with an unexplainable fear. What could be the source of her increasing anxiety? The closer they got to Janet's home, the more intense the paranoia.

CHAPTER FIFTEEN

Friday, May 4, 1979

"I thought for sure Janet would be home by now," Thad said quizzically. "Isn't she usually home from work earlier than this?"

Sherri replied, "She and I were to go grocery shopping this evening. Maybe she tired of waiting for me. I'm sure she'll be home soon."

Bringing the truck to a stop at the top of the gravel driveway, Thad threw the shifter into neutral and set the brake. Leaving the engine idle, he said, "I would come in with you, but since Janet isn't home I better head on home."

Sherri delighted in his sincere commitment to their earlier agreement to never allow themselves to be in a compromising or questionable situation.

Thad had suggested, "We'll probably be spending a lot of time together on this case. Do you suppose we ought to set some boundaries early on? Especially, in light of First Thessalonians 5:22, that tells us to abstain from all appearances of evil."

She thanked Thad and bounded from the passenger's seat. She had taken only a few steps toward the house when Thad jumped from the driver's side and ordered, "Sherri, wait. The front door is ajar."

Sherri froze in mid-stride. Her mind raced, imagining some thug waiting to ambush her or Janet.

"Get back in the truck," he commanded. "Be prepared to speed away." Pointing to the nearest farmhouse he said, "Uncle Jake and Aunt Wilma live right there. Go there and call the Sheriff's office if anything goes awry while I'm checking it out." He kept his eyes peeled toward the house while drawing his off-duty revolver from a concealed holster in his waistband. He further demanded, "Lock the doors as soon as you get in."

Several anxiety-filled minutes passed before Thad returned to the front deck and motioned for Sherri to come. As soon as her feet hit the ground, he asked, "You didn't see anyone unfamiliar out here, did you?"

She hadn't detected any excitement in his voice although he still held his gun at the ready. "No. Not even a *familiar* face. Why?"

"I don't think there is anyone around now, but the place has been ransacked."

She warily followed him into the house. "I can't believe the audacity of these scumbags! They had to have done this in broad daylight… Oh, Thad," she gasped, "you don't suppose whoever did this kidnapped Janet? Why would they take her Jeep, though? No, I can't allow myself to think of such horror."

"I certainly hope she hadn't gotten home yet. Stay right here with me, while I phone the Sheriff's department. Then we'll try to determine what all is missing."

While Thad talked with the Sheriff's dispatcher, Sherri visually surveyed the living room, not daring to leave Thad's side.

"Okay," Thad sighed, "a deputy is already on his way. Stay close by me, for caution sake."

Sherri nervously laughed. "Are you kidding? You'll think I'm glued to you."

They finished their assessment and waited in the driveway until Deputy Stone arrived.

"What are you doing up here in God's country?" Stone teased as he shook Thad's hand.

"Well," Thad replied, "right now, trying to find out who is doing the devil's deeds."

The barrel-chested deputy reached his hand toward Sherri. "Hi, I'm Warren Stone. You must be Janet."

Shaking his hand, she said banteringly, "No, sir. I'm Sherri. I'm still pleased to meet you, though."

He apologized, and then got down to business. "I understand you've been burglarized. Is that correct?"

"Vandalized, at least," Sherri answered. "There seems to be nothing missing, except a notebook containing incriminating notes of evidence on one of Monongalia County's former assistant prosecutors and his friends."

Thad opened the back screen door and led Deputy Stone inside.

"Goodness!" Stone exclaimed, as he stepped into the living room. "Somebody sure wanted to leave a message. When did this take place?"

Sherri pressed her index finger across her upper lip, and then asked Thad, "What time did we leave this morning?"

"Right around seven."

She glanced back at Deputy Stone who grinned menacingly. "Somewhere between seven this morning and six o'clock this evening." She then rebutted, "Thad arrived, *from his house*, about fifteen 'til seven to pick me up."

"I didn't say anything," he defended.

"Just be sure you don't conclude that anything unseemly is going on," she enjoined.

His fair complexion reddened, accentuating his light freckles. "Ah, I know Thad is a very religious man. However, I *did* intend to tease him, since he failed to make that distinction… You are pretty perceptive."

Thad lightly laughed. "Don't worry, this girl will keep you straight."

"I can see that. She is apparently as forthright as she is attractive."

"Thanks," Sherri said, "I think."

Deputy Stone flipped open a thin silver metal contraption revealing a writing tablet and then began writing. After jotting something, he asked, "Do you have any idea who might have done this?"

Before Sherri could answer, a male voice from outside asked, "Anything wrong over here?"

"Come on in," Thad called back.

The short and stout curly-haired gentleman no more than stepped through the doorway when Thad introduced him as 'Uncle Jake.'

Looking stunned and saying not a word, Jake slowly took in the large wrecked living room.

"Sir," Deputy Stone asked Jake, "were you home at anytime between seven this morning and six this evening?"

"I left this morning around five-thirty and got home from my construction job around five this evening."

"Had you noticed anything unusual when you arrived home?"

"No. I saw Janet's Jeep parked in the driveway. That is typical enough. She usually gets home from work around that time…I did notice an unfamiliar black Ford Bronco pull in behind Janet's Jeep. I was at the lower barn checking on an injured calf. I just supposed it was one of her friends or co-workers, and went about my chores. I didn't see either vehicle leave."

"About what time did the Bronco pull into the driveway?"

"I guess it must have been about five-fifteen or five-thirty. I got a glass of water as soon as I got home and then headed to the barn."

Sherri restrained from expressing her fear *or* her suspicions. She certainly didn't want to unduly alarm Jake.

Thad pulled a notepad from his shirt pocket. "Hey, Warren, make a note of this information," he said, turning the notepad from Sherri's view.

While Stone copied the notes, Thad explained that he had run the license plate number Janet gave to him a few days earlier. "The Pennsylvania Department of Motor Vehicles' records indicate that the Bronco in question belongs to a Gregory Grant; last known address—Pittsburgh. The Allegheny County Police checked for me and advised that Grant had moved a few months ago, leaving no forwarding address."

Jake, now looking more concerned, asked Thad, "So, what's the story behind this Ford Bronco? I just talked with Janet yesterday and she didn't even hint that she had any trouble with anyone."

"Uncle Jake," Thad said caringly, "I'll explain it all later. Let

Deputy Stone finish his work, here. Do me a favor… Take Sherri with you and wait at your house. I'll be along in a while to update you. Meanwhile, Sherri can fill in some of the blanks for you."

Sherri gently took Jake by the arm. "I guess that is Thad's way of saying, 'get out of the way of the professionals.'"

Jake, looking sullen, walked slowly toward the door with Sherri. "Maybe we *better* go to my house and invite my wife, Wilma, to join us as we seek the Lord's intervention, while these boys do their part."

Jake groaned as he rose from his front porch swing. "Heads up, girl."

Sherri rose from the large wooden rocking chair and spun around to see what Jake alluded to. She stiffened as Thad briskly approached, anger distorting his handsome face.

"I wonder what his ears are all pinned back about," Jake said, while scratching his unshaven chin.

"I'm sure he'll tell us, soon as he gets in earshot," answered Sherri.

"I tell you what," Thad threatened from thirty yards away, "these punks are going to pay, and pay big."

Sherri labored unsuccessfully to form a lucid question from the many rushing through her mind. So she resolved to wait for his explanation. She hastened to his side, clasped his right arm and marched alongside him in silence.

Thad plopped onto the second of four porch steps. Inhaling deeply, then exhaling as if to expel his rage, he said heavily, "Somebody, pray."

Sherri hesitated, and then bowed her head. "Our heavenly Father, I don't know what to pray for right this moment. May the Holy Spirit intercede for us, as your Word tells us He does in times like this?" She paused to await His inspiration.

Several seconds passed as a gradual comforting peace swept her into confident audible praise of God's majesty and His care for His children.

Thad joined in, "Thank you, Lord. Please be with Janet, Joseph, and Mr. Fenton. I ask for your comfort and guidance as Sherri and I continue our battle against the evils of this world—especially, in these present troubles."

Jake then prayed that wisdom, grace, and spiritual strength in great measure be given to them all, as well as His protection.

They ended their prayer with joint thanksgiving.

Thad lifted his head and responded to Sherri's admiring smile, "Thanks, Sherri. You are very special." He scooted closer to Sherri and said, "Uncle Jake, come sit on the steps with us. I have some worrisome news to share."

Jake lowered himself to the step and said, "I knew something gnawed at you when I saw you stomping across the field. I figured it must have been awfully upsetting."

Sherri rubbed Thad's back while assuring him all will turn out okay.

"There is no easy way to tell you this," he said. He blew a blast of air. "Deputy Stone picked up the kitchen phone to call the station. A small, tightly folded note, taped to the receiver's earpiece, scratched his ear."

"What does it say?" Jake asked impatiently.

"I'd rather not divulge the whole thing, but it is basically a ransom note."

"How much are they asking for?"

"They aren't requesting any money. They demanded that Joseph Short's 'dogs' back off—or else."

"Or else, what?" Sherri asked angrily.

"That's just it. They only said, 'or else' in the note."

Sherri burst into weeping. "What have I done? If only I had not come here. It's all my fault." Looking pleadingly to Jake and then to Thad, she cried, "Please forgive me. I didn't mean to jeopardize Janet's safety. I'm such a terrible friend. How could I let this happen?" Feeling helpless and ashamed, she turned and prostrated herself across the steps, buried her face in the porch floor, and sobbed. She felt Jake's thick strong hand on her shoulder as he pleaded for her to not blame herself.

"Yesterday," he consoled, "Janet told me that she encouraged you to come back here to help her set things right for Reverend Short. She told me that she would have taken on the task alone, eventually, if need be. She said that you simply provided the unction to accelerate her intentions."

Sherri sat upright and looked Jake in the face and entreated, "Did she really say that?"

"She sure did. She asked me to pray for Reverend Short and all those allied with her to set things straight in his behalf."

"I just wish they would have taken me hostage, instead of Janet. I'm the one who stirred things up. It's *my* big mouth that challenged them."

Jake held her hand and insisted, "Don't you take the blame for these hoodlums' doings. These kind of jerks need no invitation to do evil."

"I know, but I can't dismiss my guilt so easily."

"You must, girl. You have no right to accuse you any more than anyone else has...By the way, Janet told her Aunt Wilma and me something else interesting about this whole situation. It took us both by surprise."

Sherri wiped away the tears streaming down her face. "What's that, Uncle Jake?"

"I figure you may know this already, but she carries a torch for your uncle. She said she has secretly loved him for several years. No wonder she never got married. I think she has waited all this time, hoping that somehow she and Reverend Short would become sweethearts."

Sherri smiled sheepishly. "She only told me of this recently. I honestly had no idea. If I had known this when we were younger, I would have played matchmaker until it hurt. There is no one on this earth I love more than those two."

Thad cleared his throat, rose to his feet, stepped forward on the fieldstone sidewalk at the bottom of the steps, and faced Sherri. "Now, that ought to be enough to convince you that you are not responsible for Janet's involvement in this case. I don't want you to ever again allow Satan to plant the notion that you're to blame for any of this mess. You let the punks who started all this be the ones who take the full blame. I mean that, Sherri. Stop being so hard on yourself. It distracts you from thinking clearly and certainly is of no benefit."

"Okay," she said, in thankful surrender. "So, what do we do now?"

"That's more like it," Thad cheered. Then more solemnly, he said, "The deputies will dust for fingerprints, take photos of the place, and systematically search for other clues and pieces of evidence of what all happened at the house. Deputy Stone already issued an all-points-bulletin for Gregory Grant and his vehicle. The dispatcher immediately sent it over the Teletype to law enforcement agencies, nationwide. Before I left Janet's house, Stone also telephoned the Clarksburg office of the FBI."

"Thad," Jake said urgently, "we can't let this girl stay at Janet's, until all this is cleared up."

"I know. Sherri, I am sure I can get you a safe place to stay. I called a friend who is more than willing to help out. I didn't tell her the whole situation—only that I had a very dear friend who needs a safe haven, indefinitely. She and her husband are very good Christians. You'll like them."

"I'm so much trouble!"

"And every bit worth it."

"Thad," she said reflectively, "if Deputy Stone used Janet's phone, could he have smudged the fingerprints of whoever taped the note to it?"

"Relax. He took the applicable precautions. That's pretty insightful of you, though."

She stared off, toward Janet's driveway. "Something doesn't quite make sense."

"What?" Thad inquired.

"Well, they took Janet's Jeep CJ instead of my Oldsmobile. How did they know the Oldsmobile no longer belonged to Janet?"

"Who drove your car when those guys followed you and Janet to Star City?"

"Duh! I drove. Sometimes, I just talk really stupid."

"To question is not stupid. It reveals focus. That's indicative of a person who doesn't mindlessly accept things as they are. If I had allowed you time to think it over, you would have figured it out on your own."

Sherri chuckled. "Keep that opinion of me. It may serve me well as you get to know me better… One more thing… Why *would* they take her vehicle? Why not just kidnap her and leave her Jeep here?"

"I wonder the same thing. That *is* strange. That's why I suspect they're the ones who have done something to, or with, Ellis Fenton. Remember, Preston county deputies found his truck wrecked down the other side of Gobbler's Peak. And he is missing."

"Those jerks better not harm Janet," she declared resolutely. "They better hope God holds me back when we catch up with them."

"Okay, Tiger," Thad teased.

"I'm serious."

"I know you are. We'll get them. We must believe that God is answering our prayers. Meanwhile, we stay the course and He'll provide the victory."

"You know what, Thad? I said this already to Janet—Uncle Joseph is really going to like you. You two have so much in common."

"I'll take that as a high compliment."

"As well you should."

Abruptly changing the conversation, Thad said, "Sherri, stay here with Uncle Jake while I return to Janet's to assist Deputy Stone."

"Well," Thad said excitedly, as he bounced through the doorway, "we may have a break in the case, already."

"That's quick," Jake said with equal animation.

Hoping to hear of Janet's rescue, yet not daring to expect an affirmative answer, Sherri asked, "Did they catch them? Did they find Janet?"

"Not that big of a break—at least not yet. Corporal Daniels, from the State Police contacted the Sheriff's office to inform them that he recalled arresting Gregory Grant a couple days ago. It seems that Daniels issued a traffic violation to Grant on Route 7 at Purseglove. After Daniels pulled back onto the highway, he looked in his rearview mirror just as Grant threw the citation out his window and executed a U-Turn. Daniels turned around and pursued him, catching up with him at the parking lot of an abandoned coal company machine shop up Number Eight Hollow. Grant took a swing at Daniels. So Daniels subsequently charged him with reckless driving, resisting arrest, assaulting a police officer and littering."

"Why is he not in jail, then?" Sherri asked irritably.

"Once he posted bond they had to cut him loose until the trial date. That's how the system works."

"It's a mighty poor system."

"I agree, but we have to work within those confines."

"Okay," Sherri more calmly asked, "how does that information benefit us, now?"

"Its significance is in the fact that, although at the time Daniels gave it no thought, he recalls seeing an unoccupied new white Cadillac parked there. There are no businesses or residences within a half-mile or more of the old cinder-block building."

"I still don't get it," Sherri said impatiently. "How is that a break for us?"

"I'm getting to that."

"Well, take a short cut. You're unnerving me with all the details."

"Daniels and another trooper are checking the building and the area. If the Cadillac had no one in it, they must have been inside the abandoned building. What were they using the building for?"

Sherri's heart leaped with expectancy. "Do you think that is where they took Janet?"

Thad cautioned, "Don't count your eggs before they've hatched. However, there is a chance that *is* where they're holding her."

"If that jerk got out on bond so soon before, what is to prevent him from posting bond again and going free to create further havoc?"

"I don't think he'll be afforded that opportunity this time, Sherri. Kidnapping is a federal offense. I don't imagine local authorities will let him go without first cooperating with the FBI. They wouldn't dare risk being charged with obstructing justice for these low-life."

"Will they contact you when they get these guys?"

"We'll stay on top of the situation. First, I want you to follow me to my home. We'll park your car in my garage. Then, we'll go to the Sheriff's office to monitor what all is happening. After that, I'll take you to the friends' house I told you about. We need to get you settled into a safe place until all this is wrapped up."

CHAPTER SIXTEEN

Friday, May 4, 1979

Thad pushed open the heavy steel door and held it open for Sherri. They paused at the first window—formed by the open upper half of a steel door with the lower half welded to the metal door jams at either side. Thad slapped the window's wide ledge, just eighteen inches below the bars, which formed the window.

"Hi, Thad, my lad," chimed a male voice. "What kind of trouble are you stirring now? Come on in here and confess."

Sherri barely caught sight of the man in a blue uniform shirt as he rode a chair across the room and punched an electronic control button. At the clicking sound, Thad dodged to another metal door and pushed it open. "Come on, Sherri."

They entered the small four-foot by six-foot space between the door and the barred entrance to the jail. The man then unlocked a metal door on the right to let Sherri and Thad into the control room. "Get in here and explain why you are with this gorgeous creature," he teased. Before Thad could utter a word, the man asked Sherri, "What is a beautiful girl like you doing running around with this ugly mutt?"

"You don't have to answer that," Thad intercepted. "He will use it against you. Sherri, this is the county's jailer, dispatcher and chief troublemaker, Al."

Al locked the door behind them and clipped the huge brass Folger-Adams key to his side. Shaking Sherri's hand, he said, "I'm pleased to meet you. You know this man is jealous of me, don't you?"

"Is he?"

"Oh, yes," Al replied. "I have him figured out though. He brought you in here to make *me* jealous of *him*, for once."

"Thanks for the compliments, Al, but there is no need to be jealous of him."

"Really? What is she saying, Officer Thad?"

"We're just friends working on a case together. If you want to fire her up and see what she's made of, just keep on drawing the wrong impressions and verbalizing them."

Al threw his hands up and declared, "I think I'll stay on her good side. If she can spook ole fearless Thad Ashbury, I don't think I want to earn her wrath." Al reached to shake hands again with Sherri, and said, "Let's start over… Hi, I'm Al. What can I do for you and your fellow investigator?"

Sherri couldn't refrain from laughter. "Why, you can climb out of the holes you dig as quickly as you fall in."

"Yes, ma'am. This job is good training ground for foot-in-mouth folks like myself." Sitting back at the desk, Al insisted Sherri and Thad have a seat.

Thad and Al conversed about everything but what Sherri had come for. She desired to waste no more time and considered interrupting their jovial chatter to attend to more serious and pressing matters.

Suddenly, both men stopped their prattle.

"Do you know where else to look for them?" Al asked Thad.

"Not right at the moment."

Sherri marveled at their having heard the news over one of the many pieces of communication equipment in the ten-foot by fifteen-foot room. She imagined that only a well-trained ear could separate the barrage of constant chatter coming across the airwaves. She soon tuned in with them to the state police radio traffic as the troopers announced their failure to locate Gregory Grant or anyone else at the old building. Fearing she would miss further transmissions, she refrained from voicing her heartrending disappointment.

"Unit Thirty to dispatch, Unit Twenty-eight and I are ten-eight from that location and will be canvassing the area and interviewing residents up the hollow."

"Ten-four, Unit Thirty."

"Meanwhile, contact the Sheriff's office and obtain whatever additional information they may have available."

"Ten-four, Unit Thirty."

Sherri asked, "Who is Unit Thirty?"

"Corporal Daniels, state police," Thad answered.

The black phone, on the right side of the desk, rang. Al promptly answered it. At that very second a voice came over the main console radio to Al's right rear side. Without interrupting the phone conversation he answered, "Go ahead, Unit Six-one."

"That's Deputy Stone," Thad advised Sherri.

A red phone at the left edge of Al's desk then rang. Al asked the phone caller to hold on for a second and keyed his main microphone, "Ten-four, Unit Six-one. You are ten-seven, State Police barracks at twenty-one hundred hours." He quickly penned the information while speaking into the red phone, "What is your emergency, sir?"

Writing feverishly, he repeated the caller's response. "Thanks, Mr. Lucas." Spinning his chair, he punched a series of buttons on another console, keyed the microphone and announced, "Cheat Lake you have a vehicular fire, Route 857 North, just before dropping over the hill to Darnell Hollow." He repeated the message and instantly resumed his conversation with the caller on the black phone.

Sherri listened intently to Al's side of the conversations, gleaning from them what she could. In spite of the escalating suspense, she clung to a measure of hope that she concluded to be God's grace. The methodical professionalism and coordinated efforts of the various law enforcement agencies impressed Sherri to the point of rapture.

A loud hand slap atop the barred window's wide steel ledge caused Sherri to jump.

A deputy, sporting a sharply pressed tailored black and gray uniform threatened, "Ashbury, you need to mind your own business."

Thad stepped to the center of the room and replied, "Well, good evening to you, too, Trent."

Sherri gazed dumbfounded at Trent.

"What are *you* gawking at?" Trent growled with no noticeable change in his granite-like face—his hazel eyes dulled by his hate-filled glare.

Sherri drew a quick deep breath and then replied, "I don't know. Is there a name for it?"

"I guess you're with Star City Police Department's goof-ball who thinks he is a real detective."

Thad quickly replied, "Ignore such ignorance, Sherri. He is only trying to yank your chain. Don't give him the satisfaction."

"Yeah," Trent snarled. "Follow his lead. Stir up things like he does and then cower away in the background while the Sheriff's deputies clean up the mess."

"Look out, everybody," Thad said snidely. "Deputy Trent must have been required to actually do some police work, for once."

"Isn't this kidnap victim related to you, Ashbury?"

"She's my cousin. Why?"

"So, what does she have to do with your fugitive preacher friend's case? Never mind...Birds of a feather flock together."

Sherri's eyes widened as her face reddened. "In that case, why aren't you somewhere with other arrogant snobs like yourself? Or are you even too pompous for that crowd?"

"Huh. At least, while your dear friend, Thad Ashbury, is lollygagging around here I'll be out looking for his cousin. She probably deserves whatever comes to her."

Sherri ran to the exit door, forgetting it had been locked. Bouncing away from it, she demanded, "Let me out so I can teach this punk a lesson."

Trent snickered menacingly. "You got yourself a little fireball there, Ashbury."

Sherri stomped across the room and stepped up against the metal ledge. Peering through the bars at Trent, she said, "You wouldn't be worthy to lick the mud from Janet's nor Uncle Joseph's shoes."

He laughed mockingly as he turned to leave. As he opened the outside door he sneered, "You sure know how to pick 'em, Ashbury."

"Hey, Al," Thad said, "I'm going to Star City to get one of our portable radios. I'll let you know when I'm available. I've got to take Sherri to get her car, and then lead her to a friend's house."

"Okay, Thad…Sherri, keep your chin up. We'll get these guys. You've got the cream-of-the-crop working this case."

"Thanks, Al. I'll keep that in mind."

Sherri followed Thad up the winding mile-long private road. The tall manicured symmetrical evergreens on either side whispered serenely, prefacing the luxurious Providence Hill Estates. Feeling out of place in her nine-year-old Olds Cutlass, she wondered if Thad hadn't turned onto the wrong road. He surely could not have overlooked the massive glistening bronze sign, 'Providence Hill Estates', embedded in the multi-stone pillar at the entrance.

The road's end, at a 'T' intersection just after the gatehouse, gave way to numerous gardens of an astonishing array of flowers and other artfully displayed plants. The athletic-looking uniformed man at the octagon guardhouse stepped swiftly from behind the bulletproof glass to intercept Thad's truck. The magnificent structure, of the same mix of stones she had seen at the sign's pillar, set against the backdrop of the most brilliant green rolling hills Sherri had ever seen in real life, held her nearly spellbound. She barely noticed the gate rise to let Thad through as the officer waved for her to follow Thad.

They turned right at the 'T' and drove a quarter mile, parking in front of the first mansion, sporting pale pink and white brick, and surrounded by flower gardens like those near the entrance gate.

Stepping quickly from her car, Sherri, insisted, "You can't possibly have friends who live in this place. Nobody lives like this in West Virginia."

Thad laughed in apparent amusement at Sherri's awe. "Well, few do. The Stewarts own several businesses up and down the eastern United States. Tammy is from Morgantown. She met Steve at West Virginia University. He loved the area so much he insisted they settle here. Later, Steve's parents also moved to Morgantown."

"I know the Stewarts," Sherri said excitedly. "I didn't know they were the friends you were talking about… Wow! I knew they were well to do, but I didn't know they were filthy rich."

"*Filthy* rich?" Thad teased. "That is no way to talk about Christian folks."

"Oh, you know what I mean."

An elegant voice called out, "Are you two coming in?"

Sherri turned toward the young woman in time to see her dart from the huge mahogany double doors. "Sherri Mosley, is that you?"

Sherri picked up the pace to meet Tammy half way up the white brick serpentine sidewalk. "Thad didn't tell me you were the friend we were coming to see," she said as they embraced.

Tammy held her at arms length, quickly studied her face, and proclaimed, "You look so much like Reverend Short. You could pass for twins."

"Thanks, Tammy. I certainly take that as a compliment."

Grabbing Sherri by the hand and reaching for Thad, Tammy invited them inside. "I have already prepared some snacks and have coffee brewed and ready for my wonderful guests."

"Wow!" Sherri exclaimed as they stepped into the foyer. Twirling on the light blue marble floor, swiftly surveying the ornate fixtures and furnishings, she said, "What a majestic house. I don't even think I've seen anything this grand in the movies."

Tammy blushed. "I would never tell Steve, but sometimes I'm embarrassed over our extravagance."

Sherri immediately apologized for making such a fuss. "Oh, Tammy, I didn't mean for my compliments to lend to your feeling that way."

"Don't be silly, it isn't your fault."

Thad said, earnestly, "Well, it isn't like you and Steve flaunt your good fortune. And I know how Christ-like you two are. There is nothing to be embarrassed about."

Sherri gently laid her hand on Thad's shoulder. "Isn't it sweet, how he helps me get my foot out of my mouth?"

They enjoyed a good laugh as Tammy led them to the more casual dining room off from the large formal dining area. "Be seated and I'll get coffee and snacks and return in just a moment."

Sherri wondered at Tammy not having a maid or other servants she supposed people residing in such homes should have in their employ.

Returning with a large sterling platter with a variety of homemade cookies and other sweets, placed around the sparkling silver coffee urn, Tammy took three cups from the outer edge of the platter and sat them on the table. "Thad," she said, and then bowed her head.

Thad asked for God's blessing on the snacks and fellowship afforded them.

"I'll never forget the day Steve brought me to this place," Tammy said, smiling dreamily. "We had been dating for two years and were recently engaged. I knew Steve had money, but I had no idea he had amassed such wealth. When he said this would be our home after we married, I laughed until I thought my sides would split. The more he tried to convince me, the closer I got to hysteria."

Sherri giggled with her. "I bet that went over well."

"Actually, it did. Steve finally saw the hilarity of it all—a plain country girl being teased with such ridiculous luxury—and he couldn't help but laugh as well… I think that is one of the characteristics Reverend Short impressed me with, early on. He and Steve both have that gentlemanly, yet strong, nature few men possess. I find that so attractive, don't you?"

Sherri's cheeks heated. That accurately described Thad too. If only she could say so without encouraging a romance she may not be allowed. "Yes, I do."

"You've got to try my homemade cheesecake," Tammy announced, propelling Sherri into a tumult of emotions. "Put some of these strawberries over it," she suggested to Thad, who didn't hesitate to take her up on the offer.

Sherri silently prayed, "Dear Lord, forgive me. I can't even appreciate Frank's once-upon-a-time love of *my* strawberry cheesecake. I feel so guilty for having lost the zeal to make our marriage work." She then answered Tammy, "I think I'll try that chocolate cake," hoping her choice would dislodge thoughts of Frank. She surmised he probably despises her strawberry cheesecake as much as he deplores her. After all, he once loved both. Or so he claimed.

Thad said, "I hate to rush into our purpose for visiting you, but I go on duty in an hour. I still need to rush home to shower and get in uniform."

"Well, you can go anytime. We helpless ladies will manage without you," she teased. "I had planned on offering your 'friend' a nice secure apartment at an exceptionally reduced monthly fee. Now that I know who this 'special friend' is, I changed my mind."

Thad gave her a questioning look. "Would you please not talk in circles?"

"Sherri is going to be my guest. I want her to occupy the guesthouse out back." Looking to Sherri, Tammy said, "Steve and I will give you as much privacy as you desire. Treat the place as though you owned it. That would please me very much. Will you accept?"

"I…I…I don't know. Maybe you better hear the reason I need a place to stay before solidifying such an offer. No, I better not. I don't want to cause any more innocent people grief. Did Thad tell you why I need a place to stay?"

"No. Not in detail. I don't need to know why. He asked and I gladly said yes."

Sherri stared angrily at Thad.

"Why are you giving me the evil eye? I told Tammy we'd explain it when we got here."

"You can't just impose on someone like that. Especially, without first warning them of the potential danger."

"Sherri, you are making too much of this."

"No, Thad. You are making too little of it. How thoughtless of you! Tammy, please don't take offense to this; but I am going back to Janet's to stay."

"Oh no, you're not," said Thad. He then stood in her way when she started toward the front of the house.

"Get out of my way, Thad."

Thad stepped closer to her and repeated, "You are *not* leaving here."

She swiftly twisted her body slightly to the right, threw her right leg behind his right leg and drove her right forearm into his chest, sending him crashing to the floor. Immediately, she began to sob. "I can't believe I did that. Oh Thad," she cried. "Please forgive me."

His expression of shock turned quickly into an elfin grin. He bounded to his feet and said, "Tammy, how would you like a personal bodyguard?" Not waiting for a reply, he told Sherri, "Okay. If you can't stay because you think you will bring along danger, then stay to protect Tammy."

She giggled and said, "After that display of unbridled anger, I suppose the least I could do is reconsider. But, I still think we need to explain the whole thing before she decides whether the offer still stands."

Tammy hugged Sherri and said, "You can tell the whole story, but I doubt that it will change my mind. If it doesn't, will you stay?"

Sherri looked to Thad as if to invite his explanation.

"We didn't want Sherri to stay at Janet's until we think it is safe to do so. Janet has been kidnapped."

"Oh, my! Poor Janet. Oh, Sherri, you must stay here. Steve would have a fit if I didn't insist. Not to mention my own conscience would eat me up."

"But…"

"No buts about it. You are staying here until we all agree it is safe and wise for you to do otherwise."

"I really do hate to go," Thad interrupted. "As much as I would enjoy watching you two hardheads go at it, I have no choice."

"I guess I'm staying here," Sherri said graciously.

"You two stay put. I can show myself out. Sherri, I'll call before leaving the station in the morning." Thad then addressed Tammy, "Do I call your home phone?"

"You may, but there is a private line at the guesthouse. You can try either one."

Thad wrote the guesthouse number in his pocket notepad, said, "good night," and departed.

"Now, where were we?" Tammy asked. "Oh yeah, concerning the guesthouse. You are not welcome to offer any payment for staying there. Nor are you to pay any of the utilities. Steve and I would be offended at such gestures, no matter your intentions for any offer you may wish to make."

"You are just about as demanding as Janet," Sherri said lightheartedly.

"You and Janet are pretty close friends, aren't you?"

"Yes. I don't know of anyone, aside from Uncle Joseph, I trust and admire more. She is so genuine."

"I have that same impression of Janet *and* you."

"Thanks," Sherri said, lowering her eyes toward the tabletop. "I am really worried for Janet. These guys seem to be very cruel and dangerous."

"I think it would be unnatural to feel otherwise, Sherri. However, I believe God is keeping His eye on the situation. Whatever happens, I am sure He will bring something good from it to those who love Him and are called according to His purpose."

Sherri felt soothing warmth overshadow her. "Tammy, I have got to share something with you. God is so wonderful!" Gleefully, she continued, "What you just said confirms again to me that God has called me to take on the task of helping Uncle Joseph. That promise, taken from Romans chapter eight and verse twenty-eight, came amazingly clear to me at the beginning and has been repeated in my dreams and thoughts continuously."

Tammy's eyes moistened. "I don't recall ever using that scripture before. How odd, that I would suddenly grab it as if directly from Heaven."

"I think it is His way of assuring me that you are part of the team," Sherri said, as she wiped a salty drop from under her upper lip. "Thad shared with me a dream in which that verse resounded in his sleep, waking him and bothering him until he got up one night and found it in the Bible, just as it had ticker-taped in his sleep—word for word."

The phone rang and Tammy excused herself to answer it. "Hello." She cupped the mouthpiece and whispered, "It's Steve… I'm glad you called, Sweetheart. Reverend Short's niece, Sherri, is here. I've invited her to stay indefinitely in the guesthouse. Something tragic has happened…Her friend, Janet, has been kidnapped…How can you know that already?… That Bill Drake is something else…No, I can't think of anything we need at the moment. Just get home safe. We'll leave the light on for you."

As soon as Tammy hung up the phone, Sherri asked, "Did I understand, from your end of the conversation, that Steve already knows what happened?"

"He said he'd called Bill Drake about a church business matter and learned that Bill just missed you and Thad at the Sheriff's office this evening. I guess he'd stopped there to check on something about Reverend Short's case."

"It's okay with Steve, if I stay here?"

"Of course. His exact words were, 'good thinking, my little genius.' He'll be home shortly. He and the Sunday School Superintendent have been out visiting shut-ins. Then they went to dinner together… Come on, we'll get you settled in. Do you have luggage or anything that needs carried in?"

"I grabbed a few things before leaving the mountain this evening. I can get them later."

CHAPTER SEVENTEEN

Saturday, May 5, 1979

Sherri hastened to the phone, bumping her big toe on a leg of the end table. Hurling to the couch, she stretched to grab the receiver. "Hello," she said sleepily.

"Uh, oh! I woke you, didn't I?" Thad asked apologetically.

"Yeah, you did. But it's probably a good thing you did wake me."

"Why is that a good thing?"

"You stopped me, just in time, from strangling Angela Hillman."

Thad laughed lightly. "I knew I should have wished you sweet dreams before leaving the Stewarts' last night."

"Well, look at it this way; at least I nearly had *sweet revenge.*"

"I bet you were. Since I've already disturbed your sleep, let me offer to buy you breakfast."

"What time is it, Thad?"

"7:30."

"Oh, my. I'm to have breakfast with Tammy and Steve at eight o'clock. Tammy insisted I let her fix breakfast this morning."

"Actually, that works out. I'll head on home and get some shut-eye. Do you have plans for later…like, early afternoon?"

"I thought I might go looking for Uncle Joseph. I figured you ought to catch up on some much needed sleep, instead of working the case today."

"After a few hours of sleep, I'll be fine. Can you wait there until I get to talk with you? I have something very pressing to discuss with you."

Sherri reluctantly agreed. "Thad, get plenty of rest. I'm sure you need to be alert as possible as a police officer. You're too important to this case to jeopardize your health and safety."

"Trust me. I'll be fine."

"Okay. Oh… sweet dreams."

Thad chuckled and said, "Goodbye. I'll talk to you later."

"Good morning," Steve said cheerfully. "You are just in time. Only a few seconds ago Tammy told me to call you."

"Sorry, I'm late. I would have been even later had Thad not called."

"Don't stand there, yakking," Tammy yelled, from whence the beckoning smells of homemade hot pancakes and other delicious scents streamed.

Shortly after asking God's blessing and giving thanks, Steve said, "Sherri, I have a proposal I wish for you to seriously consider."

Suspending her fork halfway to its intended destination, she said nothing, giving him her full attention.

"My brother and I are co-owners of a large investigative and security agency. John is the president of that particular business, headquartered in Newark, New Jersey. A few weeks ago I requested that he assign one of his most talented snoops to assist with Reverend Short's case. He couldn't free anyone up right away. I called him last night. He and I agreed on what I am about to ask of you."

Sherri slowly lowered her fork to her plate. "I don't mean to sound unappreciative, but I…we… can't afford a professional investigator."

"Well, that is where our proposal comes in."

"Okay… I'm all ears."

"You aren't currently employed, right?"

The question evoked feelings of guilt for not having more diligently sought gainful employment. "No, but I have put in a few applications. I must admit that I haven't been particularly zealous in my efforts toward finding a job."

"You needn't be apologetic about that," Steve said. "I think it is within God's will that you haven't found a job yet. We would like for you to work for Stewart and Associates."

"I feel like I'm sponging off you and Tammy," Sherri said, as she lowered her gaze toward her breakfast. "I would love the opportunity to repay you."

"We aren't asking for repayment for common Christian courtesies. In the past, John and I had discussed opening a Morgantown area office. Some time ago we asked Bill Drake to help get it up and going. He had tentatively agreed, but with the understanding that he would quit once he satisfactorily staffed the office."

"Oh Steve, I'd love to accept your offer. I have a couple things to consider before accepting."

"Are they things you can discuss with me?"

"I think so… I've got to try to save my marriage. That would most likely require that I return to Youngstown, Ohio as soon as I'm sure Uncle Joseph is well and his name has been cleared."

Tammy interrupted, "Sherri, you can be sure that we will support you in your endeavor to reclaim your marriage. God's will must always have precedence over our earthly concerns. Steve has built all his businesses on that principle."

"Meanwhile," Steve added, "you can train and work as an investigator for us. Your first assignment would be Reverend Short's case, under Drake's supervision. You would also be afforded formal training in the form of correspondence courses and may be expected to attend related seminars."

Sherri choked back the tears of appreciation. Would she dare not accept this generosity? She still felt like a bum. "Well, the other thing is concerning Ellis Fenton. He had his lawyer draw up a partnership agreement giving me half ownership of *Scoop Weekly.* Of course, I don't know what is to come of that, now that Mr. Fenton has vanished."

Steve bowed his head and mumbled, "Oh, boy."

"I guess I better explain that situation to you," she quickly asserted. "Mr. Fenton recently got saved. Upon his conversion to Jesus, he decided to transform the *Scoop Weekly* into a Christian publication. He even suggested we might need to change the name of the paper."

"Wow!" Tammy gasped. "Are you serious, Sherri? Fenton actually got saved?"

Sherri's recounting of the events of Ellis Fenton's conversion captivated Tammy and Steve. The news jerked tears of joy from them as if one dear to them had been born again.

Upon Tammy's prodding, they agreed to postpone further discussion of Steve's offer until after breakfast.

"Steve," Tammy called from the kitchen, "can you get the phone? Sherri and I are busy."

"I'll get it in the library," he trumpeted.

Moments later, Steve stood in the doorway, smiling.

"I take it that the phone call amused you," Tammy said.

"Yes, it did. That was Dugan on the phone. Since he hadn't been notified of John's coming, he wouldn't let him past the gate."

"I didn't know of his coming either."

"Neither did I… I could hear him complaining in the background."

"He shouldn't complain," Tammy replied. "He ought to be pleased that Dugan is on the ball." Then, turning to Sherri she said, "The security personnel are employed by Stewart and Associates."

"Don't they know John?"

"I don't think any of them ever met John. Steve took care of hiring them and he keeps the records, periodically sending them to the main office. Dugan may have thought that John's visit amounted to a test of the security system."

"Oh, no!" Sherri exclaimed. "To add insult to injury, I'm probably occupying his place in the guesthouse."

"Hardly," Tammy answered. "I doubt that he plans to stay overnight. The few times he did stay over, he slept in one of the five spare bedrooms here at the house."

"Hey, Sherri," Steve said with a boyish grin, "help me play this up."

"I don't know. What if he gets upset and withdraws your offer?"

"He enjoys a good prank. He won't get mad. I must warn you, though, he does get even." Walking swiftly across the kitchen floor, he grabbed a full-length apron from a drawer and tossed it to Sherri. "Put this on. When he rings the doorbell you answer it and pretend to have orders to not disturb us until noon. I'll be nearby to bail you out at the right moment—after he has become duly annoyed."

Sherri giggled at the thought of it. "If I can keep from laughing. How about, I answer him through the intercom system—that way he won't see if I crack up?"

"Good idea," Steve and Tammy simultaneously cheered.

The door chimes briefly played the tune of "Jesus Loves Me," announcing John's arrival. They rushed to the foyer barely controlling their laughter.

Watching John in the monitor, encased in a decorative walnut cabinet, Sherri pressed the talk button. Feigning a German accent, she asked, "May I help you?"

"Hi," he replied as he gazed into the camera up to his left. "I'm John Stewart; Steve's brother. He is expecting me… Who are *you*?"

"Mein name is Gretta. I'm sorry; I cannot permit you to come in. I don't see your name for appointment with Herr Stewart und Frau Stewart. How did you get past security at gate, please?"

John's face registered his agitation. "Officer Dugan just talked with *Herr* Stewart on the phone and cleared me."

"I have been instructed to let no one in unless authorized. I am sorry. You must make an appointment."

He fidgeted with his wallet, retrieving his Stewart and Associates' identification card. Thrusting it toward the camera, he growled, "I am the president of the security company employing the guard at the gate. See?"

"I cannot read English, well. How do I know you are Herr Stewart's brother? Besides, I am not to disturb the Stewarts until after noon." Then with pretend ire, she asked, "Okay, if you are head of security—what is the password?"

"What password?" he yelled. "Go get Steven."

"Do not boss me. I am the *Stewarts'* maid. I am calling security."

"Just forget it," he griped. "Just forget it." Turning quickly he stomped off while grumbling, "This is ridiculous!"

Steve quickly jerked open the door and yelled after him, "Where are you going?"

John spun around and charged through the open door. "You conniving jerk," he snarled, while wrestling the taller and thinner Steve to the floor and pinning him. Leaping to his feet, he twirled toward Tammy. "You sorry thing. You orchestrated this, didn't you?" He then, ran to her and hugged her, picking her off her feet.

Steve regained his composure and head-gestured toward Sherri. "John, meet Sherri Mosley, Reverend Short's niece."

John smiled widely. "Also known as Gretta, the mysterious servant, I suppose."

Shyly grinning as she shook his hand, she said, "Glad to meet you."

Stepping back and staring into Sherri's eyes, John asked, "Did Steve talk to you about our offer?"

"Yes, sir, he did."

"Good; it's done. You will answer to Mr. Drake and then to Steven. You will be on the payroll retroactively, as of yesterday. You will be paid according to whatever agreement made between you and Steven. Regarding payment for the work done by our firm, you will not concern yourself. I am sure you will put yourself wholly into this case. And of course, you will be expected to maintain the same level of industriousness in subsequent cases."

"I will endeavor to satisfy you," Sherri said.

Addressing Tammy, he said, "How about a cup of celebratory coffee and a taste of one of your delightful homemade pastries? And don't even try to tell me that you have none."

His ability to jump from one conversation to the next, while seemingly not taking time to think what to say, astonished Sherri. Finally, she met someone else who could speak so rapid-fire.

"Hello," Sherri said anxiously after the first ring.

"Good morning," Thad said. "Or rather, good afternoon. I'm sorry, Sherri, I didn't even hear my alarm clock. When I awoke and glanced at the clock, I couldn't believe it's after one already."

"Thad, you probably ought to go back to sleep for a while longer."

"No, no. I need to see you, right away."

"Can you come to the Stewarts' home? Steve and his brother want to meet with you, Deacon Drake, and me about all that's happened."

"I'll be there in about forty-five minutes."

"Wait, Thad. Don't hang up."

"I'm still here."

"You are to call Deacon Drake before leaving home. He wants you to pick him up."

"Okay. See you, soon."

Steve opened the meeting with prayer, and then rushed into the discussion concerning the opening of the Morgantown office. They shared information on Joseph Short's case and the abductions of Janet Pixler and Ellis Fenton.

"When I arrived at the Star City police station last night," Thad said, " Officer Deberry told me to contact Preston County's Deputy Burk. He had left his home telephone number asking that I call him, no matter how late."

Steve explained to John, Deputy Burk's role involving Ellis Fenton's disappearance. He then asked Thad to continue.

"Yesterday evening, Preston County arrested Ramona Fenton for shooting her boyfriend, Bobby Stafford, at a motel in Kingwood. Bobby received emergency on-scene treatment of a superficial wound from the bullet grazing the left side of his head. A subsequent search of the motel room, prompted by marijuana in open view, uncovered a large quantity of various illegal drugs. Ramona and Bobby are being held in the Preston County jail.

"Deputy Burk wants to have a meeting, as soon as possible, with the FBI, the State Police, and Monongalia County's Deputy Stone for a joint interview with Bobby Stafford. It seems that Bobby is anxious to cut a deal and is implicating Ramona in the disappearance of her dad."

Steve asked, "Do you think Bobby is really willing to sing? Or does he have much to sing about?"

"I'm not sure. Burk must think it is worth our efforts to be there." Thad then spoke directly to Sherri, "Evidently, he implicated Ramona in Ellis Fenton's abduction. He claims firsthand knowledge of her trying to get the authorities to focus on you, as a diversion."

"Surprise, surprise," Sherri mocked. "Does he have knowledge of Janet's whereabouts?"

"*That*, we don't know yet. We can only pray that if he does have that kind of information, he is willing to give it up. You never know about his kind; they're unpredictable."

"When will this meeting take place?" asked Bill Drake.

"Burk tentatively scheduled it for 10 o'clock, Monday morning at the Sheriff's office. Stafford refused to talk without his attorney. His attorney is out of town until Monday morning. The prosecutor's office will have someone there as well. Burk agreed to let you attend the meeting, Bill. He did say that you may be restricted somewhat since you are not currently representing a law enforcement agency."

"I understand," Drake replied. "Will you be there, Thad?"

"Yes. Thank God, I am in the loop. In fact, I would like for you to ride with me."

"I certainly intend to accompany you, then."

Sherri asked, "Will they let me sit in?"

"I'm afraid not. Burk already denied that request. I must respectfully concur."

Sherri ached with disappointment, but silently prayed for temperance.

Thad drew a deep breath. "I have another matter to discuss with Sherri before discussing it in this forum. Do you gentlemen mind if she and I step out of the room for a few minutes?"

"Go ahead," Steve said. "We aren't going anywhere."

"Thad," Sherri said, bravely, "if it involves anything concerning me personally, it's okay to talk about it openly."

"It's about Frank," he said. His statement sounded more like a question.

It perplexed her that the mention of Frank's name elicited feelings of disdain.

"Who is Frank?" John asked.

His question pulled her back into the discussion. "Frank is my cowardly, unthankful, womanizing husband… It's a long story, but he once had an affair with Angela Hillman, during the time she and Uncle Joseph were separated, before their divorce."

"This Angela is the one who you all suspect to be financing the current events in this case, right?"

"I'd stake my life on it," Sherri said angrily. Her jaws tightened. "It's okay, Thad. I don't have a problem with us talking about Frank. I'm certainly curious to hear what you might have to say regarding my darling husband."

"Well, until last night, I had deliberately postponed any sort of judgment of him… He is in the Morgantown area."

"You're kidding. Please tell me you're kidding." Sherri couldn't calm the shaking of her innards. Nor could she control the quiver in her voice.

"At least the man said he is Frank. About five feet ten inches in height, around 190 to 200 pounds, drooping left eye—maybe blind in that eye, dimples and a square chin?"

"Oh, my!" Sherri cried.

"One o'clock this morning he called the Sheriff's office requesting that Star City's Officer Ashbury meet him in the Holiday Inn lobby. He wouldn't identify himself on the phone."

"Why would he ask for you? He doesn't know you, does he?"

"Around eleven last night, Uncle Jake intercepted him as he drove toward Janet's house. Uncle Jake told him of Janet's kidnapping and that you were being kept in a safe-place to avoid meeting the same fate. I called Uncle Jake this morning and learned that he had told Frank to contact me regarding your case, after requiring Frank to produce a picture I.D."

"Maybe I better contact him," Sherri said, though not sure she wanted to.

"I would have suggested it myself, but something doesn't add up. Judging from his failure to act surprised at Janet's abduction and the imminent threat of the same happening to you, I hardly believe he has come out of love for his wife."

Sherri's eyes widened. "As much as I wish he had come to beg me home, I have a funny feeling about this."

"And rightly so," he added. "He acted awfully nervous while we were talking. His posture seemed a little unnatural. That made me more suspicious of him. I observed him closely, trying to figure out why he seemed distracted and fidgety. Finally, I noticed a small bulge under his shirt, just about at his sternum—indicative of someone wearing a recording device. Then, a minute or two later, I caught a glimpse of a heavy-faced bearded man peeping from around the drawn curtain in a second floor end room."

Bill Drake asked, "What do you think he is up to?"

"Well, he said he came to get his wife and that he is not leaving without her. He tried to act sincere when he claimed he misses her and loves her. He even offered a pharisaic plea for me to 'do the Christian thing' by convincing her to return to Youngstown with him."

"Couldn't he be sincere, though?" Drake asked.

"I seriously doubt it… Sherri, I don't mean to sound so negative, but I really trust my gut-feeling about this, as well as the powers of observation."

"I told you all that he is a coward. He is probably being threatened to get me out of town."

"After I left the Holiday Inn, I called the night auditor from the station. She told me that Frank Mosley rented the room. That information proves him a liar, at best. He had told me that relatives in the area had put him up in their home. He said he would contact me at the station this evening."

"He sure *is* a liar," Sherri squealed. "He doesn't have any relatives in West Virginia. His nearest relatives are parents and brothers who all live in Ohio."

Steve rubbed his forehead and engaged Sherri's eyes. "Maybe you should remain in the background and out of sight for a while, Sherri. It would not affect your wages. You can compile information and keep files on the case as things progress."

"I appreciate your concern. But I must see this through—officially or unofficially."

He looked around at the rest of the team and asked, "What do you guys think?"

Thad leaned back in his chair and sighed heavily. "I wish she would comply with your suggestion. However, I have already learned that she is too strong-willed to argue with in this matter."

Steve then asked, "Drake, what do you say? After all, you are the boss on this one."

Drake told Sherri, "You agreed to be under my supervision in this and any other case we take on. For the time being, I'll permit your direct involvement. However, I will expect your cooperation if we later decide that you must become inactive, or that you be hidden away."

The thought of retreating or going into protective hiding rubbed her spirit like steel wool on an open sore. "No offence intended to any of you, but I will not be deterred. Nor will I cower. These punks have picked a fight that I must win—or die trying."

"See, what I mean?" Thad asked.

Steve asked, teasingly, "Was David a ruddy person, too?"

"I don't know," Sherri said stoically. "I do know I must have the same kind of faith he had when facing *his* giant."

John tapped the tabletop and declared, "Hey, folks, I must leave the rest up to you. I promised to take my wife and kids to a movie this evening, and then to a late dinner, out. Please, excuse me. I'll see myself out. I love you all. God bless."

CHAPTER EIGHTEEN

Saturday, May 5, 1979

"Miss Sherri," a whisper wafted from over the riverbank.

Sherri and Thad froze in motion for a moment, and then silently searched to see who called.

"Miss Sherri … Down here."

"Lanky," Sherri answered, "it's okay. This is Thad. He's Uncle Joseph's friend—he wants to help him."

Lanky cautiously climbed the riverbank, keeping a suspicious eye on Thad. "Are you okay, Miss Sherri? Did the bad men hurt you?"

"No. What bad men, Lanky?"

He kept a wary eye on Thad while bending to pick up a broken tree branch. Holding it at port-arms he warned Thad, "You better not hurt Miss Sherri."

Sherri spit a giggle, not sure what struck her the funniest—Lanky's uncertainties or Thad's swift alarm-ridden move to a self-defense position.

"Easy big guy," Thad pleaded, "I'm her friend."

Sherri stepped closer to Thad and wrapped her arm around his forearm. "Thad really *is* my friend, Lanky. He is nice like you. He protects me."

Lanky relaxed his posture and converted his club to a walking stick. "I'm sorry, sir… I didn't mean to scare you. I… I'm… I'm glad you are taking care of Miss Sherri, because Joe the Baptist said she is very special and she loves Jesus." His eyes softened even more as he asked, "Do you love Jesus too, Mr. Thad?"

Thad stepped slowly toward him and offered his hand. "Yes, sir, Lanky. I'm glad to meet you, my dear brother."

"You talk nice, like Joe the Baptist does," Lanky said as he shook Thad's hand.

"Well, I consider that a great compliment... Did you think some bad men might have hurt Sherri?"

"Twitchy Face told me to tell Joe the Baptist to meet him at the Courthouse Square at midnight, tonight. He said they have a girl very close to Joe the Baptist. He said to tell Joe the Baptist that they will kill her if he doesn't show up." He paused and earnestly said to Sherri, "I'm glad they didn't hurt you, Miss Sherri."

"Lanky," Thad coaxed, "these bad men kidnapped my cousin. Janet is Sherri's best friend. Do you know where they might be holding her?"

"No, sir. Twitchy Face wouldn't tell me. I thought they had Miss Sherri. But I'm still really mad... Joe the Baptist told me not to let people make me mad, but I'm mad anyhow." He shuffled nervously, and with widened eyes looked all about. "I... I can't tell Joe the Baptist," he whispered. "He is away preaching."

"Where?" Sherri asked anxiously. "Where is Uncle Joseph preaching?"

"I don't know, ma'am," he said lowly. "Don't talk so loud, Miss Sherri. The bad people might be listening."

Lanky's paranoia fastened itself to her psyche like a giant hungry leach. Eyeballing the railroad tracks northward, then southward, then scanning the buildings and the landscape above and the river below, she quietly asked, "When will he return, Lanky?"

"I don't know. He sometimes goes a long ways off. Sometimes he just goes to Fairmont and comes back the same day. He didn't come back last night."

"Well," Sherri asked impatiently, "where does he preach? Who does he preach to? How long does he usually stay? We have to know, *now*. We don't have much time."

Lanky bowed his head and sullenly apologized for making her mad.

"Oh, Lanky. I'm not mad at you. I'm sorry. I didn't mean to hurt your feelings."

Thad asked, "Who is this Twitchy Face?"

"He is a bad man that gives devil pills and goofy grass to other people for stealing things and stuff like that."

"What do they steal, Lanky?"

"Cars and trucks and other stuff like rings and radios."

"Do you know where we can find Twitchy Face?"

"Yes, sir. He lives in the Hotel Mountaineer."

Thad glanced at Sherri and stated, "That must cost a pretty penny."

Sherri checked her watch. "We only have eight hours. Lanky, we have to hurry. Where can we meet you later?

"If you come back here and wait I'll see you."

"What time can we meet you here?"

"Whatever time you come. I'll see you." Lanky then asked Thad, "Are you going to make sure nobody hurts Miss Sherri?"

"Yes, I will, Lanky."

Sherri hugged Lanky, who stood rigidly straight and blushed. "Thanks, Lanky."

"You're welcome, ma'am," he replied, shifting his weight to one foot then the other.

The tall, slender desk clerk, with baby smooth dark skin, inquisitively watched Sherri and Thad as they approached. "Hi. May I help you?" he asked affably.

Thad flashed his police I. D. and replied, "We need to know the room number for one of your long-term guests, Doby."

Doby took a step back from the counter, and studied Thad, then Sherri for a few seconds. "How do you know me?"

Thad chuckled and pointed to Doby's blazer. "I just figured you were wearing your own nametag."

"Of course. How silly of me. Can I see your I.D. again?"

Thad laid it on the counter and turned it so that Doby could read it.

"What do you need to know, Officer Ashbury?"

"I understand that you have a resident who is known on the street as Twitchy Face. I am looking for a proper name and where he is staying?"

"Oh, that would be Mr. Martel. Richard Martel."

"Can you tell me his room number?"

"Actually he is leasing a suite. He just left, about twenty minutes ago. Should I take a message for him?"

"No thanks. In fact, I'd appreciate you not telling him we were here. What suite does he occupy?"

Doby scribbled the information on the top page of a pink note pad, handed it to Thad, flashing the many rings on his right hand. He whispered, "I don't know where you got that information," and winked. "Good luck catching him in his suite. He seems to have no set schedule."

Thad turned to leave, then paused. "Does Mr. Martel get many visitors?"

"Very few. Always the same people."

"Do you know who these visitors are?"

"Sure. Everybody knows that he and Angela Hillman keep company."

"Really?" Sherri asked. "Everybody?"

"Sure. Even Marcus Hillman knows." Limply waving his right hand downward, Doby added, "What odd people!"

Thad asked, "Who else comes to see him?"

"Mr. Hillman, Gregory Grant, and a couple other guys whose names I don't know."

Thad pulled his wallet from his back jeans pocket and drew out a twenty-dollar bill. "Thanks, Doby," he said as he palmed it atop the counter.

"Oh, no sir. I can't take that. I'm simply doing my civic duty."

Thad and Sherri walked away as if they didn't hear him.

Sherri lowly asked, "Why did you do *that*? Especially since he didn't want it? He already gave the information freely."

"Consider it a small price to pay for loyalty. Besides it will fortify his conviction to cooperate with us. I suspect he'll have more to offer when we need it."

"Aren't you a sly one?" Sherri teased.

"Okay," Sherri said excitedly as she hopped into the truck. "Mr. Drake is on his way. No luck yet, huh?"

"No," Thad replied, maintaining a devoted gaze toward the hotel's front entrance. "As soon as Bill relieves us, we need to call Fairmont P.D. and the Marion County Sheriff's office to ask them to keep a look-out for Joseph."

"Are you sure that is a good idea? After all, there *is* an outstanding warrant for his arrest. Wouldn't they have to arrest him?"

"That's why I have to talk to them. I need to explain the situation to them. I suspect that if they know the urgency of the situation they'll arrange to get him to us without making an official arrest at this time."

"No offense intended, Thad, but I think that is a little too risky."

"Well, I guess it *is* risky. If you have a better idea, let's hear it."

"I wish I did have a better idea. If only we had more time."

Sherri leaned across the truck seat and unlocked Thad's door. "Who are those guys?" she asked, referring to the two men Thad had approached on the courthouse square.

"Just a couple local jailbirds who hang around here seeking donations for the purchase of cheap wine or whiskey." Pointing to the short skinny man, Thad said, "The little bald guy is known as 'Streak' because of his occasional naked runs around town."

"How does he get by with that?"

"He doesn't. He usually gets the customary thirty days in jail. The jail personnel tell me that he occasionally gets sent to Weston State Hospital to dry out."

"Do they have anything that will help us?"

"No. Rudy, the pudgy guy, said that Joseph hasn't been seen around town for several days. He thought he had been arrested… However, I did call from the Sheriff's office and talked with Marion County's Deputy Stern. He saw Joseph yesterday, near the Union Mission homeless shelter."

"Deputy Stern knew him?"

"Yeah. Evidently, everywhere Joseph goes, he is known as Joe the

Baptist. Stern says that he has quite a reputation as a Christian ambassador to the lowly."

Sherri's chest swelled with pride. "Isn't God's grace truly amazing? I guess I ought to at least be thankful that Uncle Joseph is making the best of his situation. Is it any wonder I think so highly of him?"

"It is no wonder to me. I suppose if I were to hear any ill report of him, though I have never met him, I'd have to consider it untrue."

She gazed straight ahead and exclaimed, "Oh, Thad, I can't wait for this mess to be resolved. You are really going to love Uncle Joseph. And I do believe he will quickly bond with you in Christ. You both are such good men."

"Thanks," Thad said, blushing. "Anyhow, Stern said that he became acquainted with Joseph when he responded to a mugging call one Saturday evening, a couple months ago. Two young men had mugged an elderly homeless man near the Mission. When Stern arrived on scene, Joseph limped away hurriedly. At first, Stern mistook Joseph as one of the perpetrators. Stern darted from the cruiser and ordered Joseph to stop. The victim, bleeding and sitting on the sidewalk and leaning against a stone retaining wall, called out, 'No. No. He came to my rescue.' The man then pointed to a row of hedges up the street, and said, 'Those two did it.' When Stern diverted his attention to where the man pointed, Joseph vanished."

"The muggers weren't too bright, hanging around."

"They weren't still there voluntarily. Joseph had tied them together with their own belts. He then tied their feet together with their own shoelaces after shoving them to the ground in front of the hedges. Stern said the homeless man explained that he's a recent convert to Christ under Joe the Baptist's ministry."

Sherri smiled sheepishly. "Why do I worry so much about Uncle Joseph's situation? I am a bit ashamed at my lack of faith in God's provision for His children… Why didn't Stern arrest Uncle Joseph, though?"

"Apparently, Marion County had no notice of the warrant. Stern said that he might have been tempted to ignore it anyhow, since he knows the Hillmans and is certain that the charges are trumped against Joseph.

"Is Stern going to try to locate Uncle Joseph?"

"Yes. He will also pass the word to other agencies in the Marion County area. The Harrison County authorities are being contacted as well as the state police detachments throughout north central West Virginia."

"How about Preston County?" Sherri asked.

"And Preston County. We are asking that if they locate Joseph, he not be arrested, but detained and told that his niece is looking for him and that it is urgent that he cooperates with them in their efforts to get him to Morgantown. I'll monitor my mobile scanner in case we succeed in finding him."

Sherri swallowed hard and asked, "Do you think we ought to try to make contact with Lanky and have him to intercept Uncle Joseph in case he returns to his hide-out? We can be sure that Lanky isn't going to reveal the place to us."

"That's good thinking. Let's hope Lanky sees us. We *are* running out of time."

Sherri crossed her arms and rubbed her triceps with her hands. "I don't know if it is the dropping temperature or nerves, but I can't stop trembling."

"Maybe both," Thad replied as he stepped closer, wrapped his right arm around her, and pulled her to his side. "Maybe this will help."

She started to resist his grasp, but reconsidered. Countering Thad's gesture, she wrapped her left arm around his waist. She wondered if she found this a little too comfortable. Could she be confusing her appreciation of Thad's kindness with romance? But it felt so right! Immediately she recalled Uncle Joseph's warnings that people must be careful to not trust their feelings. He had often admonished that one must not equate feelings with the blessings from the Holy Spirit. "Not all that *feels* good is good," he often stated emphatically.

Loosening his caress, Thad exclaimed, "Here comes Lanky," interrupting her self-examination.

Sherri grabbed his arm to slow his pace. "Don't approach him too quickly. You may send him running in a state of paranoia."

Thad halted as if obeying a drill command. "Yes, ma'am."

Lanky walked briskly toward them, rolling his head side to side as to search out any hiding eavesdroppers. "Hi, Miss Sherri and Thad," he said, with a more trusting tone than he had exhibited during their earlier conversation. "Did you get Twitchy Face?"

"Not yet," Sherri answered. She pleadingly reached toward him, causing him to step back nervously. "Lanky, we need you to go with us to file a report supporting conspiracy-to-kidnap charges against Twitchy Face."

"I… I can't, Miss Sherri. Joe the Baptist don't trust them authorities around here. They are bad people, too."

Sherri desperately wished she could dispute Uncle Joseph's statement. "Lanky, they aren't *all* bad people. Only a few are bad. Thad will help us identify who can be trusted."

"She's right, Lanky," Thad added. "We can't have Twitchy Face arrested without your help. You have to tell what Twitchy Face told you about having someone close to Joe the Baptist in captivity. Please, Lanky, we are running out of time. You don't want these thugs to hurt Sherri's best friend, do you?"

Lanky shifted his feet restlessly. His eyes darted repeatedly left to right. His body tensed like a sprinter awaiting the starter's gunfire. "I don't know what to do," he said excitedly. "I have to talk to Joe the Baptist."

Fearing he would run for safety, Sherri beckoned, "It's okay, Lanky. It's okay… Did Joe the Baptist teach you about prayer?"

"Yes, ma'am."

Sherri, capitalizing on his confidence in her, calmly instructed, "Well, when we are not sure what to do—that is when we really need to pray for the Holy Spirit's guidance. Right?"

"Yes, ma'am. I think so."

"Do you trust Jesus, Lanky?"

"I think so. I don't know Him like Joe the Baptist does. Joe the Baptist talks to Jesus about everything. I never heard Jesus, but Joe the Baptist hears Him. One time, I coughed real bad and started coughing up blood—a whole bunch of it. I don't trust doctors, so Joe the Baptist asked Jesus to heal me. And Jesus did it." Snapping his fingers, he proclaimed, "Just like that, He did it. I felt this nice feeling, like warm oil, in my chest and throat. Right away, I quit coughing and even felt real strong."

Sherri's heart swelled with praise. Without forethought she closed her eyes, lifted her hands toward heaven, and cried, "Oh God—my Heavenly Father, hear my plea and answer according to your will. Intercede for us in these many troubles. In Jesus' name I pray. Thank you, Lord." Lowering her eyes and not seeing Lanky, she looked at Thad, whose countenance registered the same amazement that gave her goose bumps. After several silent seconds, she asked, "How did he slip away so quickly and so quietly?"

Thad replied, "Maybe I shouldn't have closed my eyes to pray along with you. That is incredible! Not a sound. We should have at least heard him running."

They both rushed to the edge of the riverbank and looked up and down the river. "Lanky," Sherri called out. "Lanky, come on. Please, don't hide from us. Lanky, can you hear me? Come on, Janet's life may be in serious jeopardy." Spinning agitatedly toward Thad, she asked, "Now what do we do?"

"Well," Thad replied forthrightly, "we go to plan 'B' and then to plan 'C' if necessary."

"Plan 'B' is what?"

"Considering the exigency of the situation, we may have to take the law into our own hands."

"Thad, don't do anything that may get you in trouble. There has to be a way to solve this without doing anything legally unacceptable."

"It is either my reputation as a respectable law enforcement officer or Janet's life. I choose to do whatever will save her life."

"Well, let's get to it, then."

Thad nearly ran to the truck.

"Wait, Daddy Longlegs," Sherri called breathlessly, trying to catch up with him.

"Hurry, Sherri. We are going to beat these punks at their own game." He unlocked the passenger side door and jogged to the driver's side.

Jumping into the cab, he ordered, "I am dropping you off at the Sheriff's Office. I want you to ask Al to call a taxi for you. Go straight to the Stewarts'. Stay there until you hear from me or Bill Drake."

Sherri felt heat rush to her ears. "Now just wait a minute, Bossy. I have as much reason as you do to engage in whatever action necessary to secure Janet's safe return. I am not going to sit around worrying—no way. And just what do you suppose I could do at the Stewarts'?"

"Pray, Sherri. Pray like you've never prayed before. Besides, I don't want you to be privy to anything I might do that may be outside the law or beyond my legal privilege."

"Oh, great! A lot of good you'll do behind bars."

"Okay, Sherri," he yelled angrily, "what should I do? Sit back and let these jerks hurt Janet—or worse yet, *kill* her? All because the system fails… and a lunatic won't trust us?"

Her mind froze. Staring out the passenger door window to avoid detection, she arrested the pressing sobs—but the floodgates had ruptured. Hot bitter tears dropped heavily onto her blouse.

Thad scooted across the seat and laid his right hand on her left shoulder. "I'm sorry." His voice crackled as he begged her forgiveness. He then stroked her thick reddish-blonde hair, as he pleaded some more.

Sherri couldn't be sure what loosed her wailing sobs—the kiss that tenderly penetrated her left temple or the words she feared, yet longed for—"I love you."

He slid back under the steering wheel, paused, and then reached over to place his hand atop her left hand, which pressed hard against the edge of the red velvety seat.

Finally, Sherri regained enough composure to reply—albeit, tearfully. Feeling too ashamed to face Thad, she stared at the floorboard. She sandwiched his pleading hand, laying her right hand atop his. Rubbing the back of his muscular hand with her thumb, she softly said, "I'm the one who should apologize. I'm so ashamed of my outburst toward you. You don't deserve such meanness. Please, Thad, forgive me?"

He nervously chuckled, "I asked first."

Turning to face him, she said with a relief-laden smile, "Even though I don't think you did anything wrong, I forgive you. I know you're trying to look out for me. And I really do appreciate your kindness and thoughtfulness."

"Nevertheless, I should not have snapped at you. I likewise don't think *you* need to apologize for anything. However, if it will carry us forward and clear our hearts and minds so we can refocus, I forgive you, too."

"Thad," she cooed, as she engaged his gleaming brown eyes, "as much as I reservedly dare, I want you to know that I love you, too."

"You may think I'm beside myself, but I want you to feel that way toward me and yet I'm torn between wanting you and hoping that your marriage with Frank works out. I really do want God's will in my life… *and* yours. I just don't know where the line is drawn. It keeps shifting—not that God is moving it; but my spiritual vision seems a bit blurred."

"Maybe it will comfort you to know that you just conveyed my innermost turmoil. Maybe our mutual fondness of one another and our love for God will help us fulfill our present calling."

"That makes sense to me," Thad agreed, and then awkwardly returned to the matter at hand. "Now, about my plan 'B' and your part in it. I really would feel more comfortable if you weren't directly involved in what I tentatively plan to do. In fact, I'd rather you don't witness anything that you may wind up having to tell in court, later."

"I must see this through. Please, let me determine if or when I should close my eyes."

Thad drew a deep breath and then started the engine. "Okay, partner. Let's get busy."

Thad parallel parked his truck in front of Bill Drake's car. "I'll be right back," he informed Sherri as he bounded to the sidewalk and rushed to Drake's car door. Returning moments later, he explained that Drake is going to try contacting the FBI's Clarksburg office. "Maybe we better consult them since they are also investigating Janet's kidnapping. With us all working in concert we will have an increased chance of finding Janet unharmed… You and I will stay here for now, in case Martel returns to the hotel."

"How will we know him from any other man?" Sherri asked sincerely.

"Mr. Drake had taken a few minutes to ask Doby to describe him. He is tall with a muscular build, thick curly brown hair, and always handsomely dressed." Thad paused and pointed down High Street. "Speak of the *devil*."

"That's Angela Hillman with him," Sherri shrieked. "How brazen!"

"Great!" Thad griped, slapping the steering wheel. "There goes my plan; right down the drain."

"Maybe not," Sherri said confidently. Reaching into the purse at her feet, she giggled mischievously. "Let's make this really interesting," she said, offering him a glance at a small camera. "Mr. Fenton gave this to me. He insisted that I carry it everywhere, reminding me that a picture is worth a thousand words."

Doby peered over his purple-rimmed, straight-topped, half-lens reading glasses. "He is in," he whispered. "He just came in a couple moments ago… He has female company though."

Thad approached the counter, retrieved twenty dollars from his wallet and said lowly, "You didn't see us, right?"

Doby slid his hand over the money and closed his skinny manicured fingers. He looked around the lobby and theatrically said, "That's strange. I thought I heard a voice. There is nobody here but me. I must be imagining things."

Thad lightly grabbed Sherri by the arm and ushered her to the stairway.

"Feeling your oats, Officer Ashbury? There are a lot of steps to climb, you know."

"We aren't here. If we take the elevator we are likely to be seen."

"Of course."

Stopping on the fifth landing, Thad asked, "Are you sure you are up to this?"

Sherri quipped, "Do I have red hair and blue eyes?"

"Yeah. You are the most beautiful redhead I have ever seen. Now just be the fastest running redhead I've ever seen." He held open the stairway door as Sherri coolly strode into the hallway.

Her heart rocked her body like a revved engine of a racecar. The stroll to the suite door seemed ten times the twenty feet from the stairway. She inhaled deeply, and then knocked sharply. Her stomach twisted and tightened when she heard Angela demand, "Let me see."

Sherri stepped back to allow Angela a better look at her through the peephole.

"Oh, for Pete's sake! That is Joseph's niece. What should we do?"

Sherri couldn't make out Martel's reply, but heard the unlocking of the door. She took another step back and quickly brought the camera forward and rapidly snapped two shots of the pair—Angela standing to the right rear flank of Martel.

"I'll kill you, you little witch," Angela screamed as Sherri raced for the stairway.

Sherri stopped on the lower landing just as the door banged shut, and then immediately flew open again and slammed against the stairwell wall as Martel charged from the hallway.

Thad sideswiped him, driving him into the adjacent wall, pinning his face tight against the concrete blocks. "Make one wrong move and you are a dead man," Thad growled.

Just then Angela rushed through the doorway. Sherri scrambled to the top of the stairs and wrestled her to the floor, pinned her on her back, and straddled her, pressing her arms to the recently painted concrete.

Thad had handcuffed Martel and forced him to sit against the wall. Reaching to his back jeans pocket, he produced another pair of cuffs and handed them to Sherri. "Would you like the honors?"

Sherri answered breathlessly, more from the adrenaline rush than from exertion, "Oh. Would I!" Jerking Angela's left arm upward, Sherri ratcheted the first cuff. Then, bouncing to her feet, and stepping to her left, she forced Angela to roll onto her stomach. Angela volunteered her right arm, laying her wrist at the small of her back.

Thad helped Martel to his feet and warned, "One peep from you and I may feel compelled to silence you." He glared at Angela and growled, "Not a peep from either of you." Through gritted teeth, he threatened, "Second thought, please give me a good reason."

Martel snarled, "You know this is illegal. Where is your arrest warrant?" His rough gravelly voice reverberated off the walls.

Thad grabbed the back of Martel's silver silk shirt, spun him around, and slammed him against the adjacent wall so tight it restricted Martel's facial tics. "I said, not a peep, punk. For your information, you aren't under arrest. By the time I'm done with you, you'll wish you *were* arrested." Thad grabbed a handful of curly brown hair, hyper extending Martel's neck and chin. "Not another word until I tell you to speak."

"Please, Sherri," Angela whispered, "don't do this?"

"I don't want to hear your whining," Sherri replied with a low controlled tone, as she helped her petite top-heavy captive to her feet.

"Come on, Sherri," Angela begged, "you can't do this. You're a Christian and this is illegal."

Sherri shoved her against the door causing a thud. "You better pray that I haven't completely backslidden… Now shut up before temptation overcomes me."

Angela's brown eyes fixed on Sherri—whether in alarm or pleadingly, Sherri couldn't determine.

"Okay, Sherri," Thad said, while pulling Martel by the ear, "let's get them back into the room." He then peeked into the hallway. "Wait, the door is shut." He patted Martel's pockets and retrieved the key from his right front pants pocket. Handing it to Sherri, he said, "We are right behind you." Then he grabbed Martel by the hair with his right hand and Angela's with his left.

Sherri paused in the hallway. "I thought we were going to take them from the hotel."

"We were, but I feel compelled to take them back to the room."

CHAPTER NINETEEN

Saturday, May 5, 1979

The phone's first ring startled Sherri just as her eyes fell on an eerie entry in Martel's large green hardback *Record Book*. She slammed the book back onto the glass coffee table and said triumphantly, to Angela, "It's nice of your friend to keep such meticulous records for us. It appears you still owe him for silencing a Tom Duricovich."

Thad interrupted her, "Let Angela answer the phone." He then warned Angela that he is not feeling exceptionally patient.

Sherri lifted the receiver and immediately placed it to Angela's right ear and pressed her own left ear to it.

"Hello," Angela said politely.

"Is this Angela?" asked the man with a deep voice.

"Yes, this is Angela."

"Hey, Angela, this is Greg. Get Richard on the phone. I'm at the cottage. It's very urgent."

"Hold on, Greg, I'll get him for you."

Sherri cracked her on the head with the receiver and scowled a warning, and repositioned it to continue the conversation.

"He should be back soon, Greg. I forgot that he had something important to attend to, uptown. I'll have him call you."

"Oh, great! Make sure he calls me. He needs to follow up on a tip that our favorite vagabond is in the area and he's snooping around. I'll keep the line clear. Bye."

Sherri asked Angela, "Gregory Grant. Right?"

"Figure it out yourself," Angela snarled.

Sherri repeated the content of the phone call to Thad and then suggested they go get Grant.

Thad asked Martel, "Where is the cottage?"

"How am I supposed to know?"

Thad kicked his right shin.

Martel whelped and rubbed his left calf over his shin. "There must be hundreds of cottages in West Virginia," he replied defiantly.

Thad removed a hawk-bill knife from his left front pocket, opened it and began to shave the back of Martel's neck.

"Okay. Okay. It's at the backwaters of Cheat Lake."

"What's the phone number?" Thad asked, pressing the knife against Martel's left carotid.

"Come on, man. I don't know the number."

Angela snapped, "Quit trying to play tough guy and give the man what he wants."

Martel reluctantly complied, and then told Angela, "This is on you. If anything goes wrong, you'll answer for it."

Sherri dialed the number. On the first ring the same deep voice answered, "Grant."

Sherri hung up the phone and announced, "It's the right number." She commanded Martel to give them directions to the cottage.

"Never mind," Thad said. "I don't trust him that far." He then walked over to the phone and dialed. "Hey, Al, this is Thad. Do me a big favor. See if you can find the matching name and address for this phone number." Thad waited patiently for a couple minutes after quoting the number to Al. "Good. Do you have a copy of the warrant for Gregory Grant? Good. He is at that address. Tell whoever responds that there may be at least one other person with him who may be armed. I'm at Suite 53 in the Hotel Mountaineer."

For the next forty-five minutes Sherri stood guard over Martel and Angela while Thad conducted a shakedown of the suite.

Thad returned to the living room with a black leather gun belt and holster slung over his shoulder, brandishing a chrome 9mm Ruger pistol in his right hand, and clasping another large green hardback *Record Book*. He tossed the record book onto the coffee table, picked up the phone and dialed.

"Yeah, Al, this is Thad. Any word on Reverend Short or Janet?"

Sherri shuttered with anticipation when Thad gleefully trumpeted, "Praise God! That *is* great news. Is she okay?" She could hardly contain herself, hankering for Al to hurry his answer so Thad could tell her the news.

"Janet's been rescued?" she asked, before Thad could hang up the phone.

With a sparkle in his eyes, matching his flawless grin, he said, "Either she escaped or someone rescued her. Al didn't have the details. He said that an anonymous male had called Drake's house and left a message with Mrs. Drake that Bill should go to the Chateau over Cheat and pick up Janet. The caller hung up before Bill could get to the phone. Bill immediately called Special Agent Scott of the Clarksburg office of the FBI. They are to meet at the Sheriff's office."

Sherri slapped Angela on the back of the head and asked, "What do we do with these two darlings?"

Thad rubbed his forehead. "Well, we could do with them what the Morton brothers reportedly did with a couple of their vehicles a few years ago, intending to collect insurance money for those vehicles they claimed were stolen."

Sherri hadn't the slightest idea of what Thad alluded. And before she could inquire, Angela begged Thad to let them go.

"I'll do anything you want," Angela pleaded. She wiggled to the edge of the furry white couch cushion. "You name it," she begged.

Sherri almost felt ashamed of the pleasure she got from Angela's naked horror. Angela's whitened sweaty face generated too much gratification. And anon the Holy Spirit reminded her, "Rejoice not when thine enemy falleth, and let not thine heart be glad when he stumbleth: Lest the LORD see it, and it displease him, and he turn away his wrath from him."

Angela then directed her pleas to Sherri. "Please. Don't let him do this. I know enough about the Bible to know that you can't do this if you're truly saved."

"I don't know what the Morton brothers did, but it must be a good idea."

"Come on, Sherri. You can't be part of this. You can't let him do this."

Sherri scolded, "Maybe you should be pleading with God, instead of playing the 'you're a Christian' card."

Martel yelled, "Shut up, Angela, you treacherous coward. They wouldn't dare."

"Really?" Thad challenged. "By the time the evening shift quits tonight the guys at my friend's surface mine can have you buried so far beneath the spoil it would take forever to uncover you." He strode across the room and picked up the phone and started dialing.

"Okay. All right…I believe you," Martel shouted. "We can make a deal," he petitioned.

"Now, what could you possibly have that I would want?" Thad teased.

"Information. Enough information to make you a hero for solving the Spike Cottrell murder case."

Angela struggled unsuccessfully to rise from the couch, and screamed, "You do, and you are a dead man, Richard. And dare you call *me* a coward!" She then stared pleadingly at Martel and said, "Think about us, Richard. How about us?"

Martel snickered. "You two-bit piece of store-bought trash. Do you really think there is an *us*? You are as gullible as you are rich. And there are some things even *your* money can't buy, Angela."

Angela's jaw muscles throbbed as she turned toward Sherri. "Would you like an opportunity to bust the biggest illegal drug operation and burglary ring in the history of West Virginia? I can even give you the top dog."

Martel bounded from his chair and hurled himself at Angela, but Thad sent him flying sideways across the room.

Thad jerked him to his feet and drove him back into the large fluffy white chair. He reached into his front jeans pocket and pulled out a cuff key and tossed it to Sherri. "Here, remove her cuffs then hand it back to me."

Sherri fumbled about, finally setting Angela's wrists free. "You sure you want to do this?"

"I'm sure," he said, taking the cuffs and key from Sherri. "Who are they going to tell? And they sure aren't in much of a position to cause us any immediate grief." He ordered Martel to lean forward, allowing himself easy access to the cuffs. Pressing the barrel of the pistol against Martel's left temple, he warned, "One wrong move, and I'll do exactly what I am tempted to do."

Sherri grabbed both record books from the coffee table and said, "I'm sure these will prove to be beneficial."

Thad instructed her to go first. He walked backward while pointing the gun toward Martel until he stepped into the hallway and then pulled the suite door closed behind him.

Sherri asked why Thad hadn't given Martel a chance to tell who killed Spike Cottrell. "He could have saved us all a lot of time and effort."

"If he had told us while being illegally held captive, it is doubtful the information would be admissible in court. Besides, I doubt that he would have told us the truth."

"Okay. That answers that question. Have you considered that they will call Grant to tip him off that the authorities are coming after him?"

"I suppose you didn't catch me cutting the phone line. And before you ask, I plan to stop at the front desk and instruct Doby to stall them if they ask to use the hotel's phone." He grabbed her hand and said, "Hurry, we'll call from the pay phone in the lobby."

Sherri kept a lookout for Martel and Angela while Thad called the Morgantown Police Department from the only hotel lobby phone to anonymously report that a couple in suite 53 were fighting and disturbing the peace of other hotel customers.

He then unscrewed the mouthpiece cover from the handset and removed a small circular part. "That ought to keep them from calling anyone from this phone," he said as he screwed the cover back on. "No one will hear what they are saying."

They then approached Doby, who leaned forward and whispered, "I just tried sending a call from the Sheriff's office to Mr. Martel's suite but didn't get an answer. I forget the man's name who called."

"Thanks, Doby," Thad said. "By the way, if Martel or Angela Hillman asks to use your phone, don't let them." He then pulled another twenty-dollar bill from his wallet and slid it across the counter.

"Thanks," Doby said, pushing the bill toward Thad. " But I don't have to be further bribed. If you are about to take this high-class dirt ball down, that is payment enough for me. Just don't tell anyone I assisted you."

"It's a deal," Thad said. "Oh, one other thing...in about half an hour, can you replace this in the pay phone?" He handed the part to Doby and instructed him, "Just unscrew the mouthpiece and place this inside with the short coned side pointing inward."

Thad and Sherri no more than stepped into the large office across from the Sheriff's dispatcher, when Janet jumped from a seat at the table and met Sherri half way. The two women broke into cheerful sobs and laughter as they embraced each other.

"Oh, Janet! I'm so sorry," Sherri cried. "I nearly got you killed."

"Don't be so foolish. It isn't your fault. And I will face it again if I need to. They only strengthened my resolve."

"Well, I still feel responsible."

Janet led her to a bench against the nearest wall. "You aren't going to believe who rescued me."

Sherri reasoned that there is only one person who gets Janet this excited. "I could guess, but I don't see how that person could have done it."

Janet's eyes glistened with excitement. "I didn't see his face. But I recognized his soothing voice and heard his distinctive steps."

"Thank you, Jesus," Sherri shouted. Jumping to her feet, she repeated, "Oh, thank you, Jesus. Oh, thank you, Jesus." She plopped back onto the bench and grabbed Janet by the arm and asked, "Is he here, Janet? Oh, my... Is Uncle Joseph here?"

"No. I can't imagine why, but he disappeared as mysteriously as he had come to my rescue. I called after him but he had vanished without a sign of where he went."

They were so engulfed with their reunion they barely heard Deputy Stone's requests to resume the interview.

Sherri found it nearly impossible to refrain from letting loose her emotional responses to Janet's accounts of the abduction and subsequent rescue. As Janet described her ordeal, Sherri rode the most turbulent ride she had ever experienced. She plummeted into steep sorrow, then up to elation, thrown from side to side between anger and joy, hanging onto every word.

"They kept me blindfolded the entire time, from when they forced their way into the house until Joseph liberated me. They removed the duct tape from my mouth only to let me have a couple bites of food and a drink of water."

"Can you identify the men who kidnapped you?" Stone asked.

"Oh, yes. I got a good look at both their faces when fighting with them at my house. The daylight aided in my taking mental notes of their faces, body build, speech patterns, what they were wearing, and even the skull ring with diamonds set in its eye sockets, worn by one of them."

Deputy Stone wrote each description occasionally asking Janet to slow down. "Did you hear either of the men's names mentioned during your captivity?"

"No. I kept listening for them to speak one another's names, but they were especially careful about that."

Deputy Stone grinned. "They must have sensed that you were no dummy… I suspect they still underestimated your intelligence. Tell us about the rescue."

"From the basement—where my hands were cuffed around a metal support post behind me—I heard what sounded like a person falling heavily to the floor above me. Then I heard a gunshot and a second body hit the floor about six or eight feet from the first. Things fell silent for a few seconds, and then I heard what sounded like a body being dragged across the floor and a subsequent thud. A few minutes later, I heard the door at the top of the stairs open and the flipping of a light switch." Janet paused as to ward off an ensuing sob. "I'm sorry," she said as she wiped her eyes with a tissue from the box Deputy Stone had laid in front of her.

"No need to apologize," Stone insisted. "I think you're doing very well. I would cry with you, but I'm too angry at these scumbags."

Janet giggled slightly. "That is so charming. Thanks." She inhaled deeply then continued. "Even though it has been a long time since I last saw Joseph, I very easily recognized the sound of his walk as he swiftly hobbled down the stairs. I could only grunt through the duct tape they'd wrapped across my mouth and clear around to the back of my neck, and around again."

Sherri asked, "Did you tell him that we've been looking for him?"

"I started to, but he didn't stay long enough for me to say much of anything. He first unlocked the handcuffs. As he removed them he asked that I not take off the blindfold until after he left. He suggested that when I do open my eyes, to do so slowly, only allowing myself to squint until I become once more used to the light. He told me to stay seated on the floor until after he took off the gag. He said to count to ten before moving, opening my eyes or saying anything. I nodded okay." She burst into heaving sobs.

"Take your time, Janet," Thad coached. "It's okay. Let it go. It's all right to take time to weep. We can wait."

Sherri leaned to her right and hugged Janet, who then broke into teeth-tingling wails.

After a long and laborious cry, she drew more tissues from the box and cleared her sinuses. "Okay. I think I'm okay."

"You were telling us that Joseph told you to count to ten," said Deputy Stone.

"He placed a key in my right hand and folded my fingers around it. He told me that the key is for a motorboat docked just outside the basement door. He said to drive the boat southward toward the singing bridge (the old steel bridge with the grated metal surface that hums when driven over) and beyond until I came to the Chateau, on my left. He said, 'Dock the boat at the nearby marina and go to the Chateau and ask for Smitty. He will make sure you are safe until Bill Drake comes to get you.'"

"Where did he get the boat?" Sherri asked.

"I have no idea. I guess it belonged to whoever owns the cottage or the two guys that held me captive. At least I hadn't heard it pull up. That close to the cottage; surely I would have heard it if it had been driven there during my captivity."

"So, did you have a hard time finding your way?" Sherri further inquired.

"No. Thank God for a full moon tonight. It lighted my way so well I could see even the narrow passageway from the backwaters to the main lake. Otherwise I would have run into the long narrow patch of land that stretched nearly all the way across the backwaters at one point."

Sherri exchanged looks of wonderment with Thad and then with Deputy Stone. "Janet," she said, "There is no moon out at all tonight. The sky has been dark with heavy threatening storm clouds for the past few hours."

"I'm telling you the moon shone bright all the way to the marina near the Chateau." She paused as if to reflect on what Sherri had said. "Oh, but that couldn't be… Do you suppose God somehow lit my way?"

"I'm certain of it," Thad replied.

""Wow!" Janet exclaimed. "God must have heard my prayer. Just moments before Joseph overtook the guys upstairs, I had asked the Lord to forgive all my sins and I promised Him that I would worship and serve Him the rest of my life…however long or short it may be…Well, actually I couldn't speak the words with the duct tape so tight over my mouth. Do you suppose He heard me anyhow?"

Sherri joyfully replied, "God knows our thoughts and the intents of our hearts, Janet. Of course, He heard you."

A loud knock at the door summoned their attention. Deputy Stone rushed to open it and said, "You must be Special Agent Scott. Come on in." Stone introduced the FBI agent to the others and asked him to have a seat.

Agent Scott asked, "Have we arrested the kidnappers yet?"

Before anyone could answer, Al called on the intercom. "Hey, Stone. I have good news and I have bad news. Which do you want first?"

"Give us the good news, then let us down easy."

"The state police are bringing in two men they arrested at the cottage, over Cheat."

"Okay. Now let us down."

"Morgantown Police report that the suite at the Hotel Mountaineer has been vacated. The desk clerk said that the couple practically ran from the hotel. Richard Martel, the lessee, carried an arm full of clothes and a couple suitcases with him. Angela, the woman with him, tossed the room key to the clerk and kept on going."

Thad banged his fist on the table and griped, "Uh, uh, uh! If only the anonymous caller hadn't been such a moron, and would have waited to be sure they didn't go anywhere."

"They can run, but they can't hide," Deputy Stone consoled. "You needn't get upset at yourself. We'll get them. By the time we catch up with them we'll probably have plenty of evidence to support holding them without bail, anyhow."

"I suppose you're right," Thad conceded.

Janet teased, "Thad are you picking up Sherri's temperament already?"

Sherri replied, "I'm too thrilled at your being rescued to let that remark stir me."

Janet's countenance instantly paled as she announced, "Hey guys, I just remembered that Joseph must have been bleeding bad. Oh, my... He could be seriously wounded from the gunshot I heard when he overtook those men."

"What makes you think he's bleeding?" Thad asked. "Didn't you say you kept your eyes closed while counting to ten as Joseph left the scene?"

"Yes. But when I opened my eyes I saw drops of blood on the cement floor. A small puddle of fresh wet blood had formed next to me, where Joseph had stood the longest. Oh, Dear Lord, please don't let him be badly hurt."

Thad asked that the others join him in a prayer.

Special Agent Scott reached his hands to Stone on one side and Sherri on the other. "Thank God, you all are praying folks. Indeed, let us pray."

Thad offered a brief prayer for Joseph then closed with a request that Ellis Fenton be found and rescued. As soon as he said, "Amen," Janet shrieked.

"Oh, my," she announced, "I also need to tell you that my captors bragged about killing Mr. Fenton and disposing of his body way back in the inner part of a cave near Gobbler's Peak."

Deputy Stone rushed to the intercom and asked Al to contact the Preston County Sheriff's office. "Ask if there are any caves in the area that a body could be placed into. If so, ask if they have anyone available to check for Ellis Fenton's corpse in such a cave, very possibly near Gobbler's Peak. The thugs the state police are headed this way with bragged about dumping his body in a cave in that area."

"I'm on it," said Al. "I'm dialing their number this very second."

"Thanks, Al. And let me know when the troopers arrive, will ya?"

"Will do."

Stone asked if Janet felt up to identifying the two men when they arrive at the jail.

"Sure."

Thad scurried across the room and looked out the tall rectangular window facing the small lot beside the jail's sally port. "Speak of devils—here they are."

Janet raced to Thad's side and peered out. "Oh yes, these are the guys who kidnapped me and held me captive. The taller one has the name Tina tattooed on the fingers of his right hand. The other man stutters—he has difficulty saying words beginning with the letter 'P'."

Deputy Stone laughed. "I think we need to get you into law enforcement, young lady. You are really sharp."

Al called over the intercom again. "Hey, Stone. I got hold of Preston County's dispatcher and he informs me that they already have a couple units checking Fortney's Cave near Gobbler's Peak. Evidently they received a call about half an hour ago that a young couple who planned to camp out in the cave had been exploring the offshoots of the cavern when they happened upon a battered corpse that appeared to have been there for only a short time."

Sherri plopped into a swivel chair barely able to maintain consciousness. The shocking revelation overtook her to the point of complete numbness—of mind as well as of body. She faintly heard Al's next announcement over the intercom.

"Hey, guys," Al called, "I have Preston County on the landline. They want to know if Ellis Fenton is kin to the young woman they are holding in their facility—a Miss Ramona Fenton."

Stone answered, "Yes. We are to meet with Deputy Burk, Monday morning, to interview Ramona's boyfriend who is also being held by Preston County."

"Preston County copied that. He says that Burk also plans to interview the Fenton girl while you guys are there on Monday."

"Thanks, Al."

"You're welcome. Tell Thad Ashbury this is all going on his tab."

"Don't you start with me, pal," Thad yelled toward the intercom. "It doesn't hurt you to earn your keep once in a while." He then looked at his watch and said, "Hey, folks, I have to go. I told the afternoon shift officer I'd be late. But I promised to get there as soon as possible to relieve him… I'll contact you tomorrow or get updates from you on Monday, Warren."

Warren Stone patted him on the shoulder and said, "Just be safe out there, tonight."

Deacon Drake offered to give Janet and Sherri a ride to the Stewart's home and thanked everyone for their quick and professional responses. "Good night, everyone."

The short muscle-bound security officer checked Drake's, Sherri's, and Janet's identification and requested that they wait in the vehicle while he obtains clearance from the Stewarts. Returning several seconds later, he said, "Mrs. Stewart wishes for the three of you to stop at the residence before you ladies retire to the guesthouse." He reached into the building and activated the gate's arm.

Tammy ran from the house and down the illuminated sidewalk. She hugged Janet and sighed, "Thank God, you are okay. We were so worried about you." Barely allowing herself time to draw enough breath, she said, "Deputy Stone called, just after you left the Sheriff's office. He said to make sure you were notified that Mr. Fenton has been found—alive. But," she quickly interjected, "he has been life-flighted by helicopter to the West Virginia University Hospital. He's in critical condition."

Sherri grumbled, "First I nearly get Mr. Fenton killed—he could still die because of me, then I cause Janet to be abducted—she could easily have been murdered." She burst into bawling. "And now…Uncle Joseph…he's been shot and may be somewhere dying…or already dead." Her body wilted to the white brick walkway.

Janet and Tammy simultaneously dropped beside her and embraced her.

"Who knows," Sherri screeched, "what tragedy I am bringing to you and Steve." Through gritted teeth she proclaimed, "I'm not worth the dust from which I came."

Janet shook her vigorously and commanded, "Stop it, Sherri…Stop it, right now…That's fool's talk…Now stop it."

Sherri thrust herself forward, rammed her face into her cupped hands, and fervently petitioned, "Oh, God, forgive me. I'm so sorry." Unutterable sorrows overtook her, choking her—knotting her torso until it felt like her stomach and her heart were wrapping around each other.

CHAPTER TWENTY

Sunday, May 6, 1979

The morning sun danced on the cemetery's glistening manicured lawn, hopping from dewdrop to dewdrop, reverently resting on each headstone and marker.

Sherri stood quietly, studying the majestic fieldstone exterior of Nicholson Chapel holding fast as silent witness of the God for whose worship it had been established. A gentle northbound breeze whispered hypnotically.

"You know what?" Janet asked, barely penetrating Sherri's tranquility.

"What?"

"I don't think I have ever seen greener grass or felt a more soothing sunshine or known a greater peace. Until now, I hadn't paid much mind to how Nicholson Chapel's lofty property offers such a splendid view."

Sherri drew a deep soul-filling breath. "What a perfect day!"

"What a wonderful *life*." Janet sighed. "How foolish of me not to have gotten saved before now."

Sherri smiled affirmatively, glancing off across the lower hills and valleys.

"We better get inside before they start church without us."

"Yeah," said Sherri. She slid her left hand down the necklace chain and lifted the heart shaped pendant watch to read its face. "I have ten minutes 'til ten." She brought her right hand to the piece and ran her thumb across the imitation diamonds. "Frank gave this to me our first Christmas as husband and wife. It's also a locket." She flipped it open and stared thoughtfully at the picture for a few seconds. "I barely know this couple. I've never before noticed that my smile looks phony. I now see, in this young man's face, what others had read and conveyed to me—that arrogant grin and boorish disposition."

Janet stood face to face with her, reached slowly and nudged Sherri's hands from the locket and snapped it shut. Letting it drop to Sherri's bosom, she said, "Let's not ruin such a glorious day."

Before the door closed behind them, Janet and Sherri were encompassed by those gathered in the sanctuary for adult Sunday school class. In no particular formation, they lined up to personally welcome them with hugs, well-wishes, and praises to God for keeping Janet safe and setting her free from her captors.

Just as the commotion began to settle, Janet announced, "Something even more wonderful happened."

A hush rippled through the congregation until all ears and eyes gave audience to her.

With a glow in her countenance and a sparkle in her eyes, she cheerfully proclaimed, "During my captivity, I repented of all my sins. I asked Jesus to forgive me and to send his Holy Spirit into my heart…and—praise God—He did."

Excitement erupted once more. Some sat in their pews with uplifted hands, tears streaming down their faces. Some bombarded her with more hugs, joyfully welcoming her to the Body of Christ. Others dropped to their knees at the altar and bathed it in tears with jubilant thanksgiving.

Sherri joined those who knelt in prayer and soon felt Janet's arm around her. By the time Sherri and Janet—the last to leave the altar—rose to find a seat, an impromptu choir had formed around the piano, singing, "There's Victory In Jesus". The singers had barely caught their breath when the piano player led them into another hymn and then another.

Before the singers had all reached their seats, the pastor began enthusiastically preaching about a number of biblical characters' perseverance through trials of imprisonments, being cast into a fiery furnace, beatings, death threats, and the murders of fellow believers, to victorious fulfillment of God's calling and to the glory of God. "Can we not see His power for the modern-day saints being displayed?" he repeated numerous times, evoking shouts from the congregation.

No Adult Sunday school class that morning!

"Sherri," Janet said. "Do you mind if I take time to visit my parents' grave?"

"Of course not. I'll accompany you, if that's okay."

They finished saying goodbye to the other worshippers as they came out the front door. Janet pointed to a place farther up the mountain. "See that lone farm house and part of the meadow up there, surrounded by woods?"

"Yeah."

"Can you guess whose home that is?"

"I would suspect it is your Uncle Jake's if I could see your house beyond it."

"Well," said Janet, "if you were to guess it is Uncle Jake's, you'd be correct."

"That's interesting—how that from here, one might suppose that Jake's is the only house up there."

Janet turned somber. "Does it look to you like there are several vehicles up there?"

Sherri squinted and tried to make out what objects the noon sun bounced off. "I kind of wondered what reflected the sun—almost like someone or some bodies sending Morris code. I wouldn't think your Uncle Jake and Aunt Wilma are home already. Didn't you say he is pastor of a church at Hildebrand?"

"Oh, well. Let's go visit Mom's and Dad's grave."

Janet and Sherri had reminisced for nearly an hour as they strolled around the graveyard. They saw a red Ford Pinto drive into the cemetery.

As if she read Sherri's apprehension, Janet said, "That's Mr. and Mrs. Cort. They live along Nicholson Loop, just before you turn onto Murray Road to my place."

The car came to a stop and the driver beeped the horn and yelled, "Is that you, Janet?"

"Yes, sir, Mr. Cort," she replied. "How are you?"

"Well, I reckon I'm fine."

Janet turned and started walking toward the car. "Hi, Mrs. Cort. How are you?"

"I reckon I'm fine, too. We almost didn't recognize you—all dolled up like that. I always did say that you're awful pretty. How come you always try to hide all that beauty?"

Janet blushed. "Now, I know what I like about you," she teased. "You sure are good for my ego."

Mr. Cort leaned across the seat to view them through the open passenger side window. "Everybody thought you were kidnapped. I reckon them news people up at your place are gonna hate that they wasted all that time gatherin' a story about it."

"Well, actually I *had* been kidnapped, Mr. Cort. But, thank God, my hero rescued me late last night. These news people you spoke of—are they up there now?"

"They were when we left the house to come down here. They stopped at our place, asking all about you."

Mrs. Cort interrupted him. "Now, Old Man, there you go again mixin' things up."

She then said to Janet, "It's a good thing he isn't doing the reportin'. The fella that talked with us even told us that you had reportedly been rescued. They wanted to know exactly where you lived. I hope you don't mind us tellin' 'em. They would have found you anyhow."

"That's all right, Mrs. Cort. Like you said, they would find out where I live anyhow. But I don't plan on being hounded by them. I'm glad you folks told me about them—before we drove into that mess. Well, we'd better go."

Sherri waited until they got out of earshot of the Corts, then asked, "What are we going to do? We already accepted your Aunt Wilma's invitation to dinner."

"We'll drive over to Uncle Buzz's house on Beulah Road and call her. Maybe they'll be home by then. She can let us know when the coast is clear."

On the way to Buzz's house, Sherri informed Janet that she'd probably never again see her Jeep.

"I suspect you're right. But why do you say so."

"I remember Lanky telling Thad and I that Richard Martel—Lanky calls him Twitchy Face—pays the 'bad people' that hang around town, to steal things. Then, last night Angela alluded to Martel's involvement in a sizable drug and theft ring."

"I bet my Jeep has already been disassembled or sold on the black market. A couple years ago, the local courts convicted a man from the western end of the county for possession of stolen vehicles. It wouldn't surprise me if these thugs are part of that same ring of thieves."

"You'd better make sure the theft of your Jeep has been properly reported or documented."

"Deputy Stone indicated that it's been entered into the police network computers. I think he called it NCIC. I still need to report it to my insurance agent. I have full coverage—I'm certain theft coverage is included."

Janet pulled open the screen door and announced, "Aunt Wilma, your famished guests are here."

"Come on back to the kitchen," Wilma answered. "Dinner is almost ready."

They followed the aroma of fresh baked bread to where Wilma stirred a large black iron skillet full of her nearly famous homemade brown gravy. She turned sideways while maintaining her cadence. "I reckon you had quite an exiting few days, Janet."

Wilma possessed an admirable humility and a knack for putting others at ease. In Janet's eyes, no one, except maybe Uncle Jake, exhibited as genuine a spirit of meekness as Aunt Wilma. "Enough to do me for a while," Janet replied.

Wilma declared, "Well, Jake and I sure are relieved that you're okay. Jake talked with Thad early this morning. He'd called and asked Jake to be present when he talks with you girls this afternoon."

"We were going to call Thad in a little while," Sherri said.

"I don't think you'll get hold of him now. He promised to try to make it over to eat with us."

Janet grabbed a crock of butter from the refrigerator and set it by the hot loaves of bread on the kitchen counter. She pulled open a drawer beneath the counter and withdrew a tablespoon, and started buttering the top of the loaves. She glanced over her shoulder at Sherri leaning against the archway between the dining room and kitchen. "Don't stand there looking like you don't know what to do in a kitchen," she teased. "Get over here and mash the potatoes."

"Ah, Janet," Wilma politely scolded, "You don't talk to guests that way."

"Oh, but I do. Besides, she isn't a guest. Why, she's nearly kin."

Sherri felt her cheeks redden, but refused to rebut her. She walked toward the cook stove, intending to check the boiling potatoes on the back burner.

Wilma asked, "Is she picking on you, Sherri?"

"She's just being her own goofy self."

Wilma chuckled. "She's bad isn't she?"

Sherri immediately simmered down. "Yes, she's bad... Do you have a fork I can use to check these?"

Wilma pointed to the drawer from which Janet had gotten her tablespoon. "There should be one in there... You don't have to listen to Janet. I can mash those. You'll get your church clothes all messy."

Janet teased, "Oh, that's how it is, huh? Don't worry about your precious niece getting *her* clothes messy."

Wilma giggled as she scurried across the room to a utility cabinet and lifted a mixer from it and sat it on a sturdy hand crafted oak table. "I can do this," she reminded Sherri.

"No, ma'am. I want the bragging rights that I helped prepare a meal with the woman who Janet has, on more than one occasion, declared to be the best cook in the whole county."

The women gathered in the living room after doing the dishes and were discussing the complex case involving Joseph, when Wilma said, "Come on in, Thad. You know you're in trouble, don't you?"

Jake had fallen asleep in his recliner and Wilma's statement startled him awake.

Thad entered the house without replying and looking troubled. Sherri knew from the glances he exchanged with Jake that he bore terrible news.

Sherri focused her attention toward Wilma who had curled up in her recliner. Her small stature and pleasant countenance suggested a much younger age than her confessed forty years. Sherri hoped somehow to draw from Wilma's steady quiet demeanor. Thad sat on the couch beside Sherri; the only remaining seat in the room. She scooted toward Janet; purposely allowing a respectable distance between herself and Thad, fearing the others might discern her secret feelings.

An awkward silence fell over the room preying on Sherri's consternation.

Finally, Jake broke the spellbinding stillness. "Thad," he said, "You have some chilling news to report that happened early this morning on the job. Do you want me to tell the girls or would you rather handle it?"

Thad's eyes turned watery and in a shaky voice he said, "Let me try, Uncle Jake." He leaned forward resting his elbows on his knees, folded his hands, and pleaded for someone to pray.

Janet surprised Sherri by immediately praying aloud. What joy it gave her to witness the Holy Spirit's empowerment of such sincere utterances by her best friend—a pleasure cut short by the thought of an impending announcement, promising to be full of sorrows.

Janet closed her prayer with the typical 'Amen,' and the petitioners returned to their muted state. Everyone gave undivided attention to Thad.

Thad, frozen in his forward leaning position, slowly shook his head and squealed in anguish, "Oh God, help me. I can't tell her." He bawled for several seconds. Still with his head bowed toward the hardwood floor, tears splashing heavily between his feet, he muttered, "Uncle Jake… I can't…I can't…I'm such a wretch." He paused as to get his breath between tormented gasps. "Oh, Sherri… I'm not even worthy to beg your forgiveness."

His comment about *her* forgiveness altogether passed Sherri by. She knelt on the floor and laid her head against his. "Whatever it is,

Thad, we'll get through it. I know you are doing everything you can," she pleaded, barely controlling her own anguish at seeing his deep hurt.

Jake crossed the room and laid his thick calloused right hand on Thad's shoulder. "Thad," he said in his usual compassionate tone, "Do you want the women to go outside to leave us alone a bit?"

Thad answered not a word. He seemed too desperate to catch his breath to form a reply.

Sherri rose to her feet and started for the door and realized that Janet and Wilma were at her side. They slowly, without conversation, walked to an old box elder tree and sat on a wooden glider beneath its wide leafy branches. Wilma, sitting between Janet and Sherri, reached to hold their hands.

"Aunt Wilma," Janet said, "do you know why Thad is so torn?"

"No, Honey. When he called your Uncle Jake, I answered the phone but I didn't ask him why he called. I did ask Jake what Thad had to say, since Jake looked so troubled when he hung up the phone. But he just grunted and shook his head. I figured he'd tell me in his own time. I could tell he would cry if he spoke. So I just left him be. I try to not let things get to me, but that boy is really hurting about something. Janet, you know how strong and stoic he usually is. He's really worrying me."

Janet turned sullen and stared out across the lower hills and valleys.

Sherri wondered if Janet suspected the same thing she did. Silently she prayed, "Oh, Lord, please, don't let it be that Janet's dream about Uncle Joseph's death be a reality—not now—not this way."

Wilma stretched her legs and feet toward the earth beneath them and, with the tips of her toes, set the glider in slow rhythmic motion.

Janet said, as if thinking aloud, "Surely not." A slow small stream spilled over as she lowly continued, "It wouldn't be fair. No, I prayed too hard and too long." She paused and then sighed, "Oh, Joseph."

Sherri interrupted her. Lovingly, she said, "Janet, surely you don't think that stupid nightmare… No. I refuse to believe it could happen. Oh, Janet, I pray you are mistaken."

"Me too," Janet said softly.

Wilma asked cautiously, "What are you girls talking about? What nightmare? You two are upsetting each other with this nightmare talk."

"Oh, Aunt Wilma," Janet pleaded, "I dare not speak it."

"Hey Wilma," called Jake from the back deck, thirty yards away.

"Come on girls," she said.

Sherri lagged behind, semiconsciously hoping Wilma and Janet would serve as buffers between her and the dreaded news.

Jake gestured for them to enter at the back door. He waited until the women were on the deck, and then whispered, "Give Thad plenty of time to explain what happened. He'll need you to be patient. Try to hear him out." He held open the door as they filed into the dining room.

All three women hesitated, mulling around the dining room. "Go on into the living room and have a seat," he solemnly instructed.

They sat together on the couch in the same order as they had on the glider—Wilma in the middle offering unspoken support to the other two.

Sherri wondered where Thad had gone. Seconds later, the answer came. She tensed with each sound of dry heaving from the bathroom down the hall.

After a few minutes—what seemed to Sherri, several—Thad shuffled into the living room, avoiding eye contact with the others. He slumped into Wilma's recliner.

His grief stricken form broke Sherri's heart. Intending to lighten his burden, she asked in a low but assuming tone, "It's about Uncle Joseph, isn't it?"

Thad glued his gaze to the floor about midway between himself and the women. He nodded—a slow, almost undetectable, no. He tried desperately to clear his throat. "Worse," he mumbled.

"What could be worse?"

Thad spoke in measured response, as to prove each word before uttering it. "I did something this morning I'd hoped to never have to do… Around 4 a.m. I responded to a reported fight in the Holiday Inn parking lot… Seeing no one, I drove under the front entrance canopy, parked my cruiser and went inside to ask the night auditor who called in the report… She knew nothing of the matter." He paused to clear his throat again and, with the back of his hand, wiped away a tear from the tip of his nose. "Returning to my cruiser, I heard what sounded like someone moaning in the direction of a residential yard across the road… I barely made out a movement from behind the bushes and walked briskly across the parking lot, asking a couple times if the person is okay. The unlighted area from the other side of the bushes made it difficult to actually determine who or what had moved a few seconds before. Just as I stepped onto the street a shot rang out from behind the bushes. I ran and dove behind a nearby tree. A second round hit the tree. I returned fire, firing two quick rounds and waited, expecting more shots from the ambusher. Just then Deputy Randall whipped his cruiser into the parking lot and brought it to a quick stop behind me. Taking cover behind his open door, he reached inside the cruiser and turned on his spotlight. Even then we could only faintly make out that a person lay behind the bushes… We cautiously approached." He stopped speaking for several seconds as in a struggle to get his breath, and then cried out, "I killed him… Oh, God help me—I killed him."

"Thad," Sherri consoled, "apparently you had no choice. I thank God *you* didn't get killed." She bounded from her seat to comfort him and exclaimed, "You did what you had to do. God knows you had no choice."

He sprang to his feet, sidestepped her, and scampered to the front door. Turning abruptly back toward her, he bellowed, "You don't understand, Sherri…"

"Stop torturing yourself over this," she blared.

In a deliberately stoic tone, he said, "You'll despise me for the rest of your life. I hate *myself* for it."

"I could never…"

He threw his hands out beckoning her to not finish and interrupted, "You don't understand, Sherri. I shot *Frank.*" He angrily reiterated, " I killed *FRANK*, Sherri."

The statement hit her like the suffocating blast of an angry furnace. Instantly, her body and mind went numb. As if in slow motion, she regained her balance, weightily bypassed Thad, and stumbled outside. She wandered aimlessly around to the backside of the house, through several hundred feet of sloping pasture, and into the wooded rocky hollow far beyond.

CHAPTER TWENTY-ONE

Saturday, September 8, 1979

Sherri eased her blue Oldsmobile Cutlass around the hook from Murray Road onto the rocky lane to Janet's house. The four months spent in Youngstown, settling Frank's estate, had dragged her from naivety to somewhere between wise caution and near crippling suspicion.

The arduous task of selling Frank's home, his woodshop machinery and tools, and even his pick-up truck, to pay creditors—none of them receiving full payment—served to reinforce the rumors. But how could she not have known of his gambling addiction. She still couldn't understand how he had managed to secure the various loans, amounting to ten's of thousands of dollars, without her knowledge.

How could she have let a wedge be driven between her and Janet? Even now, she couldn't be sure Janet would welcome her. Why should she? Sherri had told her over the phone a few months before that she didn't want to hear anything more about Thad and how he had no choice, but to return fire, killing Frank. How could she have been so stubborn as to break off all communication with Janet?

She turned off her headlights and trusted that the dim pre-dawn light would illuminate the way up Janet's driveway. She would sit in the car until she saw signs that Janet awoke on her own. She felt like a stray pet crawling back home to beg its master's forgiveness.

Suddenly, the whole mountainside lit up. "So much for trying to go unnoticed," she exclaimed. Unsure whether she should get out of the car, she rolled her window down and looked around. For a hundred yards in every direction everything lost the concealment of darkness: a deer and her two spotted fawns eating fallen apples in Jake's and Wilma's small orchard; a family of raccoons in a meadow, feeding on something near the barn.

The sighting of Jake with a rifle resting across his right shoulder and walking toward her compelled Sherri to slowly exit the car so that she could be identified. "It's just me—Sherri."

"Good morning," he replied in a low tone carried by a subtle breeze.

"Wow! That's some lighting system."

Jake walked several more yards before responding. "The Stewarts wouldn't let Janet return home until they had an elaborate security system installed." He grinned boyishly. "Why, you even got your picture taken."

"Well," she teased, pointing to the rifle, "it must be nice to have one's own bodyguard."

"Ever since Janet's return home I've carried ole Nelly with me while I'm out doing my chores around the farm. Thad said that some of the gang members are still at large. That's why we've all been worried about *you*, since Janet lost contact with you."

"I've got a lot of apologizing to do. That is entirely my fault. I've been pouting."

"We know you've been through an awful lot lately. I just wish we could do more for you."

"My behavior has been contemptible at best. I've come to apologize to everyone. I don't deserve Janet's friendship. But I need her forgiveness, nonetheless. I've had time to think on what all has happened and I know I owe Thad a really *big* apology." Her eyes stung with self-ire. "I can be so self-centered."

"Uncle Jake," Janet yelled shrilly, causing Sherri to flinch. "Yeah, you better jump, you ruddy little renegade. You just as well get up here and get it over with. You have a good ole mountaineer butt-whipping coming to you… Uncle Jake, Aunt Wilma just called. She wants us to join you for breakfast."

Sherri turned back to tell Jake she would be honored to have breakfast with them, only to see him already nearing his porch steps.

"I hope you like whole hog sausage," Wilma said, as she placed a patty-laden plate in the center of the dining room table. "Jake swaps some of our beef for some of his cousin's sausage."

Sherri said, "Forgive my ignorance, but what is whole-hog sausage? The only time I ever heard that phrase is when Dad use to describe Mom's ranting. He'd say, 'she's going at it whole-hog.'"

Jake gave her a fatherly grin. "So she gives it all she's got, huh?"

"Oh. I get it. Instead of cutting the hog into specific things like pork chops and bacon, all parts of the hog are ground into sausage. Right?"

Janet nearly spit, trying to contain her laughter. "You've still got it," she teased.

Wilma returned from the kitchen with a plate of fried eggs and asked, "Sherri, is Janet picking on you, again?"

"Yeah. She is just tending to my Gomer Pyle syndrome."

Janet explained, "She's got this real knack for charming folks with her pretend ignorance."

Wilma took her seat as she replied, "Janet is so bad." She reached her right hand to Jake and the others followed her lead. On cue, Jake asked the blessing on the meal.

As soon as Jake said, "Amen," Sherri recalled the last time she shared a meal at their home. She felt unworthy to behold their faces but wanted them to see her sincerity. "I owe you both an apology for the way I behaved the last time you saw me."

"You didn't do anything wrong," Wilma insisted. "You handled the situation much better than most people would have. I nearly went into shock myself, when Thad told us what had happened. I became so sick with worry over you and Thad both that I nearly stayed home from church that Sunday night. I can only imagine the shock you must have endured."

"I guess I hadn't thought how the news affected anyone else. I don't mean to be so self-centered. Of course, I'm working on such flaws."

Wilma lifted the plate of eggs and slid one off onto her plate and passed it around. Jake sent the plate of sausage in the same direction.

"So," Janet said, "Thad tells me that you have at least kept in touch with Mr. Drake. The deacon kept his word to you, evidently. He would only tell Thad that you were staying in touch."

Even though Sherri had apologized for angrily severing ties with Janet, following their argument over Thad's unavoidable shooting of Frank, she still felt guilty and ashamed. And the mere mention of Thad's name evoked the same jumbled thoughts she had involuntarily entertained over the past four months. She hung her head and stammered, "I… I sure haven't made it any easier for him. I know he did what he had to do. But I guess I've been worried about how it looks to others, when they see that Thad and I were spending a lot of time together."

"He understands that, Sherri. But I think you should know that he is considering leaving West Virginia. He has made application to a few out-of-state police agencies."

Sherri's throat tightened and her chest contracted. "Would you all excuse me for a minute," she pleaded, nearly erupting.

"Of course," Wilma answered in her natural loving tone.

Sherri rushed to the front porch and wept silently. She feared that her feelings for Thad were altogether inappropriate. But she also dared not keep her feelings a secret. She couldn't bear the thought of losing him—even as a friend. She prayed for God's intervention and requested His peace. Soon, she began to softly sing "Farther Along". It surprised her that she had memorized the entire song. Or had she? She hadn't heard Wilma come outside.

"Did anyone ever tell you that you have a beautiful singing voice?"

Wilma's genuineness comforted her even more than the compliment. "Thanks, Aunt Wilma… Is it okay if I call you Aunt? You and Jake really make me feel like family."

"Sure you can call me Aunt Wilma. Speaking of *Uncle* Jake—I asked him to talk with you. I hope you don't mind. He is good at talking to people about their turmoil."

"I'd like that. It seems that when Janet and I talk we end up feuding."

"Janet means well. She is just a little blunt, sometimes."

"Yeah. But, so am I."

"Come on. Let's go finish breakfast. Then you can talk to Jake while Janet and I do the dishes."

After breakfast, Jake invited Sherri to sit with him on the front porch. He sat on a sturdy homemade bench and motioned for her to sit on the adjacent porch swing. "Wilma asked me to talk to you. She didn't say what we were to talk about."

Sherri grinned at the thoughtfulness of the couple. "I suppose she has me figured out—seeing I'm too proud to ask for guidance. She sure is easy to like. So are you."

"Thanks for saying so. We've become fond of you, too. It means a lot to Wilma and me, that you're such a good friend to Janet. You know, she doesn't have many *close* friends."

"I'm a lot like her. I guess that's why we butt heads so much. Of course, neither one of us will tolerate anyone else fussing with the other."

"Janet has pretty much said the same thing."

Sherri looked intently into Jake's clear soft blue eyes, recalling Granny Short's often-stated analogy: "They say that the eyes are the windows to the soul. Always observe the eyes, they'll tell you the truth about the soul."

"Well," said Jake, "we can talk about anything you want. Then again, if you don't want to…"

"Oh, but I do!" she interrupted. "I do want to talk. The problem is, I have so many conflicting thoughts that my mind is caught up in a perpetual whirlwind."

"Just say what is on your heart and mind. Even if it doesn't make sense at the moment, it will become clear as we talk it out."

She drew a deep breath and let it out slowly. "I'd like to know how Thad is doing. I'm reluctant to ask Janet, for fear she'll be encouraged to play matchmaker."

"I think Thad will be okay. He's torn between remaining on the force at Star City and the idea of relocating. He has even considered leaving law enforcement to pursue another career. He is wisely awaiting God's leading. He just returned to full duty last week. They had him on administrative leave until the state police completed their investigation of the shoot-out with Frank. I guess that is police protocol."

"I'm afraid I haven't made things any easier for him… Uncle Jake, can I ask your advice about a very personal matter?"

"Sure."

She felt embarrassed about it, but she desperately needed to talk to someone who could be objective and Spirit led—someone besides Janet. "You might have already figured it out. I have romantic feelings toward Thad. I try to deny them, but to no avail. I don't know if I'm permitted to love Thad. I don't want to do anything that could be sinful and discrediting to the Lord. Nor do I wish to tempt Thad to do so."

He rubbed his thick right palm back and forth across his mouth and chin. "I don't know much about your life. I mean, about your and Frank's marriage."

"It may sound like I'm making excuses to justify my feelings for Thad. Maybe I *am* trying to justify them. But, the truth is—I learned that Frank had been cheating on me for quite some time. Immediately after I came to Morgantown to look into Uncle Joseph's difficulties, Frank moved his girlfriend into our home. I knew our marriage had become shaky, but I must have blinded myself to his blatant unfaithfulness. And I dare not put all the blame on him. My quick temper and sharp tongue didn't lend to a peaceful existence for either of us. Frank had filed for divorce, further frustrating my plans to try salvaging the relationship. Sometimes I feel guilty about growing so fond of Thad."

"You sure have been through a lot, lately."

Unable to summons a subtle introduction, she blurted out, "Is it a sin for me to love Thad? And if he chose to love me back, would he be sinning?"

Jake blushed and squirmed in his seat. "Oh, my! I feared you might ask me such a question."

"I'm sorry. Maybe I shouldn't have asked. You needn't bother answering. It's unfair of me to even put you in such a spot. Please, forgive me?"

"No, no. You shouldn't be sorry. It is just that I have never had to consider such a complex question about romantic love." He stared off thoughtfully. "I can't think of any scripture that prohibits your feeling that way. Now, if your husband were alive there would be more to consider. Even then, I suppose Frank's infidelity might be considered in debating the issue. The only forthright advice I'll give you for the moment is that you don't act in haste. When all is considered, you are the only one who can make that final call. Just be prayerful."

Janet opened the screen door and announced, "Uncle Jake, you're wanted on the phone."

"Tell Wilma to take a message."

"I think you should take the call."

Jake grunted in disapproval. "Excuse me, Sherri. Let me see what's so important."

Janet joined Sherri on the porch swing. "I know you hate Thad, right now, but…"

"No, I don't," Sherri snapped. "You don't know *how* I feel."

"Bite my head off, why don't ya!"

"Well, don't make such ridiculous statements."

"Anyhow," Janet retorted, "Thad is on the phone. He called to talk to Uncle Jake. When I told him that you were back he asked if he should come over."

"Why on earth did you tell him I'm here in the first place?"

"Quit carrying a chip on your shoulder. Do you think you are the only one torn to pieces over all that's happened? You haven't a clue regarding the endless tumult others have endured on your behalf. Now, stop lending yourself to the devil's devices." She bounded to her feet and stared angrily into Sherri's eyes. "Thad is waiting for an answer. I'll tell you what your answer is—yes, a thousand times, yes. Now, stay put."

A strange sense of satisfaction swept over Sherri as she watched Janet stomp across the porch and into the house, slamming the screen door behind her. She marveled at her own appreciation of Janet's decision—the same decision she would have made if only she had the fortitude.

A few minutes later, Janet returned with a bushel basket. "Come on. Wilma and Jake already went out the basement door. We are going to help them dig up potatoes."

Sherri walked briskly to catch up with her. "So? What about Thad? Is he coming or not?"

"Yes. And you are going to behave yourself when he gets here."

"Yes, Mother."

"I mean it, Sherri."

"You can retract your claws, now. I said, 'okay.'"

"He is going to see if Deacon Drake can accompany him. They have a lot of information to share with us… By the way, did you tell Mr. Drake you were coming home?"

"Oh, yeah. I forgot to tell you. I accepted an invitation for us to join him and Mrs. Drake for lunch at their home, following the morning worship services, tomorrow."

"Why do you do things like that? Who are you to plan my day without first consulting me?"

"Don't get testy with me. Who just planned *my* day for *me*?"

"The difference is, I forewarned you that we were going to have Thad come up."

"Okay. I'm foretelling you that we are joining the Drakes for lunch."

Sherri heard an approaching vehicle crunching the gravel beneath its tires. Shielding her eyes with soil-covered hands she looked up toward Janet's house. "Thad is here." She wiped her hands on the apron, before removing it, and dropped it beside the nearly full basket.

Janet made her way to the basket to unload the potatoes from her upturned apron. "We'll be right there," she yelled, as Thad and Mr. Drake slid from the truck. Turning to Jake and Wilma, she asked, "Would you two like to join us? Thad and Deacon Drake are going to update us on their investigation."

"You girls go on," Wilma replied. "We'll get the information from you, later."

Sherri clumsily followed Janet, keenly aware that the awkwardness of the moment had attached itself to her stride.

Thad and Mr. Drake stood up, courteously acknowledging Janet and Sherri when they stepped onto the cedar deck.

"Please, be seated," said Janet, as she and Sherri walked around the table and sat on the opposite bench.

Sherri had purposely chosen to sit across from Drake, not knowing how to act, wishing to avoid any unnecessary discomfort for herself, or for Thad.

Bill Drake lifted a large black briefcase from the deck's floor and plunked it atop the table. Thumbing the three wheels of the built-in combination lock, he asked, "How much time do you ladies have?"

Janet shrugged and looked to Sherri. "I have no solid plans for the rest of the day."

"Neither do I," Sherri agreed.

Drake opened the brief case and left it open. He turned it sideways as to keep it from blocking his view of Sherri. "Before I go any further," he said, matter-of-factly, "I am going to ask Thad to absent himself for a few minutes." He looked directly at Thad and said, "Go take a walk or something. I want you out of earshot."

Thad looked surprised. "I thought we were going to do this together."

Drake jerked his head toward the steps.

Thad rose and walked around the table and quickly bounced down the steps behind Sherri and Janet.

Sherri tried to sneak a peek at Thad as he jogged toward Uncle Jake's. Her heart beat in cadence with his footsteps. "He sure is a fine young man," she muttered.

"Young lady," Drake said solemnly, "it would be kind of you to tell *him* that. He really needs to hear it from *you*. He has whipped himself over and over these past four months."

"When the time is right. I really want to, but I want the time to be right."

"Okay, now let's get down to business. First, I want to compliment you, Sherri, for being patient with me. I appreciate your cooperation the past four months. I know you were aching to hear what all happened in the case. I trust that your business at Youngstown has been pretty well completed."

"Yes, sir. I have only a few matters to attend to. But nothing that would require that I spend more than a day or so in Ohio."

"Thad and I have been very busy, working with the FBI, the State Police, Monongalia County Sheriff's Department and the Preston County Sheriff's Department. Collectively, we have gathered an astonishing amount of evidence against Angela Hillman, Richard Martel, Janet's kidnappers, and a host of others. The county, state, and federal prosecutors are thoroughly convinced we have plenty of information to get several felony convictions against them all."

Sherri rubbed the goose bumps on her upper arms. A sense of victory crept over her.

He became sullen. "Not all is good news, though."

"What news could be bad enough to counter what you've shared thus far?" She gasped at the thought. "Please, don't tell me something has happened to Uncle Joseph? Please, assure me that he is still alive and well?"

"Actually, we have no news at all concerning Joseph. We have checked with the hospitals throughout West Virginia and all the surrounding states. We have even searched for him at the various Veterans' Administration hospitals. We have concluded that the wound he received while freeing Janet is nonfatal. Otherwise, he would have been found by now."

"So, what is the bad news?"

"Just as you have maintained all along, Angela Hillman is behind everything that's been done against Joseph. We have obtained enough evidence and several witnesses that should win Angela a rather long prison sentence. We've learned that she is the queen of an unbelievably large criminal kingdom."

"I hate to sound vindictive, but that hardly classifies as bad news."

"Right. The bad news is that she and Richard Martel have disappeared. Even though most of their inner circle has been arrested and many of them are willing to testify against them—only if they are assured that the pair is incarcerated, but not where they could get to them, or dead—none of them are offering any help locating them."

"What have they got to fear? Angela and Martel can't get to them in jail, can they?"

"Most of these people have families to worry about."

"Oh, my!" She grabbed Janet's arm and said, "We know how ruthless these kind of thugs can be."

Janet swiped her hand across her forehead and announced, "I just felt a raindrop. Maybe we better go inside."

"You girls go on in. I'll walk down to Jake's and get Thad."

Janet said, "No need." She thrust her right hand to her mouth and pressed her index finger in one corner of her mouth and her pinky in the other and pierced the mountain air with a blood-curdling whistle.

Thad, Jake and Wilma froze in mid-motion and looked toward them.

Janet waved for Thad and yelled, "Get up here, boy."

"Sherri," Drake said hurriedly, "that boy is nearing his breaking point. He's been walking on pins and needles, worrying himself sick over you. And Satan has buffeted him with what he is about to reveal to you. It will shake your timbers, but not more than it has Thad's. Be easy on him."

Sherri whispered to Janet, "Let's keep the same seating arrangement."

Janet sneered but obliged her anyhow. She sat beside Sherri across from the vacant seat.

Thad darted into the kitchen and remarked, "It is starting to rain cats and dogs out there." He pulled out the vacant chair and quickly sat. He then asked Drake, "How much did you tell them?"

Drake grabbed a large yellow envelope from the briefcase and set it in front of Thad. "Just the basic update on arrests and that we don't know of Angela's, Martel's or Joseph's whereabouts."

Thad shoved the envelope back toward Drake. "Come on, Brother Drake," he protested. "You have less to lose. It would be better coming from you."

With a firm fatherly tone, Drake insisted, "You must, Thad." He pushed it back in front of him. "Do it any way you wish. But, you must do it… Read it to them, summarize it for them, or let them read it themselves—it doesn't matter how. Just do it."

Thad angrily scooted his chair away from the table and sprang to his feet. Pacing nervously across the kitchen he exclaimed, "I'm telling you, Bill, this is a bad idea."

Drake sat erect in his chair, defiantly crossed his arms over his chest, and resolutely looked straight ahead.

Thad banged his fist against the refrigerator and scolded, "How can you be so cold, Bill?" He returned to pacing the floor, only this time with more rapid jerky steps. "Sherri doesn't need to know all this—not about…" He wrapped his hands around the back of his neck and squeezed his head between his arms nearly touching his elbows together in front of his forehead. He held the position for several seconds, then stepped close to his stock-still friend, "Here's how it is," he snarled, "I'd just as soon she hate me for the rest of her life based on what information she has. No, sir. We aren't doing this."

Drake jumped from his chair and poked Thad's chest with the index finger of his trembling left hand. "This isn't just police work, boy… This is spiritual warfare. Hold forth the shield of faith. Perfect love casteth out fear."

Thad started to turn away.

Drake grabbed two fists full of Thad's shirt and shouted, "If you love this girl as you claim, fight Satan for *her*, if not for yourself. Don't you dare cower, now." He let go of Thad's shirt and walked swiftly to the living room and dropped to his knees before the couch.

Sherri's heart broke for Thad. Should she rush to his side? Should she go to prayer, too? She looked to Janet for advice, but Janet also appeared dumbfounded.

Thad wilted into the chair vacated by Drake, and laid his head facedown on the table, with his hands folded between his knees.

Sherri rose slowly, walked to his side, and knelt beside him. She began rubbing his back with her right hand. "Thad," she whispered, "do you love me that much, that you can be so torn over whatever is in that big envelope?" She raised her head and waited for a nod. She felt him convulse and saw a puddle of tears stream slowly along the thin crevice between the black cherry tabletop and the veneer edge molding. Finally, he nodded yes. He raised his head and peered into her eyes. His chin quivered as he spoke. "I don't know if I'm allowed to love you, Sherri… But I do. Even if I knew that you could never love me as deeply, I couldn't say anything—true or not—that I think may hurt you. I thought I wanted to share this information with you. Maybe it's best that we just forget about the big envelope and its contents."

She pulled herself from the floor and pressed her lips quietly and tenderly on the top of his head. She walked around to his right side and sat where he had sat earlier. She laid her hands on top of the envelope, gazed upon it, and asked, "If I were to explore what's in here, would I disappoint you or quench your love for me?"

"No, Sherri. Nothing you or anyone else could say or do would change how I feel toward you." He turned sideways in his chair keeping his hands clasped between his knees. "Even if you told me to get lost—I'd not push myself on you—but I'll always love you."

His proclamation flattered her. It also intimidated her. Is it possible to be loved that profoundly? Could she love *him* as intensely? He deserves nothing less. "Thad, I believe that whatever is in here, though it may be life-shattering, somehow holds the key to freeing you from whatever horror it holds over you. Sure, it may shake me. Remember what you told me early in our quest for justice. You warned that we must be strong because we were likely to encounter very difficult challenges. You've been strong for me. Now it's my turn to be strong for you."

Thad chuckled nervously. "You'll never run me off with that kind of talk."

"Maybe I'm not trying to chase you away."

He flashed a boyish grin and reached for the envelope. "We'll go through this stuff together. I'll need to explain some things along the way. If it's okay with you, we'll wait for Janet and Deacon Drake to get done praying."

She hadn't even noticed that Janet left the room. "Fair enough. If I fix a pot of coffee, will you have some?"

"Yes. I'd like that."

CHAPTER TWENTY-TWO

Saturday, September 8, 1979

Janet and Mr. Drake rejoined Sherri and Thad at the kitchen table.

Drake, sitting across from Thad and to Janet's right, fixed his eyes on the large yellow envelope that now lay in front of Sherri. "I see you are making progress, Thad."

"Yes, sir. We were waiting for you and Janet."

"Well, how do you figure on handling it?"

Thad reached for the envelope and said, "Sherri, let me share this information one piece at a time."

"However you wish," she said.

He opened the flap and pulled out a photocopy of an official-looking document. He placed it in front of Sherri and explained, "Even though this exonerates me in the death of Frank, I want you to know it pains me to reveal it to you. This is the official summary by State Police Sergeant Travis; the trooper assigned to investigate the incident."

Sherri felt astonishingly calm—not at all what she imagined she should feel. She read aloud, "'Attached, are documents and sworn statements supporting my official conclusion that the death of Franklin D. Mosley resulted from a self-inflicted gunshot to the center of the forehead.

"'The duty weapon surrendered by Officer Thaddeus Ashbury, Star City Police Department, and certified by the Star City Chief of Police as being the weapon officially carried by Officer Ashbury and from which two rounds had been fired during the herein referenced gunfight with the above named Mr. Mosley—Sunday, May 6th 1979 at approximately 0400 hours—did not inflict the wound that caused Mr. Mosley's death. Officer Ashbury's duty weapon inflicted only minor injury to the deceased. The pathologist's report indicates that one round from Officer Ashbury's gun struck Mr. Mosley in the right bicep, shattering the humerus three inches below the shoulder joint and lodging in the triceps. The second round, retrieved from the trunk of a poplar tree at the scene, matched Officer Ashbury's duty weapon.

"'Attachment 'C' documents the ballistics test performed on the .22 caliber revolver recovered at the scene. Note that the bullet retrieved from occipital lobe of Mr. Mosley's brain during the autopsy matches the .22 caliber revolver. Also, the fingerprints on the gun were those of Mr. Mosley and of a former felon named Richard Alan Martel, whose whereabouts is unknown as of this report date.'"

Stupefied by what she had just read, Sherri slouched back in her chair. She turned her face away from the others to ponder it.

Thad gently touched her left hand, which slightly trembled beside the report.

Unsure what she felt—something between relief that Thad didn't kill Frank, after all, and guilt for having been partly responsible for his death—she slipped her hand from beneath Thad's and slowly stumbled to the door leading to the deck. There she stood speechless for several seconds, then toddled back to her seat. She gazed into Thad's eyes and pleaded, "Please, tell me there is some logical explanation for Frank's insanity that night?"

Thad pulled out a photocopied hand written letter. "I'm afraid that none of this is logical. However, this, Frank's own confession of his involvement in Spike Cottrell's murder…"

Sherri beckoned with her hand, for Thad to be quiet. Immediately, she recognized Frank's handwriting. "Just give me a minute to digest what I've already learned. I have a notion that this letter is going to prove to be even more shocking than the investigator's remarks."

Thad gingerly laid the paper down and rested his hands on top as if to keep her from reading it. "We don't have to do this all at once, Sherri."

"Thad, I know this is going to sound a bit goofy. But maybe I can absorb it more easily if you share it with Janet. I'll try to hear it as if by happenstance."

Thad looked to Drake as to invoke his advice.

"It doesn't sound so far-fetched to me," Drake said. "It may create sort of a psychological buffer for her."

Janet volunteered to read the letter aloud. "Sherri, maybe you ought to move your chair back from the table. Maybe you can sit over against the sink counter."

"Yeah. I think that's a good idea." She dreaded what might be revealed, but found it impossible to defer.

"Before you read it," said Thad, "let me explain how we obtained the letter. The manager of the Holiday Inn called my police chief on Monday morning—the day after the shooting. Frank had asked the desk clerk to secure a package for him, just an hour before the incident. The clerk locked it in a safe, designated for securing guests' valuables. He had forgotten about it until he returned to work the next night. He notified the manager, who in turn, notified my chief. The chief called the state police since they were investigating the shooting. They burned a copy for us and dropped it off to the chief." He paused and gestured to Janet.

"'I, Frank D. Mosley, born February 3, 1949 at Youngstown, Ohio, and presently in my right mind, do write this confession of my own free will and having told no one of it.

"'On July 14, 1968 I brutally beat, to death, Charles (Spike) Cottrell at the urging of Angela Short (now Angela Hillman), for the cash sum of $10,000 hand-delivered to me by Angela, early the next morning. I hid the baseball bat, used in the slaying, under the building that now houses the Blue Cat Café. If it has not been removed, you need only to dislodge one sandstone from the foundation. I tossed the ball bat under the building and then reset the loose stone. It is the third stone from the corner nearest the Logan Apartments.

"'Tonight, Saturday, May 6th, 1979, I intend to murder Officer Thad Ashbury of the Star City Police Department. Officer Ashbury is about to expose Angela Hillman and me. I can't live with my conscience anyhow, but I am not leaving Ashbury behind just so he can have my wife, Sherri. After I kill Ashbury I plan to kill myself.'" Janet let the letter fall to the table as she stared blankly at Thad.

Sedated by shock, Sherri staggered to the table and picked up the letter. Silently, she read it for herself. She laid it back down and walked rubber-legged to the door. Through its window she blurrily focused on the distant hills where they became one with the dark gray sky. She rubbed her eyes, not sure if the scripture before her floated in physical view or in her mind. She maintained her glare toward the hills and fluted, "I will lift up mine eyes unto the hills, from whence cometh my help. My help cometh from the LORD, which made heaven and earth."

"Sherri," Thad called out, "you and Janet haven't read the back page. Do you wish to postpone it until you've had time to decipher everything else?"

Still transfixed on the distant horizon, she answered, "I want to know what else Frank revealed. I don't want to read it. Maybe someone else can read it aloud like Janet did."

Drake reached for the letter, and began reading, "'Angela Hillman's contract on Reverend Joseph Short's life is still in effect. There are at least three people actively hunting for him in hopes of collecting the $200,000 prize for his death…'"

Janet screamed, "Stop it." She wailed uncontrollably for several seconds and squalled, "Oh God, please… Oh God, please…Not Joseph…" She dropped to her knees with a thud and sobbed uncontrollably.

Sherri forced herself to keep staring out the window, hoping that somehow the agony would miraculously dissipate. She had nearly convinced herself that Janet would be fine without her intervention. Finally, when Janet's lamenting quieted, Sherri sat on the floor beside her and stroked her long thick black hair. Knowing words would not suffice, she chose to remain silent and just be there for her.

Eventually, Thad helped them to their chairs, while Deacon Drake poured them each a cup of coffee and sat it before them, and then poured some for himself and Thad.

Sherri asked Thad, "Has the ball bat been found?"

"Yes. It is still at the State Police Forensics Lab."

"Have we identified the three persons Frank mentioned as actively hunting for Uncle Joseph?"

"We can only guess. Hopefully, they are among the many we now have behind bars."

"I just can't reconcile the fact that I hadn't even a slight suspicion that Frank had murdered Spike. He acted so surprised at the news that Spike had been killed."

"Well, we can be sure this letter is authentic. The FBI handwriting analysis expert certified that, when compared to Frank's signature on various bank documents, his life insurance policy, and his truck registration, it is unquestionable that he penned the entire letter."

Sherri picked the letter up again and checked the signature. "That is definitely Frank's signature." Her eyes fell on the statement following the signature, and she read it aloud. "'In case anyone doubts my signature, I affix my left thumb print dabbed in my own blood.'"

Janet suggested that Frank still could have been forced to write the letter. "And we can't be sure someone didn't cut him and make him leave the bloody thumb print. After all, who in their right mind would even think to do something like that?"

Sherri's eyes widened and her jaw dropped. "Hold that thought," she exclaimed, and then ran to the bedroom. She dug to the bottom of one of the boxes and pulled out a book, then raced back to the kitchen. Throwing it on the table, she said, "Frank bought this book. Read the title."

Janet read aloud, "*With My Own Blood.*"

"Frank copycatted the closing scene in that novel. When he gave it to me to read, he said, 'Don't cheat. But I assure you that you'll love the ending.'"

Drake spoke up. "I should have caught that. I read that book, too."

Janet said, "I would never have guessed that Frank did much reading. Especially, not fiction."

"Actually," Sherri replied, "this is the only book I've *ever* known him to read."

Thad clasped his hands together and said, "Now that we have worked through the most shocking elements of the presentation, let me finish."

Sherri beheld him with great anticipation, not daring to avert her attention to anything or anyone else.

He reached inside the envelope and drew out a small hollow-barreled chrome key. He waved it past each of them and said, "Read the inscription on the orange handle of this key."

Sherri asked, "What's so significant about that? Frank had been a member of Stoney's Gym for about three years. He probably rented a locker there."

"Bill, would you like to explain this one?"

"Sure. On a whim, I had gone to the scene of the shoot-out, hoping I'd uncover something important that may have been missed by the officials investigating the case. I really didn't expect to find anything. I saw it lying there—half way imbedded in the grass about where Frank's body had lain. I picked it up and started to put it in my pocket—just in case. But I saw the inscription and reasoned that I had never heard of Stoney's Gym. Then I wondered if it could have been Frank's. I called Youngstown directory assistance and learned that there were two Stoney's Gyms—one at Dayton, and of course, one at Youngstown. I visited the Youngstown facility and asked the proprietor if I could check the locker this key fits. He pointed to the back wall and kept on reading."

"Yeah," Sherri interrupted. "But what's so important about that?"

Drake chuckled. "Hold your britches, girl. I'm getting there. I found a blue and white canvass gym bag stuffed into the top compartment. Inside the gym bag were several bundles of money. I took the zipped bag to the owner and asked if he had anything belonging to him or to the gym in locker seventeen. He grunted, 'no'. When I asked if he wanted to see what I'm removing from his premises he gave me a look that clearly warned that I better leave him alone. So, I took it with me. Once I got back to my car I sat there and counted it -- $150,000—all bills."

Sherri's mouth dropped open. "Uh...Uh...Uh. How could Frank have gotten that kind of cash? And without me knowing about it?"

Janet said angrily, "Let me guess. Advance payment for killing Thad."

Drake raised his eyebrows and shrugged his shoulders. "We have no idea. We may never know. Just so you don't get your hopes up regarding the money, Sherri, it has been turned over to the authorities. A judge is scheduled to rule whether it is to be released to Frank's widow. The ruling won't happen until sometime in the spring of 1980. The judge said that if by then there is no solid evidence that the money is connected to illegal activity, he will release it directly to a bank of your choice."

Thad gathered up the items and stuffed them into the envelope, tossed it into Drake's briefcase and announced that he had to be going.

"Me, too," said Drake. "Sherri, let's you and me pick up with this business Monday morning. We still have some work to do...Oh, and we have a few new cases to start working." He closed his briefcase and opened his arms to invite hugs from everyone. "Now, you girls get plenty of rest. God knows, you need it after what we put you through, today."

Monday, September 10, 1979

Sherri tapped her fingers on the conference table at the Preston County Sheriff's Department. Something about the small room and its drab furnishings seemed to smother her.

As if he had read her mind, Bill Drake said, "Sometimes it takes a while. She'll be here. They have a lot going on in jails that the uninitiated wouldn't suppose."

"Yeah, but if you knew Ramona Fenton you wouldn't be so sure she hasn't changed her mind."

The conference room door swung open and Ramona, with cuffs hooked to a chain that ran through the loops of her orange jumper, entered with a look of surrender. The female correctional officer ushered her to a seat across the table from Sherri and Drake. She pointed to a black phone sitting on a small corner stand and said,

"When you're finished just pick up that phone receiver. When someone answers tell them to send me to get inmate Fenton."

Bill Drake introduced himself and then Sherri.

"I know, Sherri," she said. Then with a measure of humility, that Sherri would not have thought her capable of, she said to Sherri, "I just hope you can let bygones be bygones."

"I can."

"I don't have anyone besides Dad. Can you tell me how he is doing?" A lone tear crept down her round face.

"I'm afraid he is not well. The doctors tell us he may never recover the ability to walk or to speak. The brutal beating he endured had caused a significant amount of brain damage."

A flood overtook the lone tear and Ramona sniffled in an apparent attempt to dam up her emotions.

Sherri pitied her. She now seemed incapable of the meanness that got her locked up and that led to Ellis' vegetated state.

Drake made clear to Ramona that he and Sherri agreed to meet with her only as a courtesy. "I don't know that you can offer much to our cause."

She hung her head and replied, "Well, I've had a lot of time to think things over these past four months."

"Yes. I'm sure you have," said Drake.

"Like I said—I don't have anybody. I have nothing to lose. Bobby still refuses to cooperate with the authorities, after promising them he would." She lifted her head and leaned forward, staring Sherri in the eyes. "Wanna know why I tried to kill Bobby Stafford? He's the one who got me in a jam with the guys who are responsible for trying to kill my dad. Bobby and I were too involved with their illegal drug trade. Because Bobby had himself so deeply indebted to them, I sold out my own Dad to save *his* hide." She sat back and stared at her handcuffs. Somberly, she said, "I hope they give me and Bobby both the death penalty. Or at least lock us away until we *rot*."

Drake kindly replied, "Ramona, I want you to understand that Sherri and I can't offer you *anything* for your cooperation. We certainly are in no position to help you with your legal woes."

"Yes, sir. I know that. I guess I just need to clear my conscience."

He folded his hands atop the table. "Well, Miss Fenton, you go right ahead and clear your conscience. I don't mean this in a condescending way, but the authorities have arrested or at least indicted about all the main players in Angela Hillman's many-faceted criminal activity. That is why we don't think you can offer us or the authorities a whole lot."

She said, meekly, "The staff here at the jail provide us with a daily newspaper. I have been following the news with great interest—as you might expect. I haven't seen anything about Marcus Hillman being charged with anything."

Sherri asked Drake, "Is she correct? Marcus Hillman hasn't been charged with anything—not even conspiracy to some of the illegal dealings of his wife?"

"She *is* correct. None of the prosecutors—State, County, nor Federal—are satisfied with what little evidence has been offered. They don't think they can get a grand jury to bind him over for trial."

Ramona leaned back in her chair and grinned triumphantly. "If you can promise me anonymity—not that I have much to lose, and I'm not afraid of these scum—I can hand Marcus Hillman to you, on a silver platter."

Drake reminded her that he and Sherri couldn't promise her anything. "But I will do my best to influence the powers-that-be to take into account your cooperation. I promise you that I won't voluntarily give them your name until I feel certain they will oblige your request for anonymity."

She cocked her head to the left and rolled her eyes mischievously and said, "No. Scratch that idea. Maybe they ought to know that one of their 'nobodies' gave them up. Especially, Marcus Hillman—the arrogant jerk. Yeah. Here is what you do."

Drake parked the car facing the building and waited there while Sherri visited the Magistrates' Clerk.

Sherri approached the counter and waited. Minutes later, Brenda Flowers returned from down the hall. "Sherri?" She looked around as to be sure no one could hear her conversation. "I am so glad to see you.

I've been trying to reach you but he phone number you gave a few months back had been changed to an unlisted number."

Whispering, she said, "I'm sorry. I didn't even think to contact you. Anyhow, Ramona Fenton said that you may have something for me."

"Yes. I think I do. Where and when can we meet? It will have to be no earlier than 4:30 this afternoon."

"Do you have the evening free?"

"Sure. I'm divorced and there is no serious suitor. And no children."

"Good. Come to my friend's house for supper. Do you have a piece of paper?"

Brenda handed her a small note pad.

While writing the directions she said, "You'll like Janet. I am living with her for now. She'll be thrilled to meet you—especially when she learns that you have incriminating evidence on Marcus Hillman."

"What time do you want me there?"

"Around six, for supper. But you can come as early as five."

"Perfect."

Sherri yearned to know what Brenda had obtained, but dared not ask for fear of being overheard.

After supper, Brenda excused herself and went to her car to get the surprise, which Janet asked not to be revealed until after they had eaten. She had said, "I like the suspense."

Sherri held open the door and directed Brenda to, "Set it on the coffee table."

Brenda slid open the large white cardboard drawer and lifted out a plain white department store garment box and handed it to Sherri.

Sherri lifted the top half of the box and let it drop onto the coffee table. She removed, one-by-one, the enlarged photographs, briefly studied them and passed them on to Janet. One picture—the forty-eighth of a lot of fifty—caught her attention more than the others had. "I knew that sooner or later Pete Pagone would come up dirty. Yeah, punk, we got you now!" She turned the picture so Brenda could see it and said, "I know Magistrate Pagone and Richard Martel. Who is the guy with the gaudy ring and diamond-studded wristwatch?"

"Oh, that is the illustrious Marcus Hillman. Look at the picture Janet has. See the envelope in Marcus' right hand?"

"Yeah."

"Okay, now look at the next to the last photo."

"Okay. He is handing the envelope to Pagone."

"And the last photo. Is Ramona a skilled photographer, or what? What a close-up! Huh?"

"Wow!" Janet blurted. "What a stack of green."

Sherri counted the fanned out bills in Pete Pagone's hands, "One, two, three, four, five, six, seven, eight, nine, ten. Am I seeing right? Are those all $1,000 bills?"

Janet asked, "How did Ramona manage to take such telling pictures? Why? I mean, it seems to me she had to have taken a dangerous risk."

Sherri laughed. "To look at that girl, you'd never suspect she could be so clever. But, to tell you the truth, I'm not surprised at her insane bravery."

Brenda reached into the large cardboard drawer again. She lifted out a metal box, eight inches square and four inches deep. "Check this out."

Janet flipped up the metal latch and lifted the lid. "Audio cassette tapes."

"Don't tell me," Sherri insisted. "She recorded the conversations corresponding to the various photographed meetings."

Brenda laughed. "I'm telling you, this girl is crazy."

"But how? Why?"

"Pagone had been sneaking around with Ramona, cheating on his wife. Ramona said that she tired of him always wanting to meet her in secluded and lowly places. She said she finally had enough of his empty promises."

Sherri quipped, "How does that adage go? Oh, yeah—hell hath no fury like that of a woman scorned."

"Hey," Brenda said excitedly, "Would you like to hear some of the recording that goes with that picture of Pete receiving money from Marcus?"

"I don't know… It will probably make me so mad the rest of the evening will be ruined."

"Well," Janet ordered, "go in another room or go outside. I want to hear it."

Sherri teased, "Nag, nag, nag. Go ahead, there is no way I am going to resist listening, if you play it."

Janet popped the cassette into the player, pushed play and sat on the floor in front of the floor model stereo system.

"You just make sure that Joseph Short gets locked up and that he is denied bail. Richard, here, will make sure he doesn't come out alive."

Janet quickly pressed the pause button. "So, that is Marcus Hillman talking, at the time Ramona is taking the picture?"

"Yeah. I told you, she's crazy."

Sherri strolled across the room and eased into the recliner. "What I don't get is why she thought she could trust *you.* I would have been afraid of the possibility that you were in the click at the Magistrates' office."

"Ramona and I were classmates at the West Virginia Career College. Then, after I had been working at the Magistrates' office for quite a while, I saw her at the mall. I had no idea at the time that she and Pete had anything going on. She had commented that my job must be interesting and then she asked if I liked working for the magistrates. Of course, if I had known about her affair with Pete I would not have told her how I detested him."

"Oh, my! Just think how that could have backfired on you?"

Janet ejected the cassette tape and returned it to the metal box. "Yeah, but how did *you* get possession of all this evidence."

"Fortunately, I usually get the mail for the office and distribute it. One day, a letter arrived, addressed to me. It had no return address. Across the top of the envelope, in big letters, she had printed the word CONFIDENTIAL. When I thought I could read it without anyone in the office seeing me, I opened it. Actually, it was just a note, asking me to come to the Preston County jail to visit her. And a P.S. that asked that I tell *no one* of my visit with her."

"Yeah, but I know she didn't have this in jail with her."

"During my visit she told me about it. Before she would agree to reveal where she hid it, I had to promise never to arbitrarily divulge its existence. She asked me to get it and secure it where only *I* would know of its whereabouts. She feared that Hillman or some of his cohorts might find it. She asked that I give it up only after she is dead or if she sends someone for it."

CHAPTER TWENTY-THREE

Saturday, December 15, 1979

"Hey, Sherri," Drake called over the intercom.

"Yes, sir."

"Shouldn't you be going? It is getting late. Or have you and Thad cancelled your dinner date?"

"Oh, my! I lost track of time. Thanks, Mr. Drake." She had grown accustomed to working long hours, often way into the late night. And most non-investigative time she spent either searching for Uncle Joseph or visiting with Ellis Fenton at the nursing home. Between *her* schedule and Thad's, their time together had dramatically decreased. But her fondness for him only grew stronger. She sure didn't want to dampen his liking for her by not being ready when he comes calling.

Sherri politely scolded, "You should have told me we were coming here." She had only heard talk of the luxurious Little Paris. Only the wealthiest romantics could afford such extravagance. "I appreciate the gesture, but this is a little out of your…our affordability."

"What kind of surprise would it be if I had told you we were dining here?"

"Yeah, but I could have shopped for an appropriate evening gown or other attire for such an elaborate date. I mean, this is the kind of place where the women wear only the best clothes and flashy jewelry. I'm going to stick out like a sore thumb."

He bounded from the truck and scurried to open her door. "When the other women—and the men—in this joint see my ravishing date they will all envy. Most women need all the costly help they can get and still can't compare to you. Besides I am equally poorly dressed."

Both Sherri and Thad declined dessert. Only the centerpiece bouquet, two slender white candles, and their long stemmed glasses—filled with nonalcoholic Champaign—remained.

Thad rose gracefully and stepped theatrically to Sherri's left side, and knelt.

Her heart raced as she gave him a shaky grin.

He took her by the left hand while pulling a diamond ring from the right pocket of his suit jacket.

The candlelight danced on the big shiny stone, mesmerizing her. She barely squeaked, "Oh, Thad!"

"Sherri, I practiced this at home. I had an eloquent proposal speech figured out, but..." He cleared his throat. "I'm not good at fancy talk...Will you marry me?"

She threw herself at him intending only to hug him. She knocked him to the floor and landed on top of him. Red hot from embarrassment, she quickly rolled off to a sitting position and tried to regain whatever dignity might be had. Thad's dazed look almost instantaneously washed away her self-consciousness.

He sprang to a sit-up position, looked all around at the other diners and shrugged. "I think that is a yes."

The entire room erupted with applause as he leaped to his feet, pulled Sherri up and passionately kissed her. Then stepping away, he said, "Oh, no! The ring. I dropped the ring."

An elderly gentleman at the table to his right, with a broad smile, reached toward him and said, "Here, son."

Thad whipped his handkerchief from his rear pocket and wiped his forehead. "Whew! Thank you, sir."

He slid the ring on her finger, kissed her on the cheek, and whispered, "How do we bow out of here?"

Taking advantage of another round of applause she replied, "Like this." She curtsied and led Thad by the hand, amid more clapping and celebratory whistles.

Monday, December 17, 1979

"Sherri," the secretary called from the front office, "there's a handsome young policeman here to see you."

"Well, I love a man in uniform. Send him in, Claire."

Thad closed the door behind him. "I had business at the courthouse. I thought I'd drop by to share something with you. I happened to be at the station typing a vandalism report this morning when someone called, asking for *me*. The chief motioned for me to pick up the phone. The kook had seen our engagement announcement in the newspaper."

"Huh. An old flame trying to rekindle the fire, I suppose."

"Hardly. *He* wouldn't give his name and refused to explain why he insists that you and I can't marry."

"Oh, well now. That's better. *I* must have a secret admirer."

"Hey, Sherri, this guy seemed very determined to dissuade me from marrying you. His voice sounded like that of an elderly man."

"Gee, Thad. Lighten up. It's just some weirdo. He's probably got nothing to do but make prank calls to entertain himself."

"Maybe you're right. But it really bothered me. At first, he demanded that we not marry. Then, he turned to begging me to break the engagement. He kept saying that he couldn't tell me why we couldn't marry. He said, 'It's downright immoral. It might even be illegal for you and Sherri to marry. Just do the right thing and call off this marriage.'"

Sherri snickered. "Maybe I'm taking this too lightly. But I suspect the man is just another of Angela Hillman's puppets. They're desperate to cause division between us. Get your mind on something else. Go chase some bad guys or something."

Janet folded the newspaper and tossed it across the room at Sherri, striking her square in the face.

"What?"

"I'm talking to you, but you're miles away."

"I'm contemplating whether Thad and I should forget about going to see my parents. If it weren't for Daddy I'd not even bother letting them know Thad and I are getting married."

"Maybe your mother has had a change of heart. Give her the opportunity to reconnect with you."

"That's just it, Janet. Mom and I have never connected in the first place. She has always shunned me. And Dad never had the guts to stand up for me. He'd never defended *himself*, for that matter. If it weren't for Thad's insistence, I'd scrap the whole notion and leave well-enough alone."

"Hey, Janet," Jake shouted from the bottom of the deck steps.

Janet scampered to the kitchen and yanked open the frosted sliding glass door. "What's the matter, Uncle Jake?"

"Bill Drake has been trying to call you girls for more than an hour. Your line has been busy."

"No one has been on the phone."

Sherri glanced over at the phone and saw that it had been knocked off its cradle. "Some big footed gal must have kicked it off when she laid across her recliner. I wonder who that could have been, Janet?"

"Sorry, Uncle Jake," said Janet. "I'll call Deacon Drake right away."

"No. No. He called from the hospital."

"Is he okay?"

"Yeah, *he* is fine."

Sherri ran barefoot to the kitchen and pushed past Janet and onto the snow covered deck. "It isn't Thad, is it? Please, tell me that Thad hasn't gotten in a wreck or anything?"

Jake made a feeble attempt at sounding calm. "You girls get your shoes and coats on and come down to the house. You can ride with me and Wilma." He turned quickly and trotted toward home.

Sherri stood motionless for a couple moments, paralyzed by Jake's unspoken answer to her question. "Oh, Janet, something terrible has happened to Thad—I just know it."

Bill Drake stood to greet them as they entered the O. R. waiting room.

One by one they hugged Drake and took a seat. He motioned for Sherri to take the seat next to his.

Afraid the answer would be unbearable, Sherri waited for someone else to inquire about Thad's condition.

Drake took Sherri by the hand and carefully explained, "The O. R. nurse came out about fifteen minutes ago. She said that they were able to remove the bullet from his brain. It's too early to tell whether he will pull through."

Sherri sat in stunned silence, trying to convince herself that it is all just a nightmare. This couldn't be happening. Every muffled word Drake spoke seemed to pass through a filter before reaching her numbed consciousness.

Drake continued, "He stood on his porch waving goodbye to me as I backed out of his driveway. I heard the gunshot that sounded like it came from a high-powered rifle. And then, I saw his body slam into the corner where the banister butts up against the house. Before I could get out of the vehicle he slumped to the porch deck."

Jake stood and turned toward the window and glared outside for a few seconds. "Did they get the shooter?"

"I don't know. I doubt it. I suspect whoever shot him is a professional. I looked all around as I ran to attend to Thad, but didn't see anyone. I can't even be sure where the shot came from. Other than the fact that it struck him in the left rear side of his head, which indicates that the shot came from the woods near his home." He turned again toward Sherri, "I'm so sorry, Sherri. I thought I had the bleeding stopped, but by the time I returned to the porch from calling the sheriff's office, Thad had lost a lot more blood"

Sherri cupped her hands over her mouth and darted for the restroom between her and the hallway. She heaved violently, emptying herself. Too weak to stand she dropped to her knees beside the commode and dry-heaved several times more before collapsing.

Tuesday, December 18, 1979

Sherri batted her eyes, trying to focus on the figure poised at her left side and looking down at her.

"Sherri, can you hear me?"

She tried to ask, "Is that you, Janet?" Something restricted her mouth from moving. Unable to raise up and finding it nearly impossible to move her head, she rolled her eyes around the room. She could hear medical monitoring equipment and an oxygen unit. She soon concluded that somehow she landed in the intensive care unit of the hospital.

"Sherri, it's me…Janet. If you can understand me signify it by batting your eyes twice."

She responded according to Janet's request.

"Good," Janet said. She turned away and pleadingly called, "Aunt Wilma."

Sherri couldn't turn her head or raise it to see where Janet went. Her eyes just wouldn't roll far enough.

Wilma stepped into view and stroked Sherri's hair as if to brush her bangs from her forehead. "The doctors said you had an aneurysm in your stomach, that ruptured. They told us that if you hadn't already been at the hospital they might not have been able to save you. But now you're doing fine. We sure thank God that you'll be okay."

Sherri became angry at the inability to ask how Thad is doing. How she desired to cry aloud what she said to herself in forced silence—"If Thad dies I don't want to live either."

Wilma rubbed the back of her hand over Sherri's cheek, "The nurse said that you'd probably be moved from intensive care to a private room in the step-down unit, tomorrow. You'll likely be there for a couple days before being discharged from the hospital. The doctor said that you would be restricted in your physical activities for a while."

Sherri wondered if Wilma's son and daughter realized what wonderful people their parents are. If not, she sure would like to explain to them what life with an unloving mother would be like for them. She batted her eyes twice to signal to Wilma that she comprehended what she'd said.

Wilma turned and said gleefully, "She batted her eyes two quick bats."

Janet reappeared, alongside Wilma. She bent over the bed rail and kissed Sherri's forehead.

An unfamiliar male voice beckoned from just outside the room, "Ma'am, are you Miss Pixler?"

"Yes, sir," Janet answered as she walked away from the bed.

Sherri's senses were dulled but she could faintly hear, "I'm Doctor Upton. I understand that you are Mr. Ashbury's next of kin. Is that correct?"

"Yes. I guess I am."

"Well, does he have parents still living, or maybe a wife?"

Janet lowered her voice, "Neither. His mother died of cancer just after his twelfth birthday. His dad's whereabouts are unknown. He'd left Thad's mother and him a couple years before, and hasn't been in contact with any of us. His Uncle Jake and Aunt Wilma took him in until he moved out on his own at the age of sixteen. That's his fiancé in there."

Catching onto Janet's clue, Dr. Upton spoke in lower tones as well. "According to medical records on file, Thaddeus has you listed as the person to contact in an emergency. Under these circumstances I think it is within the hospital's policy and legal guidelines to ask you to decide whether he is to remain on life support systems and, if so, for how long. I can't arbitrarily order that the machines be disconnected."

Sherri wanted to scream out, "Please, don't disconnect anything. I'm praying for his recovery."

"Do I have to decide right now?" Janet asked. "He'll continue to receive whatever medical attention is needed if I don't make a decision this minute, right?"

"Yes. But I must tell you that I have consulted other doctors on staff and we unanimously conclude that he is highly unlikely to ever regain consciousness."

Sherri's heart sank with the news. "Oh, God," she pleaded. "I know you hear my thoughts. Please, work a miracle for Thad and me. I have never asked you for something more fervently than what I'm now petitioning you."

Wilma, who had turned to listen to the doctor's conversation with Janet, looked empathetically at Sherri. She wiped the side of Sherri's face and whispered, "Your pillow is soaked." She sniffled and wiped at her own tears. "Sherri, honey, you heard what the doctor said, didn't you?"

Sherri blinked twice.

"I'm so sorry. I don't think you were supposed to hear him." She called for Janet to come.

Janet came to the right side of the bed and wiped the right side of Sherri's face.

"Take her other hand," Wilma instructed as she gently held Sherri's left hand. "Let's pray."

Janet and Wilma poured their hearts out to God and prayed everything that Sherri had silently prayed.

Seconds after they prayed, while the three women kept silent as to hear God's answer, a female voice excitedly called out, "Dr. Upton, come quickly. Mr. Ashbury is sitting up and trying to communicate with us."

Wilma exclaimed, "Oh, Sherri, I gotta go see! Don't go anywhere—I'll be back."

Between the pent up jubilation over the miracle and the hilarity of Wilma telling her not to go anywhere, Sherri thought she surely would bust a gut. She strained, trying to shout praises in accord with those from the room nearby.

A nurse came running into her room at the sound of an alarm from one of the machines behind her. A second nurse came in before the first could silence the machine, and injected something into the I. V. port in Sherri's upper left arm—and she fell fast asleep.

Wednesday, December 19, 1979

"Hi, Sherri," the nurse said cheerfully. "It's good to see you're wide awake. A technician will be here in a few minutes to remove those bothersome tubes. You are doing great. I bet you are ready to go to a regular room."

Sherri surprised herself when she so easily nodded yes. She felt refreshed and lively. She grew steadily more cheerful with the loosing of each contraption.

"The nurse told me to wake you."

Sherri sleepily muttered, "Uh, huh." Her eyes fluttered as she started to turn away from the voice interfering with her restful slumber. Her eyes slipped open slightly, then sprang wide open at the sight of the man dressed in pajamas and a blue housecoat. "Thad!" she exclaimed, sounding like a parrot with a sore throat.

He bounded from the bedside chair as she sprang to a sit-up. While she cried joyfully in his embrace he reached for the button and raised the bed to support her sitting position.

"You gave me an awful scare," she said, pressing her cheek against his. She released the headlock and pushed him away to behold his face. Except for the bandage around his head his appearance gave no hint that he had, so recently, barely clung to life.

He grabbed the chair with one hand and kept hold of her hand with the other. Pulling the seat closer to the bed, he said, "I hear you scared everybody, too."

"Yeah. I guess I did. By the way, have they figured out who shot you?"

"Not yet." Responding to her expression of alarm, he said, "It's okay, Sherri. You know that God didn't miraculously heal me just to allow someone else to complete the job. Deacon Drake's brief forceful lecture about this all being more than police work keeps resounding in my head. Indeed, he is right—we are involved in spiritual warfare."

"That's interesting…you saying that just now. You woke me from a dream wherein I kept hearing a voice like distant thunder telling me, "This battle is mine. Be faithful, my child."

"What are you doing out of bed?" Janet asked, interrupting Sherri's daydream.

"Nothing. Just contemplating."

"Well, what are you contemplating? What else you can do to scare us all out of our wits?" She sat at the foot of the bed and joined Sherri, gazing out the window at the soft rays of light.

Sherri held fast her gaze. "I have this unshakeable feeling that somehow my plans to marry Thad are going to be destroyed."

"Oh, that's just aftershock. God didn't miraculously spare Thad's life just to have such an important relationship denied him. Nor did He bring you through such a life-threatening situation only to desert you, now."

"What if it isn't God's perfect plan for Thad and me? Then, what would either of us do?"

Janet kicked the arm of the chair. "Stop this. I mean it. Stop it, right now."

"Well, change the subject to something that will keep me distracted for a while."

"Let's see…" Janet said as she pressed her index fingers against her temples.

"Did you call my parents?"

"Oh, yeah," Janet said sarcastically. "I talked with your dear sweet mother."

Sherri giggled at Janet's apparent annoyance.

"If you think it's fun talking to her, *you* call her."

"There are so few people who can rattle your chain. Yet you let little ole Alice Lance stoke your fire. Look at you…turning all reddish orange like an overheated potbelly stove."

Janet stood up and marched around the bed and toward the hallway. She curtly turned an about face in the doorway. "Hi, Sherri. It's good to see you sitting up out of bed."

Sherri laughed, admiring Janet's ability to switch tracks so quickly.

Janet plopped onto the bed, and swung her legs. With the voice of a little girl, she said, "I talked to your mommy. She's really nice, ain't she?"

The more Sherri giggled, the more Janet poured it on. "You did?" she chuckled.

"Yeah. The poor thing can't come see you, for fear she'll get sick. She has a good point, you know. Just look around this place. Most of the people here are sick."

They laughed together for several seconds.

Sherri grabbed her abdomen and cried, "Okay. Okay. Oh, now I know what it means to laugh until it hurts."

Janet blew on the bent fingers of her right hand and then rubbed them on her blouse's left lapel.

"Okay," Sherri said, "Now, I'm in a good enough mood to hear what the queen of cynicism had to say."

"I told her that you had suffered a ruptured stomach aneurysm and that you were recovering from the near-fatal episode."

"Let me guess—'That girl is too mean to die.'"

Janet leaned forward supporting herself with her fists against the edge of the mattress, and hung her head. "I hate to even repeat the meanness that woman spews out."

"I'm sure you aren't going to repeat anything that I haven't already been told by her."

"Probably not. I just have a difficult time accepting that anyone can be so cold and heartless toward her own daughter. It isn't like you ever did anything to deserve such ridicule and bitterness. Has she ever given you a compliment or shown any concern for your feelings?"

"Not really. I suppose that is why Uncle Joseph's kindness toward me always meant so much… So, what did she say? I take it that she has no intentions of visiting me."

"I guess not. She said that if you'd settle down, all these bad things wouldn't keep happening to you."

Sherri grinned and then said, "See? She still loves me… But really, Mom's bitterness blows my mind. I don't know of any woman whose husband does as much as Dad does for her. For as long as I can remember, he gave her anything she wanted or needed. I've seen him work extra long hours and weeks at a time without a day off to provide for her every whim. But I don't recall her ever saying thanks or giving him a compliment."

"Huh. Imagine what it must be like for him. Especially now that he can no longer work and earn extra money to pamper her."

"I warned Thad about what to expect when he meets her. The doctors are planning on discharging me from the hospital tomorrow—provided nothing unexpected happens between now and then. Thad wants us to go see Mom and Dad within the next few days."

"Sherri, I didn't even mention Thad to her. I just told her that you were visiting someone in the hospital when you suffered the ruptured aneurysm. I guess I didn't want her to further lambaste you."

"If it weren't for my wanting Dad to give me away to Thad and Thad's insistence that we give reconciliation a chance between me and Mom, I'd really not bother."

CHAPTER TWENTY-FOUR

Saturday, December 22, 1979

Thad turned off state route one hundred into the brick driveway and parked his truck in front of the white block garage at the right rear corner of the property. The well-kept old two-story house with its white wood siding perfectly fit the small riverside town of Granville. He shut off the engine and said, "I think I've been here before." He slid from the truck and looked all about the fifty-foot by fifty-foot back yard.

Sherri climbed slowly out of the truck and walked reservedly to his side, and wrapped her hands around his left forearm. "I doubt that you've been here before, unless you were here on police business."

"No. I wouldn't respond to a call in Granville unless summoned by the Granville Police Department or the sheriff's office." He pointed to a large black-walnut tree at the far left corner of the lot. "I used to play here, with a little girl and her older brother. We often swung on a swing made from a piece of two-inch by eight-inch board and two ropes. It hung from that long branch right there. Of course, the tree has grown a bit."

She teased, "Yes. The tree has grown over the past twenty-five years or so. But it couldn't have been here that you played with the girl and her brother. I lived here from infancy through my entire childhood. Are you sure you played with those kids in Granville?"

He looked back toward the main road and said, "Yeah. I'm telling you, this is the exact house. I remember being able to see the Monongahela River from here. Directly across the road from this house there stood a much smaller house, only about thirty yards from the river. It couldn't have been more than two rooms. I remember thinking that it resembled a playhouse more than an actual residence."

"Thad I'm telling you, it couldn't have been here. I don't have a brother. But I do remember a little boy about my age coming with his dad to visit. Mom and T. J.'s dad made us play outside while they visited. Mom said that Levi, the boy's dad, and she were cousins. But as I grew older I wondered about them. He seemed to visit only during Dad's absence. Of course, I haven't seen T. J. since he and I were around five or six years old." The more she talked the wider Thad's smile stretched. "What? I'm serious. It couldn't have been here, where you played."

"Oh, but it is. I remember one incident that stands out. The little girl, named Sally, thought I had swung long enough, so she pelted me with walnuts she'd picked up from the ground." Laughing, he said, "They use to call me T. J. since those are my initials—Thaddeus James."

With a delightful chuckle, Sherri said, "Sherri Ann Lance—S. A. L.—Sal—Sally. And, by the way, you *were* hogging the swing that day."

"But who am I mistaking as your older brother?"

They chorused, "Uncle Joseph!"

"My Dad is Levi Ashbury," Thad said, enthusiastically. "You know what? I think your mom and my dad *were* something other than cousins. I remember Mom accusing Dad of having an affair with a woman in Granville. Well, one of many affairs, as I learned later, that he had over the years."

Sherri tugged at his arm and said, "Maybe we ought to just leave. Let's forget about having Dad give me away. We may open old wounds for Dad. Or worse yet, invite Mom's wrath at the memories. She would never admit to anything improper. If anything she'll react with more venomous talk. I don't think I want to subject you to her nastiness."

"Too late," he said, looking beyond her, toward the road.

She turned to see her mother walking briskly toward them. Judging from the handful of letters she carried, Sherri knew she had been to the post office down the street. "Hi, Mom."

Alice furrowed her brow and snarled, "Well, I see you ain't wasted no time. Already got ya a new beau, huh?"

Sherri's heart broke for her mother. Her bitterness had aged her and robbed her of the beauty she once possessed. Pity for her mother outweighed the disappointment over the snide remark. She stepped forward to hug her.

Alice stood stiff as to force herself not to return the affection.

Sherri stepped back awkwardly. "Is Dad home? I'd like to talk to him."

"Hey, little girl. Come, let me look at you," Cody Lance called from the back porch.

Sherri grabbed Thad's hand and led him quickly toward the small-framed man on crutches. "Daddy, where is your leg."

"It's in the house. When it gets to acting like your mother, I take it off and make it stand in a corner. Shame I can't do the same with her."

Sherri looked over her left shoulder expecting a rebuttal from her mother. "She must have gone around to the front door. I wondered why you dared say that." She let go of Thad's hand and quickly ascended the steps to hug Cody. Then turning to Thad, who had stopped at the top step, she said, "Dad, this is Thad."

Thad stepped up on the porch and shook his hand. "Glad to meet you, sir."

"Thad asked me to marry him, Daddy."

Cody pointed to a chair in the corner of the porch and said, "Brush off the snow and have a seat, boy." Then he told Sherri to go inside to talk with her mother while he and Thad had a chat.

"I heard ya," Alice growled from inside the house. "Come on in here, Sally. You stay out there with the old man, boy. Me and Sally need to have a serious talk."

"Yes, ma'am," Thad said politely, as he brushed away the fluffy white powder from the chair.

Sherri no sooner stepped into the kitchen, than Alice yanked a chair from the table. "Sit down there." She then leaned against the sink counter. "You can't marry that boy."

"Oh, but I can," Sherri retorted. "And you aren't going to stop me. I didn't come here to get your approval *anyhow*. I came to ask Dad to give me away. You don't have to come to the wedding if you don't care to. But I'm tired of your denying me fellowship with my own dad."

"Shut up, girl. Quit being so pig-headed. Are you really that stupid, that you don't know that boy is your kin?"

"No, I'm *not* stupid, Mom. You think I don't know that you and Levi Ashbury aren't really cousins? You can quit playing me for the fool. I know Thad and I are not cousins. You can quit playing that game, too."

Alice took a couple steps forward and leaned over the table supporting herself with her palms pressed against the tabletop. "You stupid girl. T. J. is your brother… Don't look so shocked. You said you already figured out that Levi and I weren't cousins. And don't worry, the old man knows all about it."

The statement numbed her. She propped her elbows on the table and rested her head in her cupped hands as she tried to process the jumbled feelings and warring thoughts. Finally, she lifted her head and through blurred vision she stared at her mother, who had returned to her arrogant stance against the front of the white porcelain-coated sink. Blinking to dislodge stubborn clinging teardrops from her long thick reddish-blonde eyelashes, she asked, "Mom, are you sure? You could be mistaken. Just because you had an affair with Thad's dad doesn't mean that he fathered me."

"No. I am not mistaken. Your dad—by name only—is not able to father kids. He kept that little secret to himself until you were six years old. We were arguing about something and he blurted it out. That's when he threatened to kill Levi. One of our nosey neighbors had, long before, informed him that Levi had been frequenting our home during your dad's cross-country trips for Interstate Trucking and Hauling."

"Do you mean to tell me that he knew I couldn't be his own daughter all that time? And he didn't say a word about it until six years later?" She didn't know whether to pity Cody Lance for having put up with this woman, to despise him for his being a fool for her, or to bewail the unsettling revelation. Slowly, she rose to her feet and headed for the back door.

"I didn't want to have to tell you," Alice called after her.

Sherri refused to acknowledge her further. She had heard enough. Surely, her mother couldn't expect her to accept this news as something of little significance. She felt repulsed at the sight of Cody Lance sitting to her left as she passed between him and Thad and off the porch. The closer to the truck she got, the quicker her steps. She tried to not think at all, in hopes that she could derail the anger and hurt.

Thad soon came to the truck, and as he started the engine, he said, "Sherri, I'm sorry. I wish I knew what to say. How I wish they were mistaken!"

"Then, I guess you heard what Mom said. You've got to understand that Mom is a sick vicious person. She will say anything to make me miserable. This has to be her most disgusting lie yet…I hate her…Ooh, how I hate her! God help me, I hate her!"

He shut off the engine. "Sherri, maybe I better tell you about my conversation with your dad."

She looked into his pain-filled brown eyes and saw the same anguish in his soul that she felt deep within.

I learned the identity of the mysterious caller from the other day—the one who insisted that you and I not marry. The guy couldn't pronounce words with an 'S' in them without a distinctive whistle."

"Daddy? No. He is too timid to do something like that."

"Not this time. I confronted him about it soon as you went into the house. He told me that your mother seldom reads the newspaper. So, he figured she wouldn't know of our engagement. And he didn't want to get her stirred and then have to listen to her continual ranting and raving. He hoped to dissuade me, but he didn't know how to broach the subject without revealing the truth."

She turned her head and stared out the side window. "So, you and I really are…"

"I guess we are."

"But what about…"

"We can't."

"Am I ever glad to see you two," Janet chirped as Sherri and Thad entered the house. She raced from the kitchen, drying her hands with a dishtowel. Her enthusiasm dropped like a lead weight when she beheld their solemn faces. "I take it that the visit didn't go well."

Sherri plopped into the living room recliner and murmured, "I've never been so disappointed in my entire life."

Thad sat on the couch and grunted in agreement. "We are still reeling from the shocking revelation that Sherri and I are siblings."

Feeling too ashamed and confused, Sherri stared off toward the kitchen, past Janet. How could Thad so easily blurt it out like that? She would have at least padded it with some sort of introduction.

"Hey, Thad," Janet said quizzically, "that's not funny… Sherri, tell me he is kidding. Oh, that is ridiculous. There's no way…" Her voice tapered off, "Is there?"

Sherri waited for Thad to reply. She glanced over at him and realized that he *hadn't* so easily handled the contemptible disclosure. Her throat tightened when she started to respond to Janet's inquiry. Afraid to speak, knowing she couldn't talk without breaking down, she looked into Janet's empathetic eyes.

Janet sat on the floor just off to Sherri's left, about half way between her and Thad. "You two must be devastated. I'm so sorry."

They all sat in silence for several minutes. Finally, Sherri asked, "What is that inviting aroma coming from the kitchen?"

"Take a guess," Janet said. "It is something that your Granny Short often baked from something she grew just outside her back door."

"Rhubarb pie?"

"You got it. I'm baking it for somebody special," she teased.

Sherri instantly recalled how Uncle Joseph loved Granny's rhubarb pie.

"Well," said Thad, "I better be going. I certainly am not up to being sociable right now."

"You can't leave, Thad. Please stay? It's important to me that you meet my mystery guest. Tammy and Steve Stewart are on their way up here. They called about an hour ago. They'll be here any minute… Sherri, talk him into staying."

"Sorry, Janet. I feel the same way. This is not a good time for me *or* for Thad to be around others. We need time to work through our disillusionment."

Thad rose slowly to his feet and clumsily walked to the door. He snatched open the door and then paused before pushing open the screen door and asked Sherri, "Are you going to be okay? I can stay a little longer if you need me to."

"I'll be okay. We'll get through this, Thad. Go home and get some rest."

He stepped onto the porch and then grabbed the closing screen door. "Too late. Here come the Stewarts. It wouldn't be proper for me to leave just as they arrive."

Sherri hopped to her feet and announced, "I'm sorry. I'm not as versatile as Thad. You won't be lying if you tell Tammy and Steve that I'm not feeling well." She hastened to her bedroom and turned on the bedside radio and cranked up the volume to keep from hearing any jovial talk. She kicked off her shoes and stretched out across the bed.

A loud knock on her bedroom door woke Sherri from a surprisingly restful sleep. "Come on, Sis," Thad yelled from the hallway. "You'll be glad you joined us. Trust me on this."

"Thad, don't do that. The Stewarts may think I'm avoiding them or something."

His calling her 'Sis' sent her seesawing. Should she be happy to know that such a fine man is her brother? But, how unfair! Should she be thanking God that there is *some* consolation in that? As a little girl, hadn't she prayed many times for a brother?

"Janet said that she'd come in there and drag you out if she needs to."

"Stop it, Thad. I'm not coming out there. Now stop making me look unsociable." She felt an unction to read again, Romans 8:28. She sat up, turned on the lamp, and grabbed her Bible from the nightstand. She flipped through the pages until she found the reference, and read aloud, "And we know that all things work together for good to them that love God, to them who are the called according to his purpose." She bowed her head and whispered, “Heavenly Father, I am thoroughly convinced that I am called according to your purpose. And I do indeed love you. The part I don’t quite comprehend is how all things are working together for my good. Oh, Lord, I could sure use some token of that truth.” She paused in hopes of somehow hearing God’s reply.

“Hey, Little Red,” a muffled male voice reverberated from outside her room, “get out here, right now.”

She became instantly huffed at whoever dared to call her by Uncle Joseph’s pet name for her. She bounded from the bed, stomped to the door and yanked it open. Thrusting herself into the arms of the clean-shaven man with short curly red hair, she shrieked, “Uncle Joseph. Oh, Uncle Joseph. Oh, thank you, Jesus.”

Printed in the United States
49756LVS00004BA/1-96